MURDER 101

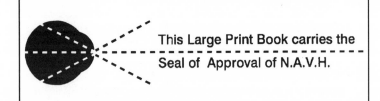

This Large Print Book carries the
Seal of Approval of N.A.V.H.

MURDER 101

MAGGIE BARBIERI

THORNDIKE PRESS

An imprint of Thomson Gale, a part of The Thomson Corporation

Detroit • New York • San Francisco • New Haven, Conn. • Waterville, Maine • London

Copyright © 2006 by Maggie Barbieri.

Thomson Gale is part of The Thomson Corporation.

Thomson and Star Logo and Thorndike are trademarks and Gale is a registered trademark used herein under license.

Thorndike Press® Large Print Mystery.

The text of this Large Print edition is unabridged.

Other aspects of the book may vary from the original edition.

Set in 16 pt. Plantin.

LIBRARY OF CONGRESS CATALOGING-IN-PUBLICATION DATA

Barbieri, Maggie.
   Murder 101 / by Maggie Barbieri.
     p. cm. — (Thorndike Press large print mystery)
   ISBN-13: 978-0-7862-9377-3 (alk. paper)
   ISBN-10: 0-7862-9377-2 (alk. paper)
   1. English teachers — Fiction. 2. Women college teachers — Fiction.
3. College students — Crimes against — Fiction. 4. Bronx (New York, N.Y.)
— Fiction. 5. Large type books. I. Title.
PS3602.A767M87 2007
813'.6—dc22   2006038070

Published in 2007 by arrangement with St. Martin's Press, LLC.

Printed in the United States of America on permanent paper
10 9 8 7 6 5 4 3 2 1

To Jim. You know why.

ACKNOWLEDGMENTS

There are many people who helped me as I wrote this book and they must be thanked: Trixie Beltrano, Sydney Blake, Carrie Brandon, Sheila Curran, Eileen D'Anna, Susan Fleischman, Annie and Michael Gelfand, Melissa Glickman, Kerry Goldberg, John and Marisa Gorman, Alice Kenny, Robin Lawrence, Kevin Mulligan, Dea Perez, Chantal Schwartz, and Kelly Thomann.

A special thanks to my dear friend and writing-group partner, Alison Hendrie, who has encouraged me during the writing process, and helped me discover new ways to say things.

Thank you to Deborah Schneider, my fantastic agent and friend. And much gratitude must go to editor extraordinaire Kelley Ragland, who believed in the entertainment value of Alison Bergeron and her struggles enough to take a chance on a first-time author. Thank you for your invaluable advice on the book and for being my sounding board. Thank you, too, to Kelley's colleague, Ryan Quinn, who was a great help to me during this entire process.

Thank you to Dr. Anna Pavlick and Dr. Daniel Coit, two brilliant and caring individuals who are a blessing to the medical community and their patients. They allowed me to have hope when hope was in short supply. Thanks, too, to Kathy Madden and Norma Sparks, my guardian angels here on earth.

To my sisters, Tricia and Colleen, my brother, Jimmy, and my parents for not laughing at me when I said I had written a novel. And for laughing when they read it.

And to my wonderful husband, Jim, and the best children anyone could have, Dea and Patrick, for listening to my story ideas, for never seeming bored, and for managing to stay conscious as I dissected every plot point for them. I love you.

ONE

"Your ass looks great in that dress."

Max is my best friend and that's her idea of a compliment. When she showed up at my office precisely at six, I was bent over the lowest drawer of my filing cabinet putting some exam booklets away. We air kissed because, as usual, she had three layers of Russian Red lipstick painted on, and I didn't have turpentine handy to remove her lip prints from my cheek. "Are you wearing a girdle?" She threw her briefcase onto one of my guest chairs and draped herself across the other one, throwing one leg over the arm of the chair. Max was in a gorgeous black dress and black shoes with red soles. She noticed me looking at them. "Christian Louboutin," she said. As if I knew what that meant.

I stood up and slammed my file cabinet shut and turned to face her. I wasn't sure if I should be flattered or insulted. "I'm not wearing a girdle." I paused a moment, not capable of lying. "Just control-top panty hose." I sat down behind my desk to tidy up before we headed off to the annual fund-raiser kickoff for the college where I teach and from which Max and I graduated. There was also to be a ceremony honoring Max — a rich alumna and proud donor of a technology classroom. Our school has an unwritten motto: "Keep your alumnae close and your rich alumnae closer."

I got a look at myself in the reflection of the windows next to my desk. I had worn my "good" dress — a sleeveless black sheath on which I had spent too much money five years earlier and felt compelled to wear everywhere in order just to get my money's worth — it's like the fashion version of amortization. I also had on nice black pumps, but I still didn't look like Max. I looked pretty good, for me. She's petite with long legs and a great body that has never been introduced to a piece of exercise equipment. She is a faithful practitioner of yoga, but I'm not exactly sure she practices it for the health benefits. She talks an awful lot about her yogi Brandon.

Max handed me a lipstick. "Just put a little bit on so you don't look quite so cadaverous." I gave her a look. "What?" she asked, indignant; comparing me to a cadaver, in her world, signaled concern. "These classrooms are leeching the life out of you."

She walked over to the tall windows at the end of my office. There is a small patch of grass behind the building, as well as a long flight of stairs that goes past the auditorium and into the building where I have my office and teach all of my classes, one of the three classroom buildings on campus. She perched on the bench that served as a covering for the radiator and crossed her legs. A group of students and a couple of professors, all male, were playing touch football on the little patch of grass behind the building.

"Is your week going any better?" she asked, referring to the fact that my car had been stolen and my divorce had become final all in the last five days. She tapped her foot to some unheard beat, admiring the bunch of twentysomethings and their bare chests.

"Who's the hunk in the striped shorts?" she said, leaning in close to the window before I could answer.

I followed her gaze. "Frank Johnson, head of the Business Department," I said, and sprayed on some perfume.

"Single?"

I looked at her. "Gay." I thought the vertically striped linen shorts and the Choose Life! tank top were a dead giveaway.

She leaned her face against the cool glass. "So? Your week?"

"I'm divorced, without a car, and walking to and from the train station. And everywhere I turn, I see my ex-husband with his newly bald head, goatee, and BMW. That pretty much sums up my week."

"Do you want me to have him killed?" she asked, losing interest in the pansexual football game and giving me her full attention. Seeing Ray, my ex, in a coffin surrounded by flowers was a fantasy I'm sure she had enjoyed for many years.

"Who are we having killed?" a male voice asked from my doorway. I turned around and saw that the voice belonged to one of a duo of men — both large, wearing guns, and holding shiny gold badges.

At five-foot-ten, I'm not used to being one of the smallest people in the room; rather, I usually tower over the little nuns and not fully developed coeds I encounter every day. These two were well into the six-foot-three or -four range, and one of them looked like he hadn't had a good day in weeks. Or a decent night's sleep. The more pleasant-looking of the two was dressed in a brown tweed jacket, khaki pants, a white shirt, and a blue-and-gold-striped tie. He held out one hand to shake and the other to show a gold badge. Not sure what to do, I took both and was then in the uncomfortable position of holding both of his hands at the same time. I dropped the one that didn't hold the badge.

"Alison Bergeron?" he asked, and stepped into my office. Designed to hold me, my stuff, and maybe one other person, it was getting tight.

I clutched the badge, not looking at it. "Yes."

"Detective Crawford, NYPD. This is Detective Wyatt." He held his hand out to retrieve his badge.

The cranky-looking one grunted some kind of greeting. He was wearing a blue suit, and, when he sat down, I could see that he had on a beautifully tailored shirt with French cuffs that had his initials embroidered on them. He had light brown skin and very short black hair. He looked to be in his early forties and seemed to be the senior of the two officers. He took eyeglasses out of his pocket and put them on as he turned in his chair and perused the books on my bookshelf.

Max seemed to be in a trance so I introduced her. "This is my friend, Maxine Rayfield. We're on our way to an alumnae dinner," I babbled. "Max is being honored by the school."

"We won't take too much of your time. Can we sit down?" Crawford asked. He looked pointedly at Max and then back at me.

I motioned to the empty chair across from my desk, which fronted the bookcase that Detective Wyatt was examining. "Oh, she can stay. Max, sit down."

She continued to stare at Wyatt. He didn't seem to register that there was anyone else in the room. She turned and looked at me, and mouthed, "Married?" But I ignored her.

After several moments of silence while he looked at the books, Wyatt asked, "Joyce scholar?"

I was surprised. "Yes."

He shook his head. "I never got him."

"A lot of people say that. I did my dissertation on him." I immediately regretted sounding like Patty McSmartypants, but it was out there and couldn't be taken back. Out of the corner of my eye I saw Max shoot me a look.

He raised his eyebrows in what was an attempt at conveying respect or disgust at my arrogance, I couldn't tell which. I asked Detective Crawford if they had found my car.

"I actually have a couple of questions about that," he said, pulling out a leather-covered notebook and a pen. He leaned forward in the chair. "When was the car taken, as far as you can ascertain?"

"I already had this conversation with a couple of police officers from the Fiftieth Precinct," I said, trying to remain polite. According to my watch, Max and I had approximately seven minutes before we had to be at the cocktail reception before the dinner. The chair of my department, Sister Mary McLaughlin, was a stickler for punctuality, and I had lost some ground with her because of my divorce. I guess I now had "loose woman" written all over me. Yes, it's the twenty-first century. Except when you work for a nun.

He smiled. "I know. Detective Wyatt and I just pulled the case, and we thought we'd go over it again."

Max came to life. "Do they always send detectives to look for stolen cars?" With the flush in her cheeks extending all the way to her red-bottomed shoes, I wasn't sure she was going to make it through the evening. I was also quite sure that if they did send detectives wearing big guns and no wedding rings to look for stolen cars, her new Jaguar would be missing by morning.

He shifted slightly. "Well, not usually." He looked at Detective Wyatt, who took a British literature anthology off my shelf and began thumbing through it. "So, when did you realize it was missing?"

"I left my office at five-thirty on Monday, and it was gone. I usually park it in the lot right at the top of those stairs," I said, pointing out my window. A group of students ran down the stairs, stopping briefly to look at the touch football game in the yard. "I came back to my office and called the campus police who, I guess, called the real police."

Wyatt let out a laugh that sounded like a car backfiring. Crawford looked at him, and he recovered his stony composure, reading the table of contents of the anthology with an intensity it didn't deserve.

"What time was that?"

"What?" I asked, not sure what event he was asking about.

"When the police showed up?"

"Are you guys IAB?" Max asked, getting more excited by the moment. As the head of programming for a cable station, she watches a lot of television. Since her station had started showing repeats of *NYPD Blue*,

I guess she thought she had the cop lingo down.

Crawford looked at her. "IAB?"

"Yeah, Internal Affairs."

"No," he said, and looked down at his notebook.

"It was by six, the latest." I pulled out my appointment book to see if I had written anything else down about whom I saw and when.

He jotted a note in his book and let out a little breath that was more of a time killer than an actual sigh. But, the look on his face told me that there was more to this than my car being gone. My stomach did a little flip.

"And where were you between four o'clock and five-thirty on Monday?"

I turned a couple of pages back in my planner and saw that that section was blank. I thought for a few moments. "I was down at the river planning for a class." I had had a class to teach on the Hudson River poets. I thought the river would provide inspiration. It hadn't. I reused a lecture I had given the year before that was a big dud and that had almost put me to sleep, never mind my students.

"Were you with anyone?" he asked as he wrote.

"No," I said, thinking that that might not be a good thing for me.

"Did anyone see you leave your office?" Wyatt asked.

I thought again. "I can't remember."

Crawford smiled again. "Try."

I felt a bead of sweat running down the indentation of my spine, even though my office was at a comfortable temperature. "I'll have to think about that. I can't think right now."

"Do you know a . . ." He flipped through his notebook, looking for information.

Wyatt stepped in. "Katherine Miceli."

"Yes," I said, and felt the blood drain from my face.

"How?" Wyatt asked, as Detective Crawford continued flipping through his notebook.

"She's in my Shakespeare class."

Wyatt looked at me. "When was the last time you saw her?"

I knew my schedule by heart because it was pretty much the same every semester. "I think it was Monday afternoon. The class meets on Monday, Wednesday, and Friday."

"Did you see her the rest of the week?" Crawford asked.

I reached into my top drawer and took out my grade book. I saw that I had marked her absent for Wednesday and Friday. I was teaching five classes this semester, including the Shakespeare class that was way out of my league. I was having trouble keeping all of it straight. "No, she was absent on Wednesday and today." My heart was pounding.

Wyatt looked perturbed. "Weren't you concerned when she didn't show up for class?"

"This is college, Detective. We don't get too concerned when students don't show up for class. We just figure they're cutting," I explained. "She also owed me a paper on Wednesday that I know she was having trouble with. I figured she cut class to avoid handing it in."

"I bet you never cut class," he said.

I ignored him and tried not to shift around in my seat to show my discomfort. "What's going on?"

Wyatt continued looking at the anthology. "Ms. Miceli is no longer with us."

"Did she transfer?" I asked. Crawford looked at me like I must be joking, but I was dead serious.

Wyatt looked up. "Would we be here if she had transferred?" He gave me an impatient look; I guess he had a point. "She's dead."

I took in a gulp of air. "How did she die?"

"She was murdered," he said. He slammed the book shut and replaced it on the shelf. Crawford pulled at his tie; the good-cop/bad-cop routine was one with which he was obviously familiar, but did not enjoy.

I heard a little squeak emanate from Max as she slid off the radiator cover. "You know what?" she asked, as she picked up her briefcase. "I think I'm going to wait outside." She slung her briefcase over her shoulder and shimmied through the three-inch space that existed between the detectives' knees and my desk, her back to them. I saw Crawford look away discreetly and move his knees to the side, while Wyatt remained fixated on her shaking ass. She faced me as she moved by them and contorted her face to convey her horror to me.

I waited until she left the room and closed the door before asking, "How?" My heart did that thing where it beats a few hundred times and then skips a beat. I took a deep breath.

"Don't know," Wyatt said. "Just found her. We're waiting for the coroner's report."

"Who found her?"

Wyatt was growing impatient with my questions. "What difference does it make?"

"What does this have to do with my car?"

Crawford, good cop — or at least, polite cop — reached into his pocket and took out a stack of photos. He held one up to my face. "Is this your car?" he asked.

I looked at the photo, and it was indeed my car. In the photo, it was dripping wet and covered in mud but, undeniably, my car. I nodded.

He put that photo on the bottom of the pile and held up another photo. I stood up behind my desk to get a better look. When I saw what I was looking at — the open trunk complete with bloodied body — a loud buzzing began in my ears.

I remember thinking about the soles of Max's shoes as I hit the floor.

Two

The Monday after Kathy's murder became public and three days after I had been questioned by the police, I returned to school with a lump on my head and a raging headache. I had sustained a concussion from the fall in my office, and while I thought the weekend would give me an opportunity to rest and recuperate, my phone rang off the hook with calls from Max — who thought an hourly phone call to make sure I was conscious was necessary — a couple of newspaper reporters to whom I refused to talk, Max's parents, and a few other concerned colleagues who had heard about my bad fortune. By the time Monday morning rolled around, I was almost relieved to go to work. I left the house around noon and got to school less than an hour later. I was commuting via Metro North; fortunately my home and school were on the same train line and I could walk to the train station from home in less than ten minutes. The walk to school from the train station was a bit longer; twenty if I wore sensible shoes, but thirty if, like today, I wasn't using my head and wore heels.

I was not eager to return to my office. Not only had I fainted at the sight of Kathy Miceli crumpled up in my trunk, I also further demeaned myself by vomiting all over "good cop's" shoes after I came to. Detective Crawford had insisted on taking me to the hospital, where he waited with me in the emergency room and filled me in on what had happened. My car had been found off the Saw Mill River Parkway, just before the Bronx ends and Westchester begins, off the road and halfway in a ditch, Katherine Miceli's body in the trunk. She had died from a head wound — the coroner was still trying to decide how it had happened exactly, but her best guess was that she had fallen against something. My car was now evidence in a murder investigation and I would never see it again. When I started to black out again, he stopped his story and held my head as I vomited all over his shoes for a second time that day. As they say, "no good deed goes unpunished."

My office still smelled slightly of vomit, but the only thing that got my attention when I entered was a note marked UR-GENT sitting on top of my desk. I picked up the lined piece of pink paper and studied it, my heart sinking when I saw that I had been called to the president's office for a meeting. I had only been in the president's office once — when I had been granted tenure — and was thankful that I had never been summoned back. There were about three layers of bureaucracy between me and Dr. Etheridge and that's the way I liked it; I hated Mark Etheridge and his snotty at-titude. The farther away I could stay from the cantankerous bastard, the better.

Maybe I wanted to remember St. Thomas as it used to be — small, private, and personal — but Mark's style rubbed me the wrong way. And the fact that I was a good six inches taller than he was probably rubbed him and his Napoleon complex the wrong way.

I felt like I was walking the plank as I trudged up to the fifth floor and across the marbled hallways to the president's office, located at the far end of the building from my office. I entered the darkly paneled of-fice of the anteroom, where Mark's secretary and my old friend, Fran Voight, sat.

"Good morning, Fran," I said. She had been the president's secretary since I had gone to school here and we knew each other well.

Fran didn't respond, but looked at me over her bifocals and motioned with her head toward Etheridge's office, her frosted helmet of hair not moving. The grim set of her mouth told me that this wasn't going to be a pleasant meeting. The triple strand of long pearls on her chest made a clicking noise as she swung around in her chair and put her back to the door of Etheridge's office. I heard her whisper "good luck" as I entered the office and closed the door behind me.

Etheridge was sitting behind his grand desk, Sister Mary in front of him. There was an empty chair for me. He stayed behind his desk and motioned to me to sit down. "Good morning, Alison."

"Dr. Etheridge," I said, smiling nervously. "Good morning, Sister."

Sister Mary avoided my eyes, and mumbled "good morning" back.

Etheridge folded his hands in front of him and stared at me. "So, this is a terrible situation," he started. "Before the police get involved with you, I'm going to give you a chance to explain yourself." He took his round, rimless glasses off and put them back on after checking them for spots. "How *did* a dead body end up in the trunk of your car, Alison?" He seemed genuinely curious rather than suspicious.

I took a deep breath. "First of all, the police are already involved with me," I said, my hands gripping the sides of the chair. "I was questioned on Friday." I stared at him, and he stared back. "And I'm not in jail, so I'm assuming that they've come to the conclusion that I don't have anything to do with this." I gave him an idiotic half smile; perhaps if he thought I was a complete moron, he wouldn't suspect me of anything more than having bad luck. "And I have no idea how a dead body ended up in my trunk." I wanted to add, "So now that we've cleared that up, can I go now?" but I could see that this meeting was far from over.

He raised an eyebrow questioningly.

"My car was stolen a week ago. I reported it to the campus police and the police from the Fiftieth Precinct who came to take the report. I explained all of this to the two detectives who came to my office." I crossed my legs and then uncrossed them.

He took his glasses off again and leaned back in his chair, folding his hands across his vested belly. "This is a terrible situation." He looked at me, and I could see his face soften a bit. "I've spent the weekend dealing with this. And thinking about what to do — what's best for the students' protection, and how to keep the media away from them and you. And from *here*," he stressed, "I think the best course of action would be to suspend you until this blows over."

I felt as if I had been punched in the stomach, but somehow, I managed to remain impassive.

He held a hand up to ward off any potential emotional outbursts, putting it down when he saw the look on my face. "But Sister Mary has talked me out of it." He leaned forward again. "So, teach your classes and grade your papers. Do not talk to the press, to your colleagues, or to anyone but the police about this." The phone on his desk buzzed and he picked it up. "Yes? Tell him I need one minute." He hung the phone up. "A Detective Crawford is here, and I need to see him. Are we clear?"

I should have gotten up and left, but I opened my mouth to speak instead. "Crystal." Sister Mary gave me a look and put her hand on top of mine, silencing me before I could say anything else. I nodded and stood.

He continued, even though I thought the

conversation was over. "Alison, let's be clear . . ."

I held up a hand to silence him. "I get it, Mark." I stood for a minute more, and when he didn't say anything, I asked, "Are we done?"

He nodded, and I left the office. Detective Crawford was standing in front of one of the bookshelves, perusing the titles that Etheridge kept there. He turned when he heard me exit the president's office. "Hello."

My face went red when I thought back to the Friday before and our conversation in my office. Then, I flashed back on my trip to the hospital and the part where I threw up on his shoes. My stomach got a little sick. "Hello," I mumbled, and strode past him and into the hallway, going too fast and misjudging the space between where the carpet of the president's office ended and the marble in the hallway began. I skidded onto the marble floor, my ankle twisting in my high heels. Just before I crumpled to a heap on the floor, I grabbed on to the door handle and righted myself. I saw Crawford start toward me and then stop, one of the books from the bookshelves in his hands. I looked at his shoes and from their high gloss could tell that they were new.

"Are you all right?" he asked from inside

the office. Fran leaned over her desk to see what had happened, her ample bosom grazing the top of a stack of files.

"I'm fine," I choked out. I managed to not lose it completely until I had put a great deal of distance between the two of us, and I raced down the hallway, cursing the janitor who had buffed the floor to such a dangerous gloss. I kept going until I reached the stairwell, thinking, My work here is done; I was completely humiliated.

I made it back to my office without injuring myself further and closed the door. Classes had been canceled and grief counselors called in, so I had no reason to stay at school other than to get out of my empty house. I swept a pile of papers off my desk and into my briefcase, which was right where I'd left it on the floor. A soft knock at the door interrupted my thoughts, and I called to the person to come in.

Sister Mary poked her head around the doorjamb tentatively and asked if she could come in. Mary isn't usually timid; on the contrary, she's officious and starchy. But being as she had to sit through Etheridge's reprimands and had probably witnessed my skid across the floor in front of Fran and Detective Crawford, she probably felt just a little bit sorry for me. She came in and sat in the chair across from my desk where Detective Crawford had sat a few days before.

"I'm not sure what to say, Alison," she said, probably the first time she had ever uttered that sentence.

Despite my best efforts, a sob slipped out, sounding like a hiccup. "If it weren't for you, I'd probably be suspended by now," I said, and continued stuffing papers into my briefcase frantically. Tears ran down my face and dropped onto my desk.

"We all know that Etheridge is a bas . . . nasty, nasty man," she said, her face flushing at the thought of using the word "bastard." "I know you had nothing to do with this. So does everyone else. Etheridge just likes to make decisions that he thinks will make him look strong to the outside world."

I stopped pushing papers into my bag and looked at her, my face tear-stained and wet. "What did you have to promise him?"

She looked back at me.

"To keep me around? What did you have to promise him?"

She ignored the question. "Let's just make sure we cooperate fully with the investigation and tell the detectives anything that we think is germane to the case." She stood. "Why don't you go home for the day? There won't be any classes until Wednesday, the earliest."

I nodded. "Are you sure you won't need me?" I asked.

She shook her head. "As long as Father McManus is here, and the grief center is open, I don't see any reason why you should have to stay on campus until classes start again." She reached out and took my hand. "Go home," she whispered, and gave my fingers a little squeeze.

I gave her a resigned shrug. "Sister, please know that . . ."

"I know, Alison. This is just a terribly tragic situation. There's nobody to blame," she said, and put her hand on the knob of the door. "Yet."

I waited until she left to blow my nose and wipe my eyes. I took out the small mirror that I kept in my top drawer and looked at my face. Terribly tragic indeed. I used a tissue to wipe away the black under my eyes and the smeared lipstick around my mouth. I took my sweater from the back of my chair, slipped it on, and grabbed my briefcase, making a hasty exit from my office and the building.

I made my way off campus and onto the avenue, walking unsteadily on my too-high heels and twisted ankle. It was after two

31

o'clock, but after what I had been through in my short time at school, I felt like it was time for bed. I passed the doorway for the Avenue Steak House and got a whiff of that old, familiar bar smell: a mixture of smoke, peanuts, and fried food. I stood for a moment, deciding what to do. After a few minutes, I turned around and went in.

I didn't think the instruction "drink martini" was on the form entitled "What to do if you sustain a concussion" which I was given when I left the hospital, but I didn't have any aspirin in my briefcase. A martini seemed to be the next best thing. I'm not usually a middle-of-the-day drinker, but the extra-strength Midol in my purse just wasn't going to cut it, in terms of stress relief. I went up to the horseshoe-shaped bar, which was empty of customers, and took a seat on one of the mahogany barstools. A television hung over the bar and was tuned to one of the cable news networks.

The bartender, a young guy with red hair and a pudgy face, put a cocktail napkin down in front of me and gave me a smile. I had been in here a few times, and, while I couldn't be considered a regular, he obviously remembered me. "What can I get you?" He closed his eyes for a minute and put one hand to his forehead. "Wait," he said, holding up his other hand. "Ketel One martini, extra dry, three olives."

I whistled. "You're good. I don't think I've been in here since before Christmas."

"I always remember the pretty ones," he schmoozed, leaning on the bar and giving me a winning smile.

I sat up a little straighter in my stool. I had about ten years on him, but after what I had been through in the past few days, I thought a little flirting might help take the edge off.

"And you look like my older sister." He turned and took a martini glass off the shelf behind the bar and began mixing my drink.

He had a lot to learn. His tip dwindled as I considered his last remark and watched him pour too much vermouth into the glass. He redeemed himself by adding an extra olive to the drink and proffering a menu. "Hungry?"

I picked up the glass and took a sip of my drink. "Actually, yes." I studied the menu and asked him for a salad with chicken. I thought I might feel less guilty about sitting in a bar on a Monday afternoon if I also ate lunch. He gave me a little salute and disappeared into the kitchen.

I took another sip of my drink and looked around. I was the only person in the bar besides the bartender, so I focused on my reflection in the mirror behind the bar. I didn't know what murderers generally looked like, but I found it hard to believe that they ever looked like the pathetic image staring back at me. I ran my hands over my head of frizzy hair in an attempt to tame it and pinched my cheeks; my face was devoid of color, my lips the same shade as my pallid skin. There was no hope. I needed a long bath followed by a long nap. I sat and waited for my food, hoping that by virtue of being the sole customer, it would come out quickly. Finally, tired of staring at myself and getting more depressed, I asked the bartender for the main section of the *New York Times* sitting at the end of the bar.

The paper was folded in half and I shook it open, staring at the main headlines, which depressed me even more; one of them screamed out about a "murder at a small, Catholic university." I had just returned to staring at myself in the mirror when the door to the bar opened and a man entered. He was of average height, and despite the fact that he looked to be in his early thirties, prematurely gray. He had on a sport jacket and khaki pants. Before the door swung shut, I caught sight of a brown car at the curb, someone in the driver's seat talking on a cell phone. The door slammed, and the man walked past me, ignoring my presence. He took a seat at the end of the bar and opened the newspaper that had been tucked under his arm.

The bartender emerged from the kitchen and told me that my food would be out in a minute. He then attended to the man, who ordered a club soda. The man focused on his paper, spread out in front of him on the bar, taking a sip of the club soda after the bartender set it down in front of him.

The bartender had returned, leaning over the bar to chat. "Terrible thing about what happened at St. Thomas."

I took a sip of my martini and tried to look suitably horrified without engaging him in conversation. I was more horrified than he would ever know, but the subject of Kathy Miceli's murder was the last thing I wanted to talk about. He turned around and looked up at the television just as a picture of my car flashed on the screen followed by a picture of St. Thomas. I sucked down the martini and asked for another one. He grabbed the remote and turned the volume on the television up so that he could hear the report.

A well-coiffed blonde was reporting live from the spot where my car had once sat.

According to the caption at the bottom of the screen, she was reporting live. I had gotten out of there just in time. ". . . Dr. Alison Bergeron, a professor at St. Thomas, and a former classmate of Gianna Miceli, mother of the murdered girl . . ." A picture of Gianna flashed on the screen, followed by a shot of me that I had no recollection of ever having posed for. It was an "action shot": in it, I was walking in the back parking lot of the Administration Building, obviously on my way to my office. And since I was wearing exactly what I currently had on, I figured out that it had been taken when I arrived at school that day. The bartender looked at the television and then back at me, his mouth agape. I looked down at the man at the other end of the bar to see his reaction, but he studied his paper, his eyes never leaving the print.

I looked back at the bartender. "I don't look as bad as I thought I did today. Your older sister must be a knockout." I returned to my paper. "Can I have that drink now?"

Assuming I must be some kind of badass or psycho serial killer, he turned around and whipped up a better drink than the first one before scurrying off to the kitchen to get my lunch. He returned and put it in front of me, backing away from the bar as if

I was about to pull out a .38 special and blow his head off. His eyes never left me as I put my napkin across my lap and prepared to dive into my salad.

"Could I have some dressing?" I asked.

"What kind?" he asked, his voice cracking.

"Ranch."

He ran off and came back with a chilled ramekin filled to the brim with dressing. He reached for the remote and turned the television off. "Do you need anything else?" he asked, his tone indicating that he hoped I didn't.

A good lawyer, maybe? I shoved a forkful of lettuce into my mouth and shook my head. He wandered off toward the end of the bar where the man sat, and tried to engage him in conversation. The man responded to the bartender's question about a recent baseball game with indifference followed by a grunt, which sent the bartender back to the kitchen. I ate quickly and downed my drink, keeping the guy at the end of the bar in my peripheral vision. Something about him wasn't right, but I didn't know what it was.

When I was done, I took a ten and a twenty out of my wallet and left them on the bar. Not seeing the bartender, I calculated in my head that I had left him more than enough for the two drinks, salad, and a tip. I grabbed my briefcase off the floor and started out of the bar.

The brown car was still parked at the curb, but it was empty. I continued down the avenue and when I reached the station road, I made a right and headed down the hill toward the river. The road doesn't have a sidewalk, so I stayed close to the edge of it even though it wasn't heavily trafficked at this time of day. I walked gingerly, careful of the clusters of gravel beneath my feet. I reached the train platform and sat on a bench.

I leaned back against the concrete headrest and fixed my eyes on a sun-dappled wave on the river. It was a beautiful spring day, and the river was calm and placid. When I thought about it, it always looked that way, rolling up toward Albany and back down again toward the Battery and the tip of Manhattan. Constantly flowing, yet static at the same time. I closed my eyes and listened for the rumble of the train coming down the tracks.

I didn't have a schedule with me, so I didn't know when a train would come. I was grateful when I heard the familiar grinding of brakes and muffled voice of the conductor calling out the window that the train would stop at Riverdale. I got up and smoothed my skirt, turning slightly to face the train. The doors opened and when I was sure that no one was getting off the train, I entered and stood in the space right inside the door. The doors closed, and I looked out the window of the train door as the train slowly started out of the station.

The train was nearly out of the station when I saw the brown car that had been outside the bar. It was parked at the edge of the parking lot, two shapes visible behind the windshield, their identities obscured by the bright sun reflecting off the glass.

The train built up speed, and I ran the length of the train car to get one more look at the car. I leaned in over an old woman who was sleeping in a two-seater; she opened her eyes and held her ticket up to my face, convinced that I was the conductor. I put my nose up to the glass and watched as the passenger-side door of the car opened and a man got out. He watched the train pull completely out of the station and continue down the tracks, his hand shielding his eyes from the sun. His jacket fluttered open, and I saw a gun on his hip.

His young face was in stark contrast to his full head of gray hair.

THREE

I leaned over and adjusted the strap on my black slingbacks. Today was Katherine Miceli's funeral — a full week after the detectives had come to my office — and her parents had decided to hold it at the chapel at school. Classes had been canceled for the day out of respect for the girl and in anticipation of the media frenzy that would surround this tragic event.

Dottie Cruz was the receptionist for all of the professors who shared that floor of the Administration Building. She had agreed to stay behind and answer the phones while most of the professors attended the funeral. She had been at the school for thirty years and was a world-class busybody. She was at her desk doing the *New York Post* jumble when I walked by. "See you later?" she asked, looking sad and forlorn. "Horrible thing, this is."

I nodded, but kept going. I didn't want to

discuss much of anything with Dottie, let alone this.

The chapel was on the same floor as my office, down a long hallway. The floors went from a worn oak plank to a highly polished marble as you approached the doors of the chapel. For a school that at its peak only had eleven hundred students, the chapel was designed to hold at least that many, including the seating in the balcony. Since the school still had a convent attached to it, the sisters used the chapel as their regular place of worship, but there were only thirty or so of them left, so the chapel was often mostly empty. The heavy wooden doors, etched with pictures of Mary and Jesus, were open to the marble foyer, and I could hear a faint buzz in the chapel.

The smell of the chapel always brought me back to my days as a student here. It was a combination of incense, burning candles, melted wax, and floor polish. When I was an undergrad, there were about sixty nuns on campus, and the holy order to which they belonged wore a habit that included a bonnet that was not unlike the one that was stamped on the plastic container of Blue Bonnet margarine. Max, in her way, called them the "bonnet heads." When she and I felt guilty about not going

41

to Mass and showed up at the Sunday 9:15 service (about once every two months), we would always sit in the back: the first several pews would be filled with old, wizened "bonnet heads," dutifully worshipping. At the time, I didn't appreciate their devotion and was puzzled by their insular world and ways. Things hadn't changed much in that regard; I was still puzzled.

The chapel was filled with about two hundred students, several hundred family members and friends from Kathy's Staten Island neighborhood, and faculty. Everyone was situated mostly near the front, but I felt more comfortable in the third pew from the back, alone in the row.

Besides the humiliating moment outside of Etheridge's office (which I didn't count as anything, trying desperately to wipe it from my mind), I hadn't seen Detective Crawford since our time together in the emergency room; but I looked up from the prayer missile that I had taken out of the holder in front of the pew and saw him sitting directly across from me with Detective Wyatt. Wyatt was thumbing through the hymnal. Crawford turned and caught my eye, giving me a faint smile.

Our chaplain, Father Kevin McManus, two female altar servers, and a priest I didn't recognize made their way down the center aisle and met the casket, which was flanked by dark-suited pallbearers, at the back of the chapel. Kathy's family stood behind the casket. Her mother, Gianna, had not changed since we had been in school together. She still had a pile of blond curls, was bone thin, and wore beautifully tailored clothes and designer shoes. She was gorgeous and always had been. She caught my eye and quickly looked away. Her husband, next to her, was the same man she dated when we were in school, but the years had not been as kind to him. Peter Miceli was short, bald, and had a paunch, despite a somewhat youthful face. He had on a black suit and shiny black lace-up shoes and was holding Gianna's arm in a death grip. My heart ached to see them following the casket of their oldest.

Max and I had been somewhat friendly with Gianna when we were freshmen and she was a junior, but the specter of her family's "business" always hung over her, making her seem a little unapproachable. When her father, a dead ringer for Michael Corleone, picked her up one Friday afternoon, Max and I shook with terror — we had seen *The Godfather* and knew what happened to people who hung out with the

Mob; they either ended up married to an abusive husband or with a horse head in their bed. Then, there was the rumor of her boyfriend — the one who had a bad reputation, even by Mob standards — who went missing. That was enough for us. We didn't want to go missing because we forgot to give her our biology lab notes. We kept our distance after that.

Today Gianna's father, Tommy Capelli, stood behind her. He didn't look much like Michael Corleone anymore but more like Don Corleone: heavy with white hair. He had on a gray suit, a starched white shirt with a big collar, and a black tie. He put his hand on Peter's shoulder and whispered something in his ear, and Peter nodded.

Gianna had gotten pregnant in her senior year, so was relatively young to have a nineteen-year-old daughter. Her two other children, a boy and a girl, were much younger — closer to being preteens than anything else. Kathy's brother and sister looked like they were in a daze as they stood to the side of their mother, holding on to a very small old woman with a black-lace mantilla on her head.

Vince Paccione, Kathy's boyfriend, was with the family, but at the back of the crowd. He had the usual snarl on his face, and his body was tensed as if ready to spring onto someone or something. I had encountered Vince once or twice when he waited for Kathy outside of class and didn't get his rebel without a clue act. He was handsome, got good grades (I had done a little snooping on that end), and seemed to have a few friends. But there was also a rumor that he was the Ecstasy connection at Joliet – St. Thomas's "brother" school from long ago — and that bothered me because from what I had witnessed, Kathy was a very nice girl and shouldn't have had a drug-dealer boyfriend. As girlfriends go, she seemed to have had that blind devotion and dedication to him that I recognized from a seven-year marriage that was dysfunctional from the beginning. I looked over at the cops in the pew and noticed Wyatt giving Vince the once-over, as if he thought something might happen.

Vince must have sensed my gaze at him because he caught my eye and held my stare. The organ sounded, and everyone focused on the procession down the aisle, and I finally looked away, a chill going through me as I saw Vince shoot me one last look over his shoulder.

Father Kevin and the other priest said a

few prayers over the casket and turned to lead it and Kathy's family up the aisle. As they processed, Father Kevin swung an urn of incense back and forth, filling the church with its pungent odor. The organist started playing, and I picked up my hymnal. Since I was raised Catholic, taught in a Catholic school, and went to church semiregularly, I knew most of what the organist played, but holding the hymnal and reading the words gave me something to do. I looked over at the detectives. Wyatt was looking around, seemingly at every face in the crowd, while Crawford was singing softly, his hands clasped in front of him. He apparently knew all of the words by heart.

I didn't know how Father Kevin was going to be able to find anything to say that would bring the family comfort; but his sermon was beautiful, invoking the idea of resting with God for all eternity. I didn't know if I believed it, but it sounded good.

When it was time for communion, Father Kevin brought the hosts down to the pews and had Kathy's family receive communion from where they were sitting. Everyone else formed two lines, side by side, and made their way up the center aisle. I found myself elbow to elbow with Detective Crawford.

He leaned over and asked how I was feeling.

"I'm better," I whispered. I think the close proximity of the two lines had him thinking that he might have to duck for cover if the body of Christ made me nauseous.

He nodded and looked straight ahead, preparing to receive communion. I looked back, but Wyatt was still in the pew, sprawled out with elbows resting on the back of the pew and his right hand resting on his gun. He stifled a yawn as he watched everyone first proceed up the aisle and then back down.

I returned to my pew at the back of the church and knelt to pray. I didn't know quite what to pray for: happiness in heaven? A swift resolution to this mystery of the murder? Retribution? So, in the end, I said good-bye to this young girl who never did understand what constituted plagiarism or the correct form of the bibliography. And when I thought about her that way, in the only way I really knew her, I was overcome by profound sadness. Tears leaked from the corners of my eyes and dropped onto the pew in front of me. I put my face in my hands and rested my elbows on the top of the pew.

The Mass ended, and the sound of sobbing girls — Kathy's friends — was loud and echoed throughout the building. I recognized a couple of the girls from my classes — Fiona Martin, Mercedes Rivas, and Jennifer Garrison. As her family followed the casket out of the chapel, her grandfather, Tommy, began to wail — a low, pitiful moan that filled the chapel and reverberated around us. I saw Crawford fold his hands in front of him and look down, his discomfort with the loud displays of grief obvious to me. Wyatt looked over at Capelli in disbelief. I sat in my pew and waited until everyone had left. Outside the chapel there was a buzz of activity as every major media outlet was covering the funeral. I wasn't sure if it was Kathy's family that generated the interest, the circumstances of her death, or a combination of those two things, but the campus had been crawling with vans filled with crews and reporters since the beginning of the week. President Etheridge, hoping to maintain some kind of normalcy for the students, arranged for uniformed officers from the local precinct to patrol and monitor traffic coming into the school. The president's affiliation with the mayor and his latest campaign seemed to ensure that there were at least fifteen officers on campus at all times. Too bad that hadn't been the case when someone was stealing my car, murdering a young girl, and dumping both alongside a parkway on the border of the City and Westchester County.

As soon as I was sure that the hearse and the limousines had left the front of the building, I left the chapel and stepped onto the cool marble floor of the foyer. The foyer was circular, with benches on either side, and a balcony that overlooked the main floor. Ray sat on a bench looking out of the circular rose window that overlooked the river. When he heard my footsteps, he turned to face me.

He held his arms out to me and by habit, I went to step into them before I remembered that I didn't have to and didn't want to. I would have liked a hug but I couldn't do it and his arms hung awkwardly in the air before he dropped them to his sides. "Are you OK?" he asked.

"Yes." I took a step toward him. "Were you at the funeral?"

"I was," he said. "I had Kathy in class."

"Me, too," I said, and studied his face. Funny . . . I didn't remember ever having seen him cry when we were married or even when we were in the throes of divorce, but now, tears were coursing down his cheeks.

"I heard that they found her in your car."

49

"Apparently."

"How are you getting to school then?" he asked, running his hands across his wet eyes.

"I'm taking the train and walking from the station."

"If you ever need a ride, just call me on my cell, and I'll pick you up," he said. Even I had to admit it was a nice offer. "You know I'm still here for you."

I had no idea what he was talking about. He was never there for me during our marriage, but now that we were apart, we were best friends? The man lived in an alternate universe where his logic actually made sense, but only to him.

When I didn't respond, he shrugged, resigned. He started for the stairs on the right side of the chapel. "Do you need a ride today?"

"No, I don't. But thanks for thinking of me," I managed to say, and started down the stairs on the left side, picking up my pace as I descended each creaky riser. Because as hard as I had tried to hold on to him for all those years, now I couldn't get away from him fast enough.

FOUR

I returned to my office and stopped by Dottie's desk to look in my mailbox, which was in a row of boxes behind her. I saw that I had two phone messages from Max — one dated three days before — a late paper from a student with a Post-it note of apology on the front, and a business card from a publisher's rep who wanted to sell me a new literature anthology for my intro class. Dottie swung around in her desk chair and looked at me pointedly, one of her tattooed-on eyebrows raised questioningly. I figured she wanted details of the funeral, which I would refuse to give. But she persisted in looking at me until I met her eye. She threw her head to the left as if she were having some kind of seizure. "Are you all right?" I asked. Normally, I like just about everyone I meet; Dottie is the one person with whom I have no patience. She's nosy, lazy, and a crappy secretary. She tried to bond with me over my divorce, but I didn't think Dottie could provide any solace during one of the worst stretches in my life. Right now, we had an uneasy alliance; she worked for everyone on the floor, including me. I had to be, at the very least, polite.

I followed her gaze and thrusting head. Detectives Wyatt and Crawford were standing outside my office. Wyatt was looking at the Modern Language bulletin board, seemingly mulling over a junior year abroad in La Rochelle; Crawford spotted me and gave me the same wan smile that he had greeted me with in the chapel. So I had been spotted. I could try to run away, but slingbacks wouldn't provide any traction. Running away could also get me arrested. I strode over to the door of my office and greeted them with a grimly resigned, "Come on in."

I put the key in the lock of my office door and opened it. Both refused to enter until I went in. I walked around to my desk and motioned to the two chairs. "Have a seat."

Wyatt had on a starched white oxford shirt that had at least an eighteen-inch neck. His jacket was a black-and-white-herringbone, and his pants a black lightweight flannel. I still couldn't tell what nationality he was — slightly Asian, slightly African-American, kind of white . . . it was hard to tell. He was a bit of a dandy for a large, imposing behemoth of a man, but he obviously made an effort with his appearance. Crawford, with his chiseled Irish-American face, looked like every guy whom I had gone to college with, had had a crush on, and been too intimidated to talk to. He was in khakis, a white oxford, and a blue blazer. Wyatt's look said "I have a wife, and she shops at Brooks Brothers," while Crawford's screamed "I'm single and I get the Lands' End catalog."

Wyatt jumped right in with the questions. "Did you talk with Mrs. Miceli today?"

"Why, hello, Detective. So nice to see you," I said, trying to affect a nonchalant sarcasm that I was incapable of pulling off. When he continued to stare back at me, eyes narrowed and beady, I decided to answer his question. "Gianna? No." I neatened a stack of papers on my desk. "I didn't think today was the day to do that. I sent a Mass card to their home."

"Anybody else in the family?" he asked.

I shook my head. Boy, these papers were really disorganized. I continued neatening, giving the desk my undivided attention.

"Did you and Mrs. Miceli have a relationship in college?"

I thought back. "Relationship? We were

53

friendly. We lived on the same dorm floor during my sophomore and her senior year so we saw each other until she left school. She was dating Peter at that time, I think."

Even though he had closed the door on the way into my office, Crawford's voice was barely above a whisper. "What is your relationship with your ex-husband?"

My face reddened. I hadn't expected any questions about Ray, and I was taken off guard. "Amicable," I managed to say through almost-clenched teeth.

Crawford waited to see if I had anything else to say. I did, but I decided to say it in the mirror to myself later that day, when I was home. Alone. It had to do with goatees, infidelity, and new cars.

"You must see each other a lot." He looked directly at me, probably hoping to read something on my face.

"We team-teach a course together three times a week, so we see each other on those days. What does Ray have to do with any-thing?"

Wyatt changed the subject. "Do you have any other connections to the Miceli family besides your history with the mother?" He leaned forward in his chair and laced his fingers together between his knees.

"How did you know?" I asked, flippantly. "Yes. I'm a headlining exotic dancer at one of their clubs. Who happens to read Joyce while she's giving lap dances." I held Wyatt's gaze.

Crawford looked down but couldn't contain a slight smile. He did his old tie-pull time killer and looked around, focusing on a spot behind my head.

When Wyatt didn't respond to my attempt at humor, I decided to give a straight response. "I knew Gianna eighteen years ago. I never saw her from the day she left school until the first day of school this year, when Kathy was moving in."

"What about Mr. Miceli?" Crawford asked.

"I haven't seen Peter during that entire time until today."

"Did you see him when you were in school with Mrs. Miceli?"

"He had a souped-up Trans Am with twin exhausts. He was hard to miss."

Wyatt leaned back in his chair and shifted his hands up to his stomach. "What do you have to do with this, Professor?" he said, using my title almost condescendingly. "Why your car, for instance?"

I could feel my armpits dampen. This dress was a goner. "It's 'doctor,' and I don't know what I have to do with this, Detective," I said.

"Doctor." He smirked a bit. "Face it. Twelve-year-old Volvos aren't really a hot commodity for car thieves these days. Unless they've become vintage and I didn't realize it. Are they vintage, Crawford?" he asked, looking over at Crawford.

Tie pull. "Not that I know of."

I still had the remnants of a concussion, and my head was starting to pound. I felt my face go from red to ashen in the space of a few seconds, and I saw Crawford get the same panicky look he had on his face the second time I vomited on his shoes. I opened my bottom desk drawer and rooted around for a water bottle. It might have been my weakened, almost-hallucinogenic state, but I could have sworn I saw Wyatt instinctively put his hand on his gun. He relaxed when he saw the water bottle, and I was sure then that he had planned on killing me.

"Detectives, I'm going to have to do this another time. I'm not feeling well, and I have to go home," I said, one aspect of that statement being true. I opened the bottle and drained it in two swigs. "Maybe I could come to the station house or precinct house or whatever it is you call it so we don't have to do this here. Pick me up in your cruiser. I don't have a car."

"We don't drive cruisers," Crawford interjected. As if it mattered.

Wyatt persisted. "You didn't answer my question."

I looked at him.

"Why your car?" he repeated, as if I had forgotten the question in the last twenty seconds. "It doesn't make sense."

If he didn't know, then I surely didn't. I was exhausted with thinking about a possible answer. "I . . . don't . . . know," I said, as slowly and clearly as I could. I tried to stare Wyatt down. "Do I need a lawyer, Detective?"

He shrugged. "I don't know. Do you?"

"I don't think so, but the way these questions are going . . ."

Crawford took over. "How well do you know Vince Paccione?" he said in his same, whispered tone. He acted like we were still in the chapel and he was conducting the interrogation there.

"Not at all. I see him every now and again on campus, but that's it. I don't think we've exchanged three words all year." I needed more water, but I was afraid if I opened my desk drawer again, Wyatt and his itchy trigger finger would shoot me dead.

"And how well did you know Kathy?" he asked.

"I already told you, remember? She was in my class. I knew her a bit better than most of my students but only because I had known her mother. I would ask how her mother was, and she would give me her mother's regards. Nothing more."

Crawford stared at me expectantly.

"Ginkgo biloba is a wonderful remedy for memory loss. It's all natural, too," I said, and tried to hold Crawford's gaze. He stared right back at me. I had to face it: I wasn't tough, they knew it, and that was the end of that. What I was was a trembling, scared, insecure English professor who was now linked to a tragic death. He continued to look at me until I spoke. "There's nothing else. We've been over this."

Wyatt returned from whatever reverie he had entered momentarily. "Did you know that Kathy was in your husband's — sorry," he said with gravity, "— ex-husband's introductory biology class?"

"Yes, Ray mentioned that." And was crying when he did, I thought, but again, held back.

"She never mentioned it to you?" he asked, dubiously.

"No," I said, emphatically.

58

And with that, they stood up. I stood, too. "Thank you for coming by," I said, forgetting for a moment that I had just been interrogated and didn't need to thank them for anything. I mentally slapped myself. If nothing else, I had been taught to be unfailingly polite. I recalled thanking Ray for signing and submitting his divorce papers on time.

Crawford gave me a bemused smile. "Why, you're welcome," he said.

Wyatt followed Crawford out and closed the door behind him. When I thought that they were a safe distance down the hall, I pulled out my garbage can and puked into it.

FIVE

As is often the case with Max, I heard her before I saw her. "Detectives!" she called out in greeting as she entered the office area. She arrived just as they were leaving. I heard some mumbled responses from them and then the clickety clack of her high heels on the wooden floors. I quickly pulled a wad of tissues from the box on my desk and blotted my mouth.

She knocked softly and came in. I hadn't been expecting her and asked her why she was here. "I'm taking you to lunch," she replied. "God, it stinks in here!" she said, thrusting her tongue out all the way in an exaggerated gesture of disgust. I still didn't know why she had picked this day to come get me for lunch, but I was happy to see her. Maybe after all these years, we had some kind of telepathy between us; whatever it was, she had come when I needed her, and that was all that mattered. "What were they doing here?" she asked, taking stock of my sickly pallor. "And what happened to you?" she asked. She leaned over, took in the garbage can, and crinkled her nose.

"I just got interrogated again," I said, and poured some water from a new bottle onto another wad of tissues. I pressed it against my forehead and around my mouth, hoping to bring myself back to life.

"You've got to stop puking every time you see him." She picked up the garbage can and handed it to me, smiling as she came to a conclusion. With Max, you can practically see the lightbulb go off over her head, signaling some kind of epiphany. "You've got a crush on the detective," she sang.

I was queasy and short of temper. "I don't puke every time I see him. I puke every time my name comes up in connection with a murder case." I didn't feel the need to dignify the crush remark; I was a mature woman who didn't get crushes on men I had just met, especially those who thought I could murder a coed and stick her in the trunk of my car. I took the garbage can and left the office, going into the coed bathroom three doors down. I cleaned out the garbage can, sprayed it with the Lysol in the medicine cabinet above the sink, and dried it with a clump of paper towels. I rinsed my mouth out a few dozen times. When I returned to my office, Max was sitting in one of the chairs across from the desk, her feet on the edge of my desk, picking at one of her cuticles. I closed the door and sat down, a few tears spilling onto the front of my dress.

"Oh, come on," she said, rolling her eyes. She hated crying. "What's the matter?"

"Max, I'm a suspect in a murder case!" I said, now into full-blown hysteria, my nose running. "They think I have something to do with this. What am I going to do?"

"Now, why would you be a suspect?" she asked. She got up and patted my shoulder awkwardly.

I rolled my eyes. "I don't know . . . maybe it's the dead girl they found in my car," I said, stating what I thought was obvious.

"If they pay attention at all, they'll figure out that you had nothing to do with this. You're guilty of nothing more than driving a shitty car that was easy to steal."

"Do you think it has something to do with Mob business?" I asked, innocently. Although I had nothing to go on besides the fact that it was rumored that Peter owned a strip club in addition to a couple of race-horses, the Capelli-Miceli union had the stink of Mafia around it.

Max snorted. "Mob business?" She laughed. "You watch too much cable." She sat down again, her comforting skills having no effect on me. "Didn't you tell me that she had a crazy boyfriend? My money's on him."

I thought for a moment. She had a point. Although I didn't know Vince very well, I had heard things around campus. Possessive. Jealous. Druggy. Except for the druggy part, those adjectives described me when I was married to Ray. Kathy had seemed young, naïve, and scared a lot of the time, but that was just my perception, and I really didn't have anything to back up that feeling. If I saw a movie of myself during the time I had been married, I probably looked the same way most of the time.

"I don't even know if the police are looking at him. I could be their only suspect," I said. I put my head into my hands. "Why would I kill her? And why would I dump her in my car? I know I'm not a criminal mastermind, but you'd think the police would give me some credit for being intelligent."

Max continued chewing on her cuticle, deep in thought. "You didn't kill her, did you?"

"No!" I screamed. "Jesus, Max!"

She put her hands up. "I had to ask." She went back to thinking, and I saw her eyes widen. "Vince goes to Joliet, right?" Joliet was a school about twenty blocks or so down the avenue and our two schools had a cooperative agreement. Students could take classes at either place, depending on the course and department schedules. "Can you get into the admissions records on your computer?"

I looked at her. "I don't know. I've never tried." My eyes narrowed. "What are you getting at?"

"We need to find out where Vince lives."

"OK," I said slowly. "Why?"

"So we can look around his room." She stood up. "Who knows what we'll find? Maybe he's so stupid that he kept your keys after he stole your car."

"You're really convinced it was Vince?"

She nodded. "Yep. If he's as much of a psycho as everyone says he is, then it's definitely possible that he killed his girl-friend, stole your car, and dumped the body."

"Who's been watching too much cable?" I asked. There were moments when I sus-pected that Max might spend a little too much time in the fantasy world of cable television. "I hope you can line up Jane Sey-

64

mour to play me in the cable movie version of *A Murder on Campus: Love, Lies, and Deceit.* I've always liked her."

"Well, that scenario is a little better than crazy college professor loses her shit and goes on a killing rampage, dumping bodies in her shitty car."

"Stop calling my car 'shitty.' "

She ignored me. "Think about it. Crazy boyfriend, cheating . . ." She stopped when I protested and then repeated the word emphatically so that I would follow her train of thought. ". . . *cheating* girlfriend, crime of passion, unpremeditated murder." She threw up her hands. "Voilà! Case closed."

I tried to keep the sarcasm out of my voice, but couldn't. "You should have been here when the police were here, Max. You could have solved the whole thing and saved the New York City Police Department a tremendous number of man-hours."

"It's the only thing that makes sense to me."

"Why would you think that she was cheating?"

"What else would make a guy like that snap?" she asked.

I shrugged. "I honestly don't know. Just about anything, I guess." My husband had cheated on me, and I hadn't gone off the deep end. Maybe Vince wasn't as evolved as I liked to think I was. Or rational. Or as much of a dullard when it came to one's loved one cheating. I thought for a moment. The police seemed to be spending an awful lot of time on me; did they even consider Vince a suspect? As harebrained as it sounded, maybe Max was onto something. It was definitely a stretch. But Vince was sure to be at the cemetery and get-together after the funeral for a few hours so we had a window of opportunity. "I have a friend at Joliet who works in the housing office." I picked up the phone and called Diane Berlinger. She picked up after the second ring. "Diane? Alison Bergeron."

"Alison? Hi!" she said, happy to hear from me.

We chatted for a few minutes and then I got to my question. "Diane, let me ask you something. Do sophomores at Joliet still live in La Salle Hall?"

"Yes. Why?"

I hadn't expected that she would want to know why, so I came up with a lie on the spot. I sounded contrite. "I'm way behind on grading and I've got a few research papers to deliver. I've got a couple of Joliet sophomores in my creative writing class and

I'd like to hand-deliver their papers. I'm on my way to the City and thought I'd stop by and stick them in their mailboxes."

Max looked at me and stuck her finger down her throat in mock disgust. I was a terrible liar, and she knew it; fortunately, Diane couldn't see my face turn scarlet as I concocted this untruth.

"Wow, that's really nice of you, Alison. I don't think any of the professors here would be so considerate," she said, making me feel even worse. "Yes, any sophomore who is a resident will be in that hall. Males are on one and two and females are on four, five, and six. A group of displaced juniors are on three." She paused for a moment. "I can look up the names of the sophomores you need if you want to save some time."

I hesitated a moment. I didn't have any Joliet sophomores in my creative writing class, so I would have to come up with other names besides Vince's on the spot. But getting his room number would save a lot of time in the long run. "Well," I said, "I've got Vince Paccione . . ."

I heard her punch some keys on her computer keyboard. "One twelve." She paused for a moment. "Didn't he date that poor girl from St. Thomas who was murdered?"

I noisily rifled through some papers on my desk, ignoring her question. "And . . ." I called out to an imaginary student at my door. "Be right there!" I returned to Diane. "Oh, Diane, I've got a student. Gotta run. I'll find the others when I get there. Thanks so much for your help!" She was still talking as I hung up the phone.

Max looked at me. "That was pathetic."

"Thanks." I stood up. "So what now?"

"Now, we break in."

We left my office through the back door and went to Max's car, which was parked in the lot at Regis Hall, right behind my building. I had no idea how we were going to get into Vince's room, but I was determined to find something that would either implicate Vince or exonerate me. Max drove down the avenue, cutting through the posh neighborhood that separated the two campuses. She drove to the back of La Salle Hall and parked her car next to a Dumpster, illegally.

We got out of the car, and she hit the button on the key tag that chirped, flashed the lights, and locked the doors, all at the same time. Max stared at the back of the building. "One twelve, right?" she asked.

I nodded. We walked up and looked in the window closest to us. Each room had two sets of double-hung windows that faced the back parking lot. Max said that she had dated a guy in La Salle when we were in school and his room was the first one to the right — 102. She counted down the windows until she pointed at what she thought was one twelve.

"How did you remember that?" I asked.

"I climbed in and out of that window a hundred times." She stood with her hand on her hip. "Back in the day, they didn't allow visitation after nine. Remember?"

I didn't. I didn't date a lot in college, and the guys that I did date always dropped me off before visitation ended. Rule-following nerds seek out other rule-following nerds; it's one of life's sure bets. Too bad I hadn't stuck to that in choosing a husband.

"Go inside and wait for me." I didn't move fast enough for her. "Go!" she said, and pointed to the door.

I was getting cold feet. I stood rooted to the pavement until she gave me a push. I went in through the back door and looked down the hallway, first to the right and then to the left. I didn't see anyone, so I made a left and tiptoed in my heels down the hallway. I stopped in front of 112 and waited. I didn't know what Max had in mind, but I did as I was told.

The hallway had the smell of stale beer,

Doritos, and feet. I stared at the cinder-block wall in front of me and prayed that nobody would come down the hallway. I was so paralyzed by fear that I didn't even have the ability to produce sweat.

I heard Max's entrance. She came through the back window, rolled over onto something, cursed like a sailor, and landed on the floor. A few seconds later, she opened the door. She studied the bulletin board to my left. "Hey, Rufus Wainright is playing here next Saturday," she said. "Do you want to go?"

I looked around nervously, and hissed, "Focus!"

"Get in here," she said, and grabbed me by the collar, dragging me into the room.

Vince's room, like every room in this dorm, was a double. Beds were on opposite walls, with built-in shelves above them. At the top end of each bed was a desk pushed against each wall and to the side of each window. The screen of the left window was open: Max's mode of entry. At the bottom of each bed was a closet. Max looked at me, and mouthed, "Vince?" as she pointed to the bed on the left. The bed was covered with a chenille bedspread and had two pillows.

I shrugged and went to the desk. A day

planner lay open and I turned to the first page. Vince had scrawled his name in the front of it, along with his Staten Island address. I looked over at Max and nodded. I flipped to the day when my car was stolen, but Vince didn't have any entries for that day or any of the days that followed. Unfortunately, it didn't say anything like "kill Kathy, steal professor's car," or anything to that effect. Either Vince didn't see the advantages of using a planner, or he led a very empty life. Or both.

Max picked up Vince's mattress and looked underneath it. "See anything?" I asked.

She dropped the mattress and shook her head. She went into the closet, burrowing in like a pack rat. I could see her rear end and feet and nothing else. She tossed the closet in no time flat and came out. "Nothing."

I looked at the articles on the desk: a picture of Vince's family, his books, a bong, and his car keys. Not a thing that would link him to the murder or let me off the hook. I opened the top drawer gingerly and found a mess of papers, pens, pencils, and other detritus, but again, nothing incriminating.

I heard voices in the hall. I froze in place

and looked at her, wild-eyed. She was by the closet, standing still and holding her breath. We stood looking at each other until the voices got softer and whoever it was moved down the hall.

"Let's go!" I whispered as loudly as I could. I was definitely going to confession — or jail — when this escapade was over.

She looked at me and pointed at the window. I jumped up onto Vince's desk and threw myself out the window and onto the pavement, rolling a few inches, ripping a huge hole in my panty hose, and scraping the hell out of my shin. Max, better prepared for the break-in than I, in black pants and black-cotton turtleneck, hoisted herself out and perched on the sill. She put both hands on either side of her feet, deftly jumped onto the pavement like a gymnast, not a hair out of place, and landed flat on her feet, high heels and all. She pulled the screen down, and we made a run for the car.

We got in and looked around. There was nobody in the back parking lot or coming down the path from the gym. When we got in the car, I smacked Max's arm. "I can't believe I let you talk me into that!" I muttered through clenched teeth.

"Oh, calm down," she said, and started

the car. "Nobody saw us." She pulled a wide U-turn in the parking lot and headed off the campus.

"Not that we know of," I said, looking out the window. I pulled a hand across my sweaty forehead. "Jesus."

"Yes, Jesus saw us," she said in a patronizing tone, and made a left.

I started to reply but couldn't come up with an appropriate response and gave up. I breathed deeply and put my head on the headrest. "Nothing there," I said, disappointed. "Max, what am I going to do?" I asked, feeling tears well up in my eyes again.

She shrugged. "Don't know." She started the car. "Hey, you want to get some wings and a pitcher at Maloney's?" she asked.

I looked at her, incredulous. With Max, there's always time for food. When we were in college, Maloney's was our place of choice — two dozen wings and a pitcher of draft beer for $3.50 on a Friday afternoon. I still visited Maloney's occasionally with Father Kevin. After fifteen years, the price of a pitcher and a dozen wings had gone up to $6.50.

I *was* kind of hungry. "Sure."

She pointed the car toward Broadway and found a parking spot a few doors north of the bar. She eased the car into a very tight spot, parallel parking like a pro. The el rumbled above us as a train headed away from this final destination in the Bronx toward Manhattan. We got out and headed south on Broadway to the bar.

It was just after lunchtime, and the bar was empty, except for the ancient bartender, Sully, and one older man at the end. They were discussing the ever-controversial topic of the designated hitter. The bar was dark, dank, and smelly, but comfortably familiar. Sully looked up when he saw me; he had been bartending at Maloney's since Max and I were in school. "Hey, Doc," he said, wiping the bar down with a dingy, yellowed rag that was probably dirtier than the bar he was cleaning.

"Hi, Sully," I said, and went over to the bar. I leaned in and gave him a kiss. "How's things?" I asked. "Do you remember Max?"

He looked at her. "Sure, I do. Max Barfly?" he asked, breaking into a toothy grin. He had given her that nickname in our freshman year and it stuck.

She snickered. "That's me."

"The kids don't drink kamikazes anymore," he said, sadly. Max had been the kamikaze shot queen for three years running; a bout with mono in senior year forced her to give up her crown. He balled the rag up and threw it into the sink behind the bar. "What can I get you ladies?"

"Two dozen and a pitcher," Max said. She turned to me. "What do you want?" She laughed; this was something I had heard a hundred times while we were in school. "Just kidding."

I led her to one of the wooden booths across from the bar. I sat and stuck my right leg out to the side to examine the damage from my roll on the pavement; my stockings were torn, and I had a nice bloody scrape on my shin. "I didn't stick my landing like you did," I explained as I got up to go the bathroom and wash up in the dark, dank, and smelly bathroom (Maloney's had found a decorating motif and was sticking to it). I pulled off my panty hose, stepping out of one shoe and then the other as I extricated myself from my hose. I didn't want to put even one bare toe on the bathroom floor; I had been to this bar enough times to know what went on in the bathroom and how infrequently the floor was mopped (never). I tossed my stockings into the garbage can and took some paper towels from the dispenser, wet them, and pressed them against the scrape on my leg, sopping up as much of the blood as possible and trying to get the area relatively clean. I ran the water in the sink and washed my face. When I was done, I emerged, cleaner and a little calmer than when I had entered.

Max was hunched over a big plate of wings when I returned and a pitcher of beer sat in front of her. She had poured each of us some beer into the plastic cups that Sully provided. Her mouth was ringed in orange wing sauce, and she had her sleeves rolled up almost to her shoulders. She took a swig of beer and left an orange imprint around the side of the cup. "So good," she murmured, as she tossed some bones onto the wing platter.

"Nice," I said, and picked up her bones with a napkin, creating a new burial ground for her discards. "Don't you remember anything? You don't mix old bones with new wings."

I picked up a wing and nibbled at it, not having as much of an appetite as I originally thought. I put the wing down and pushed my beer away. I'm not a big beer drinker; when Father Kevin and I come for wings, Sully always makes me an Absolut martini from a private vodka stash that he keeps in a locked cabinet under the bar. "So what do you think I should do now?" I asked her.

She picked up a napkin and wiped her hands as much as she could; the paper ripped off and stuck to her fingers. "Keep thinking. I think the fact that your car was involved in this was random. But maybe not. Why would someone steal your car?" she asked.

"Because they could?"

"Probably." She drank her beer and refilled her glass from the pitcher. "Shitty cars are easy to steal," she said, looking at me for my reaction, which was to reach over the table and playfully smack her cheek. "I'm kidding!" She returned to the wings, pointing one at me as she spoke. "I hope the police figure this out, because I certainly can't. And I'm pretty good at this stuff."

I didn't know what made her "good at this stuff," but I didn't argue. We ate and drank in silence, Max polishing off twenty wings to my four. She drank the rest of the pitcher and proudly belched. "Let me wash up before I go back to work," she said.

While she was gone, I cleaned up the table, putting the chicken bones and discarded napkins onto the platter. My mind was racing with the thought that I was actually a suspect in a murder case and that I had just broken into someone's dorm room. But I had to figure out a way to show the police that I didn't have anything to do with this. Waiting around and hoping that they would come to that conclusion on their own wasn't enough for me.

Max came out of the bathroom, clean, full, and ready to go. She picked up her purse from the bench of the booth and riffled around in her wallet. She pulled out two twenties and tossed them on the table. "Thanks, Sully," she said. Sully was deep in conversation with the man at the end of the bar, the two still on opposite sides of the designated hitter debate. He gave us a quick wave as we departed.

Outside in the street, squinting at the glare, it took me a few minutes to make out the shape of Detective Crawford leaning nonchalantly against Max's car, his arms crossed and his eyes focused on something north up Broadway. I threw an elbow into Max's side, and, as her eyes adjusted, she stiffened.

Crawford turned and looked at us. "Ladies."

"It's Detective Hot Pants," Max muttered under her breath, and froze on the spot. I knew what she was thinking: we were in big-ass trouble. I struggled to stay calm as I mentally considered myself in handcuffs and leg irons. Crawford eased himself off the car and ambled toward us, stopping just a few feet from where we stood.

We stood like statues for a few more seconds before Max said, "Gotta go," and went into a full sprint down the street, her legs pumping in her high heels. I was starting to think she could do just about anything in stilettos. She pulled her car keys out of her pocketbook as she was running and got into the driver's side of the car. She was out of the parking space almost before Crawford realized what she was doing; he turned and watched her maneuver out of the spot and speed down Broadway, through a yellow light, and out of sight.

I stood there, under the el, listening to the trains come and go, weighing my options. Turn around and go the other way? Go back into Maloney's? Hail a gypsy cab? Die right on the spot? There was too much to choose from and not enough time to make a decision.

Crawford was in front of me before I could do anything. He smiled slightly: "good" cop in a bad mood. "Hello, Dr. Bergeron. Long time, no see."

"Detective." I didn't think a neon sign with the words "I'm guilty" was flashing from my forehead, but it was pretty damn close. I tried to hold his gaze but cast my eyes down.

"What are you doing over here?" he asked.

I held up my fingers, which were still slightly orange from the wings, despite my best efforts with the Handi Wipes. "Eating wings," I said.

"They don't have wings up by you?" he asked, "up by you" implying that my school was so far away from Joliet. Twenty city blocks equals a mile.

I shook my head. "Not like Maloney's."

"Should I try them?" he asked.

"If you like wings, then yes." I looked around. "Where's Detective Wyatt?"

"He went to the cemetery," he said. He pulled on his tie. In my heels, we were closer in height, but he still had a good four inches on me. I had ice in my veins as it dawned on me that he had probably followed us and seen us break into Vince's dorm room. I imagined their conversation, Wyatt saying, "I'm going to the cemetery. You stick to the professor like glue." And Crawford responding, "I'll see if she does anything hinky." Or something like that. That's the way cops talk on TV.

"Anything you want to tell me?" he asked. He stared down at me, his green eyes boring into mine. This guy was good; I was about to wet my pants.

I shook my head; I guess he wanted to know about the "hinky" stuff, but I wasn't prepared to share. "I don't think so," I said.

The el rumbled above us and he looked up. "Can I give you a tip, Dr. Bergeron?"

I looked down at my shoes. "Put a five on Long Legs in the fifth at Yonkers Raceway?"

He didn't smile at what I thought was a pretty funny joke. "Breaking and entering carries a minimum five- to ten-year jail sentence, and that's if nothing was taken. And the definition of breaking and entering includes lifting up screens and going into dorm rooms." His face turned hard. "Don't ever do anything like that again."

Tears sprang to my eyes, but I kept silent.

He took me by the elbow. "Now, where is it you'd like to go?" he asked, steering me toward his brown Crown Victoria sedan, which was parked right behind the space where Max's car had been.

I managed to get out, "Train station." I waited for him to push my head down into the car like I had seen the cops do to "perps" on TV, but he just opened the door and waited for me to get in. I looked out the window and clutched my purse to my stomach. If there was a cranky cop smell, this car had it. He got into the driver's side and sighed, saying, "Put your seat belt on," rather crankily. Now I knew where the smell came from.

He refused to pull away from the curb until I did so, so I obliged. We drove to the train station in silence, me looking out the window and blinking back tears and him breathing heavily in exasperation. When we arrived at the station, he pulled the car over and threw it into PARK. He turned to me, his face and tone softer. "Please stop crying," he said, and pulled a clean, folded handkerchief out of the inside pocket of his blazer.

I took it and blew my nose, then tried to hand it back to him. "I don't want it back," he said, giving me a slight smile.

"Thanks," I said, and put it into my purse.

He leaned down and looked at my leg. "Make sure you put some antiseptic on that when you get home. And keep it covered."

"Thanks," I said again.

He put his left arm over the steering wheel and turned his body to face me. "Listen. If you think we should be exploring any other angles, just call me and talk to me about it. Don't take matters into your own hands."

I nodded.

"Don't you think it occurred to us to look at Vince as a suspect? And at his dorm room? We've been all over that place," he said.

"So, why does he still have a bong in

there?" I asked, regretting asking that as soon as it was out of my mouth.

He chuckled. "Must be a replacement bong. All the other stuff was bagged as evidence."

I cried some more.

"Would you please stop crying?" he asked again, running his hand over his face. "Do you want me to drive you home?"

I shook my head. "No, thank you." I undid the seat belt. "Thanks for the ride." I got out of the car and tiptoed across the gravel parking lot to the platform, not looking back. I sat on a bench facing the river and cried some more, using his handkerchief to blow my nose again and wipe my eyes. The train arrived five minutes later; I stood and waited for it to stop, turning around to look back at the parking lot.

Crawford was still there, in the car, watching me as I got on the train.

Six

I woke up at six-thirty the next morning to the sound of a car idling in front of my house. I got up and looked out the window, but didn't see anyone. At that point, I was fully awake, so despite the early hour, I decided to stay up.

After a quick shower, I got dressed and went downstairs to make coffee. I opened the refrigerator to find that not only did I not have any coffee but also that the milk in the container was ten days past its sell-by date and now a solid rather than a liquid. Plan B was put into effect as I left the house and began my walk into the village to Starbucks.

I was still upset about the events of the previous day — especially the scolding from Crawford. Nothing like a good dorm break-in to make you seem really guilty.

I was also upset that I seemed to be falling apart. I had always thought of myself as a relatively strong person: I had weathered the deaths of both my parents before I was thirty, endured a marriage to a man who humiliated me with his actions at least once a year, put myself through graduate school while working full-time, and gotten a doctorate in the shortest amount of time possible. Now, I was involved in something totally out of my realm of experience, and the thought of it made me sick and more than a little crazed.

The weather was beautiful: bright, sunny, and clear, and in direct contrast to my mood: dark, cloudy, and complicated. I was furious at Max for leaving me on Broadway, and I was mad at myself for allowing her to convince me to do something I knew wasn't right. Kathy's death also weighed heavily on my mind. Parents sent their children to our school thinking they would be safe: a Catholic institution, a long tradition of graduating strong, independent women (and a few men), and a peaceful setting all contributed to a feeling of safety and well-being. An occasional stolen car was all we normally had to deal with. Now, we had murder to add to the list of things people thought about when they conjured up St. Thomas.

I made a left and headed up the hill in the village to Starbucks. At a little after seven in the morning on a Saturday, it was open, but not crowded. I went up to the counter and ordered a grande French roast — black, no sugar — and a banana muffin. I paid and took a seat at a small round table near the back of the cafe.

I could feel myself coming dangerously close to sliding under a wave of self-pity as I watched couples come and go in the coffee shop. It also occurred to me as I sat there that probably none of the patrons were murder suspects. So, there I was, a divorced, carless murder suspect, eating alone in Starbucks. It doesn't get much sadder than that. Unless you're a nineteen-year-old dead girl in a Volvo casket, I reminded myself.

I shoved the remainder of the muffin in my mouth and washed it down with the dregs from my coffee cup. I crumpled everything into a little ball and shoved it into the metal garbage can by the door. A young man with a skateboard under his arm started in, saw me, and held the door open. "Why don't you go first, ma'am?" he asked politely.

Ma'am. Thanks. I managed a smile and walked out onto the sidewalk, stopping for a moment to adjust my pocketbook on my shoulder. I started down the street, taking in the river, the boats swaying gently on the small waves right beyond the train station, and the sun's rays dancing across the river's surface. I made a conscious decision to remain very angry at Max but to stop feeling sorry for myself. Being angry at Max would at least burn a few calories, but feeling sorry at myself would force me to eat the entire box of Godiva chocolate that I had in the refrigerator.

Max picked me up at ten for our day of shopping at the Westchester, a mall near my house. We got there at ten-thirty, found a spot near the elevator, and were cruising the carpeted floors of the mall in no time.

I was still feeling a little icy toward Max, but she didn't notice. She was too involved in spending more money than the gross national product of some smaller nations.

We spent an hour or so stocking up on cosmetics and hair accessories at Sephora, the large cosmetics retailer on the bottom floor. Max's hair was only a few inches long, but she bought some jeweled barrettes and some kind of turban that she said was essential to making home facials successful. I wandered around the bath aisle, finally picking up some kind of shower gel that promised, "serenity, sensuality, and a feeling of well-being." Whatever. It smelled like coconut. I also picked a lipstick called Jennifer, which was a muted peachy brown and not nearly dramatic enough for Max who stuck her tongue out in disgust when I showed it to her.

I finally let Max know how furious I was when we sat down to lunch at the City Limits Diner, located at the east end of the mall.

"I thought I would give you some 'alone' time," she said, making those stupid finger quotes, and with the misguided conviction that what she had done was justified and, actually, considerate. "I assumed he was there to ask you out." She slid into the booth and tossed her snakeskin purse and multiple shopping bags onto the seat next to her.

"Then why did you run?" I asked.

She picked up her menu and looked at it for a moment before shutting it, ignoring my question entirely. "He's very cute."

I slammed my menu shut, content with ordering the same item I ordered every time I came to the diner: curried egg salad on seven-grain bread, a chocolate egg cream, and a plate of fries. "He's not going to ask me out, Max," I clarified. "But he might put me in jail." I pulled a napkin out of the holder and wiped it across my upper lip. *"I am a suspect in a murder case."* I spoke slowly and clearly so that she couldn't mistake what I was saying for, "I'm in love with Detective Crawford," or whatever else she might possibly hear in the alternate universe in which she lived.

She raised an eyebrow at me.

"That's just what I think. They've never said anything to that effect."

"You're probably right. Cops wouldn't show up at your office twice unless you were on their most-wanted list." She looked around. "I wish I was on the other one's most-wanted list," she muttered, opening her menu again. "Hey, I'm thinking about a new show," she said, after making a new lunch decision. "It's called *Detectives* and in it we follow around two hot New York City detectives as they investigate murders. What do you think?" she asked.

I've known Max long enough to know that her ditsy façade is just that — a façade. She is one of the smartest people I know and good at what she does; she hadn't earned the title of "Queen of Reality TV" for nothing.

"Not funny, Max," I said. "You could always do *Murder 101* and follow me as I end up on death row."

The waiter arrived and we placed our

order: me, the usual, and Max, a medium cheddar burger with fries and a chocolate shake. She looked at me, and said, "I didn't have breakfast," as a way of explaining her large order. She's one of those people who eats to excess and remains a size four; if I hadn't witnessed her hedonism over the last twenty years, I wouldn't have believed it myself. But she ate and drank to excess five out of seven nights, never exercised, and still looked amazing.

"Who does the strip search if you go to jail?" she asked, only half-joking. "The cute one or my new boyfriend?"

I rolled my eyes. "This is serious, Max. What if I am their only suspect?" I looked around to see who was sitting in our general vicinity, but didn't spot any suspicious-looking private eyes hiding behind menus or large policemen lurking.

The waiter appeared with the drinks, and Max put her straw into the giant thick shake and took a long sip. She licked her upper lip with her tongue. "Look at it this way. If you are a suspect, you'll get to see Detective Hot Pants on a regular basis." She let out a laugh, obviously amused with herself.

I wasn't feeling so lighthearted. I looked around the restaurant, feeling vulnerable, exposed, and a bit sad. Max was like Teflon

— everything slid off her. She didn't seem affected by anything and found humor in almost everything. And right now, she wasn't even sensitive enough to shut her trap and notice that I was scared. I decided not to make an issue of it and dropped the subject entirely. "What are you doing tonight?" I asked.

"Sleeping over at your house," she stated, surprising me. When she saw my reaction, she explained herself. "We haven't had a sleepover in a while, so I figured we could do that tonight. Let's go to the video store and get some porn. Maybe something with 'Detective Hot Pants' in the title?" She reached across and held my hand for a split second.

I guess she wasn't as dense as I thought. She had been right there with me, all the time.

We drove home after lunch. Max told me that she had her laptop with her and wanted to check e-mail and do some work. It had been a long week; I was going to curl up in bed with the Harry Potter book that I had bought a few months earlier but hadn't had time to read. I knew I should look through my briefcase and unearth the term papers that I had to read, but I was tired and drained. An afternoon in my bed, under the covers, was just what I needed.

Max pulled up the full length of the driveway and parked right in front of the garage, a detached, barnlike structure that housed everything but my car, when I actually owned one. She popped the trunk from inside the car and got out to retrieve her packages and her computer. Based on years of experience, I knew that we would be having a fashion show later when she modeled all of her new purchases.

She went across the backyard and turned back to me. "You left the back door open." She opened the door and went inside, stopping right inside the threshold.

I wasn't paying much attention to her. My attention was taken up by a brand-new, black Mercedes parked in front of my house, shiny, sleek, and with tinted windows that made it impossible to see inside. I was distracted and didn't notice Max standing, statuelike, inside the kitchen. I walked straight into her, pushing her ahead a bit until she was up against the counter.

Peter Miceli was sitting at the kitchen table, staring at both of us, his eyes red and tired-looking. His hands were folded in front of him on the table.

I was stunned, but not too stunned to speak. "How did you get in here?"

He stood when he heard my voice. He was wearing a golf shirt, golf cleats, and yellow pants — perfect for a day on the links — but not the kind of outfit you wear when you break into someone's house. I couldn't imagine what kind of man played golf the day after burying his daughter, but I also couldn't imagine the kind of man who allegedly had access to so much cement that he could bury people at the bottom of rivers. "Alison. I'm sorry. I wanted to talk with you but didn't think we would be able to arrange a meeting."

A meeting. With Peter Miceli. Yes, that would be hard to arrange. Especially after I had put myself voluntarily in the witness protection program. I didn't say anything.

Max broke the silence. "I'm going to go check my e-mail. Peter, I'm sorry for your loss. It is so nice to see you after all these years," she said, her voice cracking slightly. She tiptoed out of the kitchen and up the stairs to my bedroom.

I stared at Peter. I hadn't been afraid of Peter in college — he was a chubby business major with a hot car and a hot girlfriend, but no game — but I was afraid of him now. He certainly was always charming and nice to me. Now, it appeared, he was also very successful. I had heard rumors about his businesses — the ones that were legitimate and that didn't include racehorses and strip clubs — but I wasn't sure if there was any truth to them; after all, he had married Gianna Capelli, she of the Capelli crime family, and it may have just been a case of "guilt by association." I wasn't sure. I didn't think he was here to hurt me, but breaking into my house could never be considered a good thing. I cleared my throat. "What do you want, Peter?"

He hooked a thumb in the space that Max had just occupied. "Do I know her?"

"That's Max Rayfield. We went to St. Thomas with Gianna."

He thought for a moment. "Max Rayfield . . . oh, yeah . . . crazy girl. Liked to drink kamikazes and dance on the bar at Maloney's." He drummed his fingers on the table. "She a dancer now?"

I shook my head.

"Too bad." He looked up at the ceiling, apparently imagining Max working at The Pleasure Cave or a place like that.

"She your girlfriend?"

"Only in the most platonic sense."

He looked disappointed again.

He motioned to the chair across from him at the kitchen table like he, not I, lived there. I pulled the chair out and sat down.

He spread his hands out on the table and let out a choked sob. "I'm sorry, Alison." He pulled a big square of cotton out of his pocket and blew his nose noisily. "This has been very hard for us."

"I can imagine," I said.

Tears poured from his eyes, and he shuddered. "I'm going to find who did this," he said, his teeth clenched.

I had no doubt that that was the case. Then it occurred to me that perhaps he thought I was the one "who did this." I felt all the blood in my veins drain and my skin go icy.

He saw my reaction and quickly amended. "I don't think you had anything to do with this, Alison. You wouldn't hurt a fly. Kathy always told us how nice you were to her. I'll always remember that." He sniffled loudly. He pointed a short, stubby finger at me. "I owe you," he said, dramatically.

I really wasn't in the market for possible Mob favors, but if Ray continued to act like an asshole and didn't get his crap out of my guest room, knowing that I could make him disappear was mildly comforting.

"How's Gianna?" I asked.

He shook his head sadly. "Not good. She'll feel better when we find out who did this."

I repeated my question. "Peter, what do

you want?"

He cried some more. He finally shook his head. "I'm not sure." He stood. "I guess I just wanted to see if you knew anything."

"I don't know a thing, Peter." I stood, too. "Leave it to the police, Peter. They'll handle this."

He leaned on the table and let out another heart-wrenching sob. I felt a tremendous amount of pity for him, despite the suspicions I had about him. He was still a father, and he loved his daughter. "She was a good girl . . ." he said, trailing off.

Peter stood suddenly and grabbed me in a bear hug — he was a few inches shorter than me, but barrel-chested and powerfully built — and squeezed me. The air was pushed out of my lungs as I was pressed against his prodigious belly. After a hug that went on longer than it should have, he finally let go and kissed me on the forehead. He grabbed my face in his fat hands and looked into my eyes. I stared back at him until he broke my gaze and walked out of the kitchen and into my backyard. A few seconds later, I heard the Mercedes start and pull away from the front of my house.

I resisted the urge to vomit and instead went for the always popular dead faint.

SEVEN

You would think that if I were going to have a somewhat erotic, somewhat sexy dream, I would be wearing something better than black Dansko clogs and a raincoat. In my dream, in my clogs, black pants, white shirt, and Lands' End raincoat I looked like a cross between a Swedish chef and a Westchester soccer mom. It had been so long since I had had sex, I couldn't even have a sexy dream without wearing sensible shoes.

In my dream, it was a few days after the funeral and the day that I had talked with the detectives. I left school and began the half-mile trek to the train station at around dusk. With their rubber soles, my clogs didn't make noise on the wet street. I realized that I was clad all in black — not a good idea for walking along a dark street on a rainy night. I shifted my leather briefcase from one shoulder to the other, cursing myself for deciding to read all of my students' Shakespeare research papers that night. The bag weighed heavily on my shoulder so I pulled the strap diagonally across my chest, hoping to redistribute the weight.

I heard a car driving slowly behind me, the lights shining on my back. The car pulled up alongside me, and I stopped in my tracks. The passenger-side door opened and two muscular arms pulled me into the front seat. I noticed the glint of a badge as the driver planted a deep, slow kiss on my mouth . . .

The train's brakes squealed a loud welcome as we pulled into the station. The conductor brushed past me, knocking my briefcase off my lap and waking me up just in time. He screamed out the name of my stop. I sat up with a jolt and tried to grab the front of my briefcase before it hit the wet floor of the train car; a stray paper floated out and I snatched it from the gray puddle of muck in front of me in which it had landed. I read the name on top: Fiona Martin. Fiona would get a good grade just by virtue of the fact that I wouldn't be able to read half of the drivel she wrote in the paper. The train stopped, and I lurched up from my seat and out the door onto the platform, not sure where I was, what had happened, or why my face was blazing hot.

I sat on a bench to compose myself. I put Fiona's paper back into my briefcase and rearranged everything else: my umbrella, my wallet, my keys, and my cell phone. I watched the train pull slowly out of the station. The river on the other side of the platform was calm and black, with a few large raindrops forming dimples on the wedge of water that was illuminated by the station's bright lights. My hair was damp from the rain, so I pulled the hood of my raincoat up over my head and prepared to leave the station, concentrating on putting one foot in front of the other and leaving dream analysis to another time.

The only road out of the station went straight up. The first few days of my walk were horrendous as I adjusted to the length and pitch of the road. Now, after two weeks of walking, I was getting used to the steep slope and wasn't even winded when I reached the top. I guess that was what was called "getting into shape." I still felt like I needed a cigarette when I reached the top, just as a reward, but I had given up that nasty habit the year I had graduated from St. Thomas. I reached the top of the hill and looked at my watch: ten to seven. The deli at the end of my street would be open for another ten minutes, and I needed dinner. I started running down Broadway and reached the door three minutes later.

Tony, the owner, and probably my future husband with the way things were going, was unplugging the meat slicer as I walked in, the bell on the door jangling and announcing my presence.

"Mi amore!" Tony cried, so happy to see me that if he wasn't so kind, I would be scared. "You just made it! I'm closing in two minutes."

"Hi, Tony," I said, and took my hood off. I set my briefcase on the counter, opened it, and reached in for my wallet. "Can you make me a sandwich?"

"The usual?" he asked, as he got out two slices of rye bread, chicken salad, and began assembling a sandwich for me.

"Sure," I said. Man, I have a usual. And a sixty-five-year-old, widowed, Italian boyfriend who knows what the usual is. But the sad fact was that Tony was more considerate of me and clearly more trustworthy than my ex-husband.

I looked around. A big bag of potato chips, probably enough for a party of four, sat on the shelf behind me, just begging to be bought. I put it on the counter. I made my way to the refrigerator and reached in to take out a glass bottle of lemonade when a large can of Foster's Lager caught my eye. The Foster's cans looked like minikegs. For your maximum drinking pleasure, I guess. I had never had a can of Foster's in my life and the only beer that I had had in the last twenty years was the one I gulped down with Max at Maloney's a few days ago. I figured now was the time to be adventurous. I grabbed not one, but two cans, enjoying the feel of their squat roundness in my hands. They were cold and a little wet. I put one of them to my head and then on the counter, along with the potato chips.

Tony brought my sandwich over and eyed the cans suspiciously. "Having company?" he asked, looking slightly jealous. He punched a few numbers into the register.

"Uh . . . no . . . well, maybe," I lied, and took a twenty out of my wallet. Just want to get drunk is more like it. Just me and a bunch of boring papers on *Macbeth;* can't a girl have something to get her through? He loved me so much that I couldn't bring myself to tell him the truth.

He put all of my items in a bag and looked at me sadly. "How are you doing, my friend? Really?"

Tony had gotten the full scoop about my divorce from my cleaning lady, Magda. I loved her, but she had a big mouth. The month I bought an ovulation kit, I swore that I saw one of her Hungarian friends in the juice aisle of the supermarket put some kind of spell on my abdominal area. Fortunately, it was the spell that made you barren when you were married to lying, cheating assholes. "I'm fine, Tony," I said, picking up my bag. "Really." I leaned over and kissed his cheek.

He pretended to swoon. "Anytime you are ready for me, I'm yours!" he called, as the door swung shut and the jangling bells sounded again. I decided that if I ever found myself considering his offer with any seriousness, I would sell my house and move to Canada.

I had lived alone for six months. Even after Ray and I had decided to call it quits, I let him stay on until he got his life in order — finding an apartment, buying a car, paying off the Visa — which was about six months as well. He had slept in my home office, which had a futon, a computer, and a closet. I kept the master bedroom, my master bath and Jacuzzi, and the king-size bed. Seemed only fair.

Even though Ray had moved out six

months ago and I had been living alone since then, I hadn't been divorced until the week before. In my mind, being legally separated and officially divorced were two different things. As long as I was legally separated, I was still married, and therefore, not alone. Officially divorced meant that I was on my own, and, after nine years with one man, it was a little frightening. In my head, the whole thing made perfect sense.

I turned onto my street and walked the last quarter mile to my house. In the air, there was a smell of steak cooking, and my mouth started to water. The chips in my bag were singing a crunchy siren song as they jostled against my hip. I couldn't wait to break them open along with my first giant can of Foster's.

I switched on the kitchen light when I entered, put the bag with my food down on the counter, pulled out a can of beer, and ripped open the bag of chips, shoving a giant handful in my mouth. My briefcase was still crisscross across my chest. I cracked open the beer and took a large swallow, instantly remembering why I never drink beer — it was bitter, sudsy, and made me burp. But a nice, smooth glow was cast over my body, and I sighed, thinking that I could become a beer drinker in my new life as a single thirtysomething. I imagined myself at singles' parties, hoisting beers, a big grin on my face, telling jokes and meeting lots of other single people. Maybe it wouldn't be so bad. As long as I had beer and a few single friends, I could live the life of a Dockers' khaki commercial: good friends, good times, and a few beers. It was not lost on me that all of the people in those commercials were men. What did that mean? I would deal with that fact later, along with my train dream.

I took out the sandwich and opened the paper in which it was wrapped. I still had my raincoat on, but it didn't matter. I was single and alone, eating over my Formica counter, standing up. I could do whatever I wanted. Ray wasn't here to tell me how many calories, triglycerides, nitrates, or general shit was in my food.

I took a huge bite of the sandwich, chicken salad dripping out of the corners of my mouth (note to self: don't buy chicken salad right before Tony closes) when there was a knock at the back door. I had been so engaged in my sandwich that I hadn't noticed a car, headlights blazing, parked right in front of my detached garage. I nearly choked. I looked through the panes of glass in the back door to find Detective

Crawford standing there. The dream from the train came rushing back, and my face went hot with embarrassment. I hastily put a napkin to my lips and tried to push in the too-big bite of sandwich that filled my normally capable-of-huge-bites mouth.

I opened the back door a crack. "Hi?" I asked. I tried to swallow everything at once, unsuccessfully. I chewed quickly and swallowed a few more times, finally emptying my mouth.

He poked his head in, dripping water from the perimeter of the hood of his raincoat. "I'm sorry to bother you, but . . ."

I opened the back door all of the way. "Come in, come in." I stepped back and motioned for him to enter. I stared at him, a little nervous. Maybe he was finally there to arrest me. When he came in and took off his hood and I saw that he was smiling slightly, I felt a little bit better. Since I wasn't in heels this time, he seemed taller than I remembered, towering over me by a good six inches. In spite of being dripping wet (or maybe because of it), he was also quite good-looking. When I was wetting my pants on Broadway after the wing fest, none of this had registered, but judging from my wet dream on the train, my subconscious had been working overtime.

He took his hood off. "I'm sorry to bother you, but I actually have a few more questions. I was just on my way home and thought I would stop by."

I looked around him to see where his partner was. "Nope," he said, "just me." He looked around, taking in the sandwich, the can of Foster's, and the potato chips, which were half-out of the plastic bag. "Sorry to interrupt your dinner."

"It's OK," I said. With my raincoat and hood on, foraging for food on my counter, I must have looked like a giant raccoon dining on garbage. "I really hadn't started."

"Are you feeling all right?" he asked.

"Tonight?"

He glanced around. "No . . . you know, the first time we met . . . I always meant to ask you . . ."

"Oh, you mean that. Yes, I'm fine. I actually hit my head pretty badly, but the concussion symptoms only lasted a few days." I felt a rush of blood go to my face as I remembered his shoes. "Sorry about your shoes." I put the sandwich down, my appetite gone.

"I shouldn't have shown you those pictures." He thrust his hands into his pockets and hunched his shoulders apologetically.

"Let's say we're even."

The silence was awkward and filled the little space that was left in the kitchen. "Hey, you want a Foster's Lager?" I asked with a little too much cheer, thinking that my Dockers' commercial days could start immediately. Big detective, big can of beer . . . wasn't exactly what I had in mind for my new single life, but it was a start. "I have two cans." I held them up to examine them more closely. "Or two minikegs. That would be a more accurate description."

He laughed slightly. "I didn't think anybody actually drank that stuff."

"Well, actually they don't. It just looked good sitting in the deli refrigerator, and I thought I should give it a try."

"No, thanks." He continued to stand in silence.

"You wanted to ask me some questions?" I reminded him.

He shifted from one foot to the other. "Were you committed to eating that sandwich and drinking that beer?"

I was puzzled; was that one of the questions? "Not in any serious kind of way." I figured if the conversation kept going in this direction, we would be at "I know you are but what am I?" in no time.

"Do you want to have dinner?" he asked.

"I could ask you my questions while we're eating."

I thought for a moment. Getting grilled about a murder could be mitigated by eating a big burger. I accepted, knowing exactly where I would take him.

EIGHT

It was a Tuesday night and Sadie's, right in the center of town, wasn't crowded. The hostess gave us a table near the bar but tucked in a corner of the restaurant. She took our wet raincoats and our drink order at the same time.

Crawford motioned to me. "What would you like?"

I thought a moment. "I'll have a vodka martini, straight up, with a twist."

The hostess looked at him. "A glass of cabernet. Thank you."

Cabernet, I thought. I would have pegged him as a draft beer kind of guy. You never know.

He clasped his hands together in the center of the table. "I'm sorry I just showed up out of the blue."

I shrugged, like I was accustomed to homicide detectives in my kitchen every night of the week. "Not a problem. Do you live around here?"

He looked down. "Manhattan."

Hmmm. Depending on where he lived in Manhattan, he was at least forty-five minutes from home. We sat in silence until the hostess reappeared with our drinks. I was relieved when she returned; I could cease examining the painting next to our table like I was an art curator and focus on my martini instead. The uncomfortable silence would be eliminated by the slurping of alcoholic beverages. I made considerable work of preparing my drink for the first sip — swirling the vodka, taking out the twist, twisting it again. I took a drink and tried not to sigh aloud at how good it tasted. "So, what did you want to ask me?" I inquired.

He reached in the pocket of his jacket and took out his notebook. After flipping a few pages, he looked at me. The close proximity allowed me to study his face. Green eyes, angular features, and short, brown, cop hair. One ear stuck out a little bit more than the other. At this late hour, a slight stubble was beginning to appear on his jawline and under his nose, but not enough to make him swarthy. He cleared his throat. "Did you know Kathy Miceli well?"

Hadn't we done this already, like, fourteen times? I guess they didn't take the ginkgo biloba advice. I took a slug of my drink. If I was going to get grilled, I might as well be baked. "Sort of. Her mother was a few years ahead of me in school, but we overlapped at the college for two years. I saw Gianna a few times while Kathy was here, so having that connection made us a little more familiar."

"Did you know her boyfriend?"

"Vince?" I asked, and winced. "A little."

He looked at me questioningly. "What's up with Vince?"

"Vince seems like a jerk." I stopped there. "What kind of jerk?"

I thought about how to phrase it. Vince went to Joliet, but spent a lot of time on our campus doing his Stanley Kowalski impression, screaming Kathy's name outside of her dorm room, either drunk or stoned. That's what I had heard, anyway. "He's possessive, crude, and coarse. She was a nice girl who deserved a nice boyfriend. She never seemed incredibly happy when they were together." And you should be happy if you're in love, I thought to myself. I was nothing if not gifted in hindsight.

He jotted a few notes in his notebook. I guess a repeat of "professor thinks Vince is a jerk . . . knew Kathy a little bit." How many times was he going to write that down? The waitress appeared with menus, and we studied them a tad too intently given there were only about six choices for dinner. I settled on the bacon burger, figuring I would need my strength if I had to walk everywhere. Crawford ordered the crab cakes and told the waitress that he wanted to see a wine list.

"This calls for conjecture," he admitted, taking a sip of his wine, "but do you think that he is capable of violence?"

"Do you?"

He looked back at me. "I asked you."

I thought for a moment. "I can't say. Who knows? If someone had asked me a year ago if my husband of seven years had had a secret vasectomy and was capable of having not one but four affairs during the course of our marriage, I would have said no, but I learned the hard way." I took a deep breath and laughed ruefully. "Did I say that out loud?"

He nodded and smiled. The waitress came back to the table with the wine list. "Do you like red or white, or does it matter?" he asked.

"It doesn't matter. Whatever you like." I took a sip of my martini. I guess grading papers this evening would be out of the question, between the martini and the wine.

He chose a nice red wine that I would have chosen myself. Either the city of New York was picking up the tab, or cops got paid better than I thought; it was on the high side of the price list. He looked down, seemingly unable to make eye contact. He focused on his place mat. "How do you have a secret vasectomy, by the way?"

I laughed. "Why? You in the market for one?"

"Nobody to keep it a secret from," he said, and drained his wineglass.

That was good information to have. "You wait until your wife goes on a visiting professorship to Ireland for six weeks, and you schedule it. She comes home, your balls look none the worse for wear, and nobody is the wiser. Particularly the wife." I put my napkin on the table. We were now into my "loose lips sink ships" portion of the evening. "And with that confession, it seems like a good time to visit the ladies' room. Excuse me." I pushed my chair back from the table. He stood as I departed.

I went into the restroom and locked myself in a stall. I put the seat down and sat for a moment. I didn't have to go to the bathroom; I just needed a break. I took my cell phone out of my pocket and hit speed dial #1 for Max. She answered after four rings, out of breath.

"It's me. Did I take you away from someone or something?"

"I was running on my treadmill."

Liar. She doesn't run, and she doesn't have a treadmill. "Hey, you'll never guess where I am and who I'm with."

"You're right. I won't. Just tell me."

"Remember Detective Crawford?"

Her sharp intake of breath confirmed that she did.

"He came by my house right after I got home from school and said he wanted to ask me some questions. Then, he asked me to go to dinner. What do you think that means?"

"He was hungry and working overtime?"

I could tell she wasn't into this conversation. I would remember this the next time she called me from the shoe store looking for advice on two pairs of Jimmy Choo pumps. "Thanks for your help."

"Maybe he'd be a good Rebound Man," she said.

"I don't need a Rebound Man," I reminded her for the fiftieth time. "Hey . . . we're breaking up," I lied, slamming my cell phone against the side of the stall. I knew where this conversation was headed. "Gotta go."

I unlocked the door of the stall and faced the huge wall of mirrors. I guess it would have helped to visit the restroom earlier in the evening, judging from my sad appearance, but what was done was done. I wet a paper towel and wiped the mascara away from under my eyes and ran the towel over my face.

I whispered to my reflection in the mirror, even though there was nobody else in the bathroom. "Did I just say 'balls' in front of the detective?" I pushed my hair back from my face, hoping to achieve some kind of tousled coif instead of a rain-soaked rat's nest.

I had been having such a good time that I realized that I had not told him about my "meeting" with Peter Miceli. I was sure that I would get a lecture for not telling him first thing, but I could deal with that. I took a deep breath and left the bathroom.

When I returned to the table, the wine was there, as was our food. My burger looked bloated and obscene next to his three crab cakes and rice pilaf.

"Wine?" he asked, and held the bottle aloft over my clean glass.

"Sure." I started cutting my burger into smaller pieces, gave up, and put a big hunk in my mouth.

He flipped through his notebook again. "Was it common knowledge on campus that the Micelis were a Mob family?"

I thought for a moment. "It's always been rumored but nobody ever knew for sure. There was the thing about Peter being involved in that strip club a few years back, but I guess regular businessmen can own them? Or am I being naïve?" I blushed as I flashed back to my Joyce-reading lap-dancer comment. "But it was the same way fifteen years ago when I was in school with Kathy's mother. We knew, but didn't discuss it." I took a sip of my wine. "Is that part of the investigation?" He didn't answer. "If you tell me, you'll have to kill me?"

He laughed. "Something like that."

I shifted in my chair, ready to tell him about Peter. "I have to tell you something."

He continued eating but looked up at me while he chewed.

"Um, I went shopping with my friend on Saturday, and when we came back, Peter Miceli was in my kitchen." I tried to make it sound like a common occurrence, but we both knew that it wasn't. I let out a ridiculous-sounding giggle.

He dropped his fork onto his plate, making a small racket. "What? Why didn't you tell me this on Saturday, or at the very least, as soon as I got to your house tonight?"

Because I'd had two pounds of chicken salad in my mouth? "Is it important?"

He rubbed his hand over his face. "Uh, yes," he said, as if I were an idiot. "What did he say?"

I wasn't sure how to phrase this part, so I just blurted out, "I think he's going to find out who did this and kill them." I grimaced. "I'm sorry. I should have told you sooner."

He was alone with his thoughts for a minute before he asked me to recount exactly what happened, word for word, or as best as I could remember. I told him about everything, including the weird bear hug, forehead kiss, and face holding at the end. He wrote everything down and continued writing even after I had finished.

He seemed to have lost his appetite; he took his napkin off his lap and placed it next to his plate. "You have to . . . Listen, you . . ." he stammered before getting his point across, "you have to tell me everything that happens relative to this case. Peter Miceli dropping by is major. That is not something you should handle on your own."

I think I understood that now. I nodded, contrite. "I'm sorry," I said again.

"It's OK. You just have to keep me in the loop on everything." He put his napkin back on his lap. "Everything."

We sat in silence for a few minutes, eating. I was waiting for the part where he would tell me why he asked me out to dinner and why he and Wyatt just didn't come to my office to ask me the questions, but that never happened. We finished, declined dessert, and he asked for the check.

The waitress came back and dropped it on the table. I made a move to pick it up, but he was faster. "I asked you." He put a credit card on top of the check and left it on the corner of the table. The credit card was upside down so I couldn't tell if I was guest of the police department or Detective Crawford. The waitress came back and swooped it up.

"Now I get to ask you a few questions," I said, emboldened by a martini and half a bottle of wine and trying to lighten the mood.

He clasped his hands again, and said, "Shoot."

"Mets or Yankees?"

"Mets."

"Rangers or Islanders?"

"Rangers."

"Paper or plastic?"

"Paper."

"Married?"

He hesitated for just a split second. "No."

"Kids?" In this day and age, the two were not mutually exclusive.

"Two. Twin girls. Not identical. Sixteen."

"Do you live uptown or downtown?"

"Uptown. Upper West Side. Ninety-seventh and Riverside. That's where I grew up."

So, he wasn't that far out of his way. As the crow flies, or if you swam down the river, we only lived about twenty miles apart. The waitress returned with the credit-card receipt. He signed it and stood up. Unlike me, he didn't have to consult a tip card and a global-positioning system to figure out the gratuity.

He stood and touched the back of my chair. "Ready?" He put his hand lightly on my back and steered me to the coatroom. We got our raincoats and left the restaurant. I went out to the sidewalk and turned my face up to the mist that was falling. He stood directly under the streetlight and put his hand up to smooth his hair. I caught a glimpse of a very big gun on his right hip under the same tweed blazer that he was wearing the day he first came to my office. I thought about asking if that was his gun or was he just happy to see me, but I thought better of it and kept my mouth shut.

"I think I'll walk home," I said.

"It's raining and" — he lifted his sleeve to look at his watch — "nine-thirty at night. I'm not letting you walk."

"It's kind of like my new hobby," I said. "You know, no car and all." I started down the hill in front of the restaurant, more than a little drunk and hoping to walk it off.

He caught up with me and grabbed my arm gently. "You're not walking."

"Hey, this is Dobbs Ferry, not . . ." I searched my brain for the name of a bad neighborhood, but couldn't come up with one, ". . . somewhere else. I'll be fine," I insisted.

He looked at me for a long time and finally relented. "All right. Thanks for dinner and answering my questions." In a move that surprised me, he pulled my hood up over my head and pulled the zipper up to my neck. He held on to the collar of my raincoat for a split second longer than I would have expected. If I hadn't been almost drunk, I would have been able to discern what the look on his face meant. In my addled state, it looked like he was going to give me a noogie.

"No, *thank you,*" I said. "This was much better than what I had planned to do to myself tonight." I mentally smacked myself in the head. Stupid. Sounded like I was going to eat and masturbate or something equally idiotic.

His car, a brown, police-issue Crown Victoria, was parked perpendicular to the curb a storefront down from the restaurant. He opened the door and put one leg in. "Thanks, again."

"Sexy car," I remarked to myself as I waved and continued down the hill. I heard the car start and go into reverse. I turned around to wave again and saw that he had put the removable flashing light on top of the car. The ground in front me turned yellow, then red, as the flasher on top of the car started revolving. He put the car in drive and followed me slowly down the hill. We continued like this for about two-tenths of a mile before he rolled down the passenger-side window. "Do you want to get in now?"

"Nope. Thanks, though!" I called and plodded, in my decidedly unsexy, rubber-soled clogs, down the street toward my block. I turned into my street and realized that I had another quarter mile of this humiliation and now, in front of the prying eyes of all of my neighbors. I stopped, and he pulled up alongside me, opening the passenger-side door. I got in. He reached across me, but instead of acting out my fantasy and kissing me like I had never been kissed, he pulled the seat belt out of the holder and strapped me in.

"Thanks," he said.

"Are you always this controlling?" I asked.

"Are you always this stubborn?" He drove to my house and pulled up in front.

"You have my card, right?" he asked. "In case you remember anything else?" he asked pointedly, referring to what was now known as the "Peter Miceli incident" in my mind.

I nodded. "What should I be thinking about?"

"Anything. Where you were when your car was taken, who you saw, anything about Kathy . . . anything."

"Got it."

He turned his face to the driver-side window and let out a sigh. "You're still a sus— . . ." I thought I heard him whisper. He looked over at me with a sad expression.

I waited a moment, hoping for the end of the sentence. But there was none. Just a long, pregnant moment in a steamy car accompanied by the slapping of the windshield wipers on wet glass.

I already knew what he was trying to say, and if I thought about it, I didn't want to hear him actually say it.

He got out of the car and opened my door, watching me as I walked up the front walk of my small Cape Cod house. I turned and waved for the last time before entering. I closed and locked the door, leaning my forehead against the cool wood of the door. That was far superior to eating and masturbating.

NINE

I woke up feeling much better than I should have, considering the only beverages I had consumed the day before consisted of coffee, a slug of Foster's Lager, a martini, and red wine. I considered that my daily two-mile walks might have been contributing to my good health and joie de vivre and that I would never buy a new car. I didn't want to lose this new sense of feeling rested, invigorated, and in shape. As I threw my legs over the side of the bed, I heard the turnover of an engine and the crunch of gravel in front of my house. I looked at my alarm clock and saw that it was six-fifteen. I walked over to the window and pulled the shade back only to see taillights twinkling in the distance. That drove home for me the reality of the situation: I was a suspect in a murder, and I was being watched. I could pretend that my dinner with Detective Crawford was just a meal between two friends, but he had a job, and he was going to do it, despite all of our witty repartee about grocery bags and New York sports teams.

I had my least favorite class, the infamous Shakespeare introduction, later that day. An image of Fiona Martin's muck-covered paper floated into my head, but I pushed it away with my mantra, "tabula rasa." Clean slate. Don't think about it. An apt mantra for many aspects of my life.

I took a quick shower and wrapped my hair and body in towels. I dried off, stepped into my bedroom, and opened my closet. I saw my trusty clogs on the floor, still mud-spattered and a little wet from my walks in the rain. I spied a Nine West box in the corner and opened it, looking at a beautiful pair of backless brown-leather mules that I bought at an end-of-season sale at Bloomingdale's in the midst of a very long winter. Today was the day. I would not wear my clogs but these beautiful shoes. I would stand tall, at six feet in my heels, and teach my classes: Professor Amazon. I pulled out tan linen pants, and a fitted, brown linen shirt to go along with the shoes.

I took the towel off my head and stood in front of the bathroom mirror to put on makeup and blow-dry my hair. I picked up a bottle of sculpting gel, compliments of

Max, thought better of it, and threw the bottle in the garbage. All I needed was to show up at school with a big mane of sculpted hair looking like the Merry Divorcee of Dobbs Ferry for the talk to start. Sister Mary would not approve.

After a quick breakfast of juice and tortilla chips, I headed out the door, marveling at the comfort of my new mules. I was at the end of my driveway when my neighbor, Jackson, pulled out of his driveway and stopped his car in front of me.

"Hey, Alison! Do you want a ride?" he asked. "I'm heading for the seven-twenty train."

I thought a moment. "Sure. Why not?" I jumped into the car and put my briefcase between my legs. "How are you? I feel like I haven't seen you in months."

I didn't know much about Jackson, except that he was a graphic designer at a publishing company. Although I had lived in my house for almost ten years, he was a relative newcomer, having only lived in the neighborhood for five years. I usually saw him and his wife, Terri, while doing yard work, but beyond that, hardly ever. They were clearly headed toward parenthood at some point while Ray and I weren't — the secret vasectomy and all — so that put us in another social circle. It seemed that we were the "career couple" on the block and nobody quite knew what to make of us as a result.

He took a breath. "We haven't seen Ray much. Everything all right?" he asked.

I hesitated but felt that he deserved an answer. "Well, Jackson, not really. We're divorced. Ray moved out about six months ago, but we had filed before that. I'm sorry. I figured everyone knew."

"It's OK. I'm real sorry, Alison. You shouldn't have to go through something like that." He made a turn into the station and looked for a parking space. He stayed silent for a moment. "I was sorry to hear about all that business at your school, too."

If "all that business" was Kathy's murder, I was sorry, too. "Thanks. It's been horrible."

"They found her in your car, huh?" he said, pulling up to a stop sign.

"Yep."

He cast me a sidelong glance but didn't say anything. He pulled into a spot about an eighth of a mile from the platform. We were late and lucky to have found a spot at all. "Are you staying in the house?" he asked, pulling the keys from the ignition.

"Sure. I really like where I am. I'm staying put." I opened the door and got out.

"That's good." He started toward the station. "I have to buy a ticket. I'll see you on the train." He jogged down the parking lot. "By the way, nice shoes!" he yelled back at me.

I headed toward the platform. "Thanks, Jackson. See you soon."

The day was turning out to be a beautiful one after all the rain from the day before. I stood on the platform with my back to the river and let the sun wash over me. I saw the train in the distance and pulled my briefcase strap over my head.

The train came right on schedule and arrived fifteen minutes later at the station close to school. I got off the train and started up the hill that just the night before had been dark, wet, and foggy. My new shoes were holding up well, but I felt a blister starting on the top of my pinkie toe. I pushed the pain out of my head and trudged up the hill, down the avenue, and onto campus.

By the time I reached the guard booth at the front gate of campus, I was in agony. I stopped at the booth and saw Franklin, the morning guard.

"Morning, Prof," he said, as he did every day, not seeming to be alarmed by my hobbling through the front entrance in obvious distress.

"Hi, Franklin." I collapsed against the side of the guard booth and took off my right shoe to massage my foot. "Listen, could you call down and have someone drive up the cart to pick me up? I can't walk another step in these shoes."

He looked down at my raw feet. Every toe now had a blister. He whistled his sympathy. "Not the right kind of shoes for walking," he said, as if he were talking to an idiot. Which apparently I was. He spoke into a walkie-talkie that was perched on the counter in the guard booth and asked Joe, one of the other guards, to bring up the golf cart. Franklin and Joe, with a collective age of 130, represented some of the younger, spryer guards on campus. The golf cart was probably used in the first Bob Hope celebrity golf classic. "Safe" and "sound" were not words that could be used to describe our campus anymore, what with the murder and the rapidly advancing age of our security force.

After making fifteen minutes' worth of weather chitchat with Franklin, Joe appeared. The waistband of his pants, stretched to the maximum allowable circumference, touched the steering wheel. He motioned for me to get in. "Where you going?"

"Thanks, Joe. Could you drop me behind the Administration Building?" I asked as politely as I could, through clenched teeth. The pain in my feet was unrelenting and throbbed to a beat all its own.

I endured a much longer cart ride than the distance required. And a dissertation on why we should "bomb the hell out of Iran, Iraq, and *Cyprius*." I wasn't sure where that was but was too afraid to ask for a geography lesson; he seemed pretty pissed off. Finally, he pulled in behind the Administration Building and pulled up as close as possible to the steps behind the building. I hopped out, holding both of my shoes in my right hand, and walked down the stairs, barefoot. Things were going my way, and the back door was open. I made a left into the main office area and hobbled back to my office, which faced the back steps.

I rocked back on my heels so that my feet wouldn't touch the ground and opened my office door. I threw my briefcase onto the guest chair and settled in behind my desk, opening my top drawer to see what kind of ancient first-aid items might be lurking therein. I found a box of Band-Aids from a drugstore that wasn't in business anymore and pulled them out. Hopefully, adhesive didn't have an expiration date.

I was putting a Band-Aid on my last toe when the phone rang. It was Max. "You're at work early," she said.

"I have a ten-ten class and papers to correct. I figured it was a good idea to get in. What's up?"

"You sound pretty good for someone who was drinking her face off twelve hours ago," she said, taking a noisy slurp of her morning coffee.

"I wasn't drinking my face off. I had a martini and a glass of wine. And a couple of sips of Foster's Lager."

"Maybe you were just giddy from your dinner with Detective Hot Pants."

"Maybe, Max," I said, losing patience. "Why did you call anyway?"

"I just wanted to touch base. We got cut off, remember?"

"Right," I lied.

"Do you want to have dinner tomorrow?"

"Sure. Remember, I still don't have a car, so take pity and make it close to me."

"That's right. I'll come up by you. When are you going to get one?"

"I don't know. Before today, I was actually enjoying walking everywhere. Today, however, it seems pretty old."

She mumbled something to someone in her office that sounded like "the fish is in the oven." "Gotta run. Let's go to the Chart House. Six o'clock." She hung up without waiting for my answer.

I had two hours until my first class, blisters on my feet, and no way to get to the cafeteria for a cup of coffee. I swung my chair around to look out the window and saw Father Kevin trotting down the steps behind the building. He looked up, saw me, and waved. I motioned for him to come in when he got into the building.

He arrived moments later, dressed from his morning run in sweatpants, a T-shirt, and running shoes. He was extremely myopic and astigmatic, so he had to wear glasses every moment of the day. Today, they were attached to his head by an elastic headband that back in the day would have made him the recipient of a good beating in most New York City neighborhoods. Fortunately for him, his Irish mother had given him Irish dancing lessons and boxing lessons simultaneously. He was graceful, knew what a hornpipe was, could run fast, and had a killer right hook. He was dripping sweat, his shaggy blond hair almost black from the moisture. "Hi, Alison. How are you?"

"I'm good, Kevin." I stood up and gave him a peck on the cheek, trying not to swallow a gallon of sweat in the process. Kevin had taken over as chaplain at the college two years earlier and we had become fast friends. We were about the same age and both loved the Rangers, an instant bond. He was also the most irreverent person I had ever met. Kevin had been the pastor of a parish in Westchester, but his outspokenness was not popular among the wealthy patrons of the church. Since the Catholic Church was not in the position to fire anyone given that vocations were at an all-time low, Kevin got away with saying things from the pulpit that would have had him excommunicated only a few years before. I think the archdiocese figured they would keep him but put him where he could do the least damage, i.e., reach the smallest population. So, Sunday Mass consisted of Kevin preaching to fifty half-deaf nuns and a smattering of college students who thought he was the closest thing to an ordained rock star. I was certain that we would lose him after he referred to the Cardinal as Mo from the Three Stooges, but he was still here. "Do me a favor?"

"Anything."

I lifted my feet and displayed my bandages. "Could you get me a cup of coffee? I'm trying to limit the amount of walking I'm going to do today." I showed him the mules, and he whistled.

"Nice shoes. Not for this campus, though. Where are the clogs?" He sat in one of the chairs, panting from his exertion.

"I'm giving the clogs a rest. They've served me well, but I was starting to feel dowdy. I needed an attitude adjustment." I reached into my bag and got out my wallet, figuring he didn't have money on him. "Coffee? Please?" I held my hands out pleadingly.

"Sure," he said, taking the money. "Muffin?"

"If they look good. And get yourself a cup, too. Let's chat for a minute, if you have time."

He was gone ten minutes and returned with two muffins, two large coffees, milk, and sugar packets. He sat down across from me and kicked the door closed with his left foot. "What's going on?"

"You did a nice job at the funeral."

He blushed slightly. "They're always hard, but that was the hardest one yet."

"Who was the concelebrant?"

"Father Minette. From Kathy's parish. He knows the family well."

"How's her family doing? Gianna?"

He shrugged. "Not good. I saw them over the weekend, and they are having a very difficult time. Peter has holed up in the bedroom and is in deep mourning. Keep them in your prayers."

I wanted to tell Kevin that Peter wasn't holed up in the bedroom for the whole weekend, but I didn't. "I do, Kevin." And I was telling the truth. "Did you know Kathy?"

He pulled the paper off his muffin and took a bite. "Yes," he said, and went silent. That, to me, meant that he had spent some time with her but was not at liberty to talk about it.

"Do the police know that you knew her?"

He nodded. "I've spent a few hours with Detective . . ." he paused, searching for the name.

"Crawford?" I asked, and felt a blush come to my cheeks.

"Yes, and the other, crabby one. Wyatt?" He continued eating his muffin. "Crawford gets why I can't go into detail but Wyatt doesn't. He keeps pressing me, but I can't tell him anything. He even threatened to subpoena me," he said, shaking his head. "Can you believe that?"

"Crawford gets it because he's Catholic."

"That's what I figured, but I don't know why I can't get Wyatt to understand it. If he subpoenas me, I'm going to have to sic a church lawyer on him. My cousin is at Catholic University studying canon law. He'd love to get into it with the police." He laughed, getting a mental image of what that would be like.

"Have you ever met Vince?" I asked.

"I never could figure out what she saw in him," was all he said. He took the lid off his coffee and poured in cream from a little plastic container.

"Me, neither. But who am I to judge?" I asked, and gave a little laugh.

Kevin ran his hands through his shaggy blond hair and put them behind his head. "You doing all right with all of that?"

I nodded. "I have to see Ray every other day for our course, so we have to be civil with each other. Things are as OK as they can be. I'm doing better with the whole divorce thing." I looked out the window. "I don't feel like Mary Magdalene anymore, which is good, right?"

We sat and chatted and ate our muffins and drank the coffee. Kevin stood up a half hour later and stretched. "Well, glad I ran, because that muffin was probably two thousand calories." He gathered up his garbage and threw it into my waste can. "Don't get up," he said, and leaned over to kiss me. "I have to go prepare a sermon for twelve o'clock Mass. Something on the ill effects of revenge or something like that. Any ideas?"

"You're asking me?" I asked, incredulously. "I'm still trying to figure out a way to key Ray's new BMW without getting caught."

He laughed. "You're no help." He opened the door. "I'll talk with you soon." He turned and looked at me with that mixture of sadness and pity that I was beginning to recognize only too well.

The day went fine, as days go when I have to talk about the significance of the three witches in *Macbeth* to a bunch of disinterested young adults. I called it quits around five. I knew that I couldn't make it to the train station on foot, but didn't want to waste money on a cab. My aversion to cabs became instilled in me when I was a broke college student here, so I gave in and called Ray's office. He answered on the first ring.

"It's me," I said. "Hey, remember when you said I could get a ride when I needed it? Well, I need a ride. Can you take me to the train?"

He was more enthusiastic than I thought he would be. "Sure. I can even drive you home if you want. Can you meet me over here within a half hour?"

I agreed and began tidying up my office. I slipped my sore feet into my shoes not sure if I was going to make it from my office to Ray's, but I figured I'd give it a try.

His office was located just a short walk but after only a few steps, the pain in my feet was vibrating throughout my entire body, so I removed my shoes and walked barefoot across campus.

The hall was lit by overhead fluorescent lights that were harsh on the complexion. My skin turned a ghastly green shade, as evidenced by my hands. I put my shoes back on. They echoed as first the toe and then the heel of each foot hit the tile floor. I saw that Ray's door was closed, but heard his and other male voices talking behind it.

I decided to wait in the hallway. He knew I was coming, so I didn't feel the need to knock. I stood for a few minutes, but the blood rushing to my feet became more than I could stand as my blisters began to throb.

I bent down to put my briefcase on the floor and as I stood up, the door opened and I came face-to-face (or face-to-neck in our case) with Detective Crawford. He looked as surprised as I was. Wyatt was behind him, and behind Wyatt was a clearly distressed Ray.

Ray motioned me into his office and closed the door. The four of us stood shoulder to shoulder in the small, windowless office. I could almost see the fear rising off Ray like the fog on the street the night before. His starched white shirt had rings of sweat under each arm, and he pulled nervously at his collar when I asked him what was happening. He reached into his pocket and handed me his car keys.

"I'm going to be a while, Alison. Why don't you take my car and drive yourself home? It's right behind the building in the parking lot," he said. He looked at the two cops. "Can she do that? Take the car?"

Crawford looked at Wyatt, and Wyatt gave a slight nod.

"Ray?" I asked, looking at him quizzically. When he didn't answer, I looked at Crawford, who gave me one of his sad faces.

Wyatt was the only one to speak. "We have to talk with your husband for a few minutes, Professor Bergeron."

Ray and I answered in unison. "Ex-husband."

"Why don't you take the car and drive yourself home, like he suggested?" Wyatt asked. He wasn't his usual menacing self, and seemed to be trying to get me out of the situation as gracefully as he could.

I reached out and Ray handed me his keys. I took them and looked at the complicated hieroglyphics on the plastic key tag. I knew I was in trouble. I didn't think I'd be able to get into the car, never mind drive it home.

Wyatt looked at Crawford. "Why don't you carry the professor's briefcase to the car, Bobby?"

Crawford took my briefcase from my shoulder and steered me out of the office. He held the door open as I walked out into the parking lot.

Ray's new BMW sedan sat in a "faculty" spot close to the door. Crawford put his hand out and I handed him the keys. He hit a button and the car made a short beeping noise, but the interior lights came on. That was promising. Crawford opened the driver-side door and put my briefcase in the back-seat.

I looked up at him. "Your name is Bobby?"

He smiled. "Yes."

It occurred to me that I hadn't known that fact. "What's going on with Ray? Is he in trouble?"

Sad face again. "I'm not sure yet. We're

taking him in for questioning." He leaned his elbow on the roof of the car, and there was that damn gun again. "Are you going to be all right driving home?"

"I think I'll be fine." I looked at the control panel. Getting an aeronautics degree from NASA would be easier than trying to turn on the air-conditioning. "I've never driven a car that didn't have window cranks, but I should be able to figure it out." I thought about Ray in a room being questioned, and I started to figure out what was going on. He was a suspect in the murder. I couldn't think of any other reason why he was going to end up at the police station. I was pretty sure that being a shitty husband wasn't against the law, even though I had given some thought to calling my local councilman on that one.

Crawford leaned down and I got a whiff of a light scent that reminded me of clean laundry. He held out the plastic key tag. "Whatever you do, just don't hit this button. That will set off the alarm. I don't think you need to set it. Everything else should be straightforward." He paused for a minute. "I don't get the sense that the car will be stolen in your neighborhood, but if so, I also don't get the sense that you'd be really broken up about it." He raised his eyebrows questioningly.

"You're absolutely right about both things." I got in the car but left the door open, one leg out. "He's an asshole, but he's harmless." I said the words but wasn't sure if I believed them at that moment. I hadn't believed that he would cheat on me, so what was to say that he wouldn't kill, too? I felt a sob rising in my throat. "You know, secret vasectomies and all." I closed the door and quickly backed out of the spot. I looked in the rearview mirror as I drove away, and Crawford was still in the parking lot looking at the car with his sad, handsome face.

TEN

I left campus and merged onto the Saw Mill River Parkway, going north. I had never had a car so responsive and had to keep myself from going eighty miles an hour all the way home. I didn't know why, but I was crying so hard that I had to blow my nose into the sleeve of my blouse. I guess I still had a soft spot for Ray that would take a long time to harden. He had hurt me worse than anyone I could imagine, but we had been together for a long time. I wondered aloud if he would be so upset if he thought I was going to end up in jail.

Ray had one of those fancy voice-activated cell phone things attached to the console. Since I wasn't Ray and I was sure he didn't have Max's number stored in his phone, I punched in her number as I was driving and hoped that she would be able to hear me. She picked up after four rings.

"Max, it's me. Listen, Ray needs help.

What was the name of that hotshot lawyer you used to date? The one who defended the guy who shot the kid on the subway?"

"Mitch Klein," she said. "What's going on? Are you crying?"

I sniffled loudly. "Yes. I went to Ray's office, and those two cops were there. They're taking him in for questioning on the Miceli thing. I don't know why." I noticed that I was going eighty again and slowed down. I came to the light at Executive Boulevard and stopped. "Call me in a half hour or so and give me the number just in case he needs it. Can you do that?"

"Sure. I'll call you in a half hour."

Ten minutes later, I'd managed to pull the car up my driveway, get out, and lock the doors without incident, priding myself on the fine execution. I let myself in through the back door, threw my briefcase on the kitchen table, and took out my remaining can of Foster's. I opened it and guzzled most of it down, some of it running down either side of my face. I found a crumpled-up paper towel on the counter and ran it over my face to sop up what hadn't ended up in my mouth. In moments, I had the golden glow that I had not been able to replicate with martinis or red wine.

I went into the powder room off my front

hallway and turned on the light. My face was red and blotchy from crying, and my mascara had run down my cheeks. I filled the white porcelain basin with water and washed my face with the antibacterial hand soap that I kept on the sink. Now my face was red, blotchy, dry, and germ-free.

I went up to my bedroom to change my clothes. I grabbed a pair of jeans and a clean T-shirt out of my drawers and shook off the mules. I took everything I had on and threw the pile into the hamper. The phone rang just as I had taken a pair of flip-flops out of the closet and put them on. It was Max.

"Mitch Klein," she said, and recited the number. "I already spoke with him and told him to expect your call."

I jotted the number down on a scrap of paper next to the phone. "Thanks, Max."

"What's going on?" she asked. "Do the police really think that Ray had something to do with this?"

"I don't know. It looked serious when I showed up at his office, and being taken in for questioning can't be good."

"Let me know what happens. Make sure you tell the police that Ray is an asshole, but relatively harmless."

I had to laugh. "I already did, Max." I

hung up and put the scrap of paper in my pocket.

The crunch of gravel outside my window, followed by the warning beeps of a commercial truck in reverse, made me go to the window to investigate. As I pulled the shade aside, I saw a tow truck backing up my driveway. I dropped the shade and raced back down the stairs.

I ran out the back door and into the yard. The tow truck was hooking the rear end of Ray's car to a winch and pulling it up onto the flatbed. Detective Crawford stood to the side of the tow truck, watching impassively, one arm hanging down and the other lazily resting on his gun. An NYPD police car with two uniformed officers inside sat at the bottom of the driveway, flashers revolving; they had been accompanied by a Dobbs Ferry car with two officers in it. Crawford looked up when he heard the back door slam.

"We need the car, Alison," he said. It was the first time I had heard him use my name.

"For what?" I yelled over the din of the winch.

"Ray is a suspect. We're impounding the car and its contents so that we can do a thorough investigation. We have reason to believe that Ray knew Kathy Miceli."

"Of course he knew her. She was in his intro biology class," I yelled. He looked at me. "Don't look at me with the sad face," I said, putting my head in my hands. I knew what that meant. She was in his class but "knew" was the operative word.

He looked confused. "Let's go inside." He walked over to the tow-truck driver and motioned to the officers in the police car. After exchanging a few words, he turned back to me. "Did you leave anything in the car?"

I thought for a moment and remembered my briefcase on the kitchen table. I shook my head.

"Can you get me the keys?"

He held open the back door and waited for me to enter. I handed him the keys, and he went back outside. After a few minutes, the noise died down as the police car, the tow truck, and Ray's car left my driveway. Crawford came back in and sat down across from me. We sat at the kitchen table, me with the can of Foster's in front of me. A happy beer commercial with swinging singles it was not.

I felt drained. "Can I get you something?" I asked, trying not to forget my manners.

"Can I have some water?" he asked.

I pulled myself up from the chair and

opened the refrigerator. There were several bottles of water on the top shelf and not much else. I handed him one and sat down. "I hope you don't want a glass," I said, and slumped back into the chair.

He opened the water and took a long drink. "I need to ask you a few questions."

"You have got to get a better opening line," I said wearily.

"You're upset."

"You think?" I rubbed my hands over my eyes.

"We have to investigate every single angle," he said, trying to justify Ray's being questioned.

"I know. Why Ray?"

He didn't answer. "Did Ray have a set of keys for the Volvo?"

I thought for a minute. "Yes. He told me that he lost them a few weeks ago."

"When did he move out?"

"Six months ago."

He took out his notebook again and flipped to a clean page. "And when was your divorce finalized?"

"The same week that my car was stolen."

His pen stopped moving in the notebook but he didn't look up and I was glad. That revelation would certainly have brought out the sad face. I was already crying; the sad face would have put me over the edge. "We're going to search the house tonight." I got the sense that he wasn't supposed to tell me that by how softly he spoke. I think the police usually like the element of surprise when it comes to searches. "Wyatt's getting a search warrant now. We don't like to break and enter if we don't have to." He gave me a knowing look, and I flashed back to the dorm break-in.

I tried to remain calm, but tears were streaming down my face. "What do you think you're going to find?"

"We're not sure, but anything that Ray left behind, anything that ties him to other women, to Kathy, in particular, is what we're after."

I took a napkin out of the holder on the table and snorted loudly into it. "Are you a really shitty cop or do you just feel sorry for me? Why are you telling me this?"

He pulled on his tie. "Because you asked. And I don't know how you got mixed up in this, so yes, I guess I feel a little sorry for you." He looked like he was going to say something else, but he pressed his lips together instead.

I wiped my eyes with the soggy napkin. Crawford handed me a clean one from the holder. "Listen, call Wyatt and tell him he doesn't need a warrant. You can look through the whole house if you want. There's nothing here," I said.

He took out his cell phone and punched in a number. He got up and walked into the hallway, his back turned to me. When he was done, he turned back around and sat down at the table. "They'll be here in an hour or so."

I nodded. "Will it be all right if I leave while you're looking through my things?"

"Only if it's all right for us to be here without you," he said. "Where are you going to go?"

"I can't go far. I don't have a car, remember?" I laughed because I was done crying, and I was in that crazy-hysterical place where laughing turns to crying and vice versa. A big blast of snot flew out of my nose, and I caught it in the napkin, but not before he caught sight of it. I got up. "I think I've demeaned myself enough for the short time we've known each other, so I'll take my leave." I put my hand on the door handle. "Will you still be here when I get back?"

"I'll call you when we're done. Take your phone."

I reached into my briefcase and got my phone. He stood up, took off his blazer, and hung it neatly on the back of the kitchen chair. The big gun looked even bigger than it normally did, strapped in a leather holster that ran under his arm and across his back. I could see the outline of his badge under his shirt pocket.

"If you don't want me in the house until Wyatt and the other officers get here, I'll wait outside." He rolled up his left sleeve to just below his elbows. I guess searching through my underwear drawer for evidence was dirty business, and he wanted to be prepared.

I waved my hand dismissively. "You? You're about the only person I trust anymore, and I didn't even know your first name until two hours ago."

"It's Robert Edward." He held out his hand.

I took it. "Nice to meet you, Robert Edward," I said. I walked out into the backyard, down the driveway, and into the street, not sure where I was going.

ELEVEN

I was sitting in Starbucks in town when my phone rang for the first time. It was nine o'clock, and I had just finished my third cup of coffee. Ray's voice sounded strained.

"Alison, I need some help. They want to hold me overnight. I cannot stay here all night," he pleaded.

I pulled the scrap of paper from my pocket. "Ray, I got Mitch Klein's number from Max. Call him. He's the lawyer who defended that guy who shot the kid on the subway."

"You don't understand. You're my one phone call. Call Klein and tell him I'm at the Fiftieth Precinct in a holding cell. He'll know what to do."

He hung up before I could respond. So they really did enforce the one-phone-call rule. I called Klein. I got an answering service but left the message with the operator, saying that Ray and I were friends with

Max and that he was involved in something related to the Katherine Miceli case. I figured that would get his attention and at least get us a call back. High-priced lawyers and high-profile cases went together like peanut butter and jelly.

I was the only person in the cafe. I asked the young woman behind the counter what time they closed. She had on a very small T-shirt and jeans that barely covered her butt crack; I prayed that she wouldn't have to bend over for anything. "Eleven," she said, and returned to cleaning the big espresso maker. "You want another? It's on me."

I pulled a five out of my jeans pocket and got up. I handed it to her. "No, it's on me. Have one, too."

"I don't drink coffee," she said, stuffing the five into the tip jar. "That stuff will rot your insides."

Great. Global warming, breast cancer, terrorism, a potentially homicidal ex-husband, and coffee that rots your insides. One more thing to worry about.

She handed me a hot cup of coffee. "Be careful. That coffee is nuclear hot."

Nuclear hot. As opposed to just hot, I thought smugly. I sat back down and prepared to take a careful sip. The door to the coffee shop opened suddenly, and a bell jangled, startling me in my overcaffeinated state. Instead of the slow sip I was going to take, the cup jiggled a bit in my hand, and coffee spewed out of the top of the cup. The scalding liquid dribbled from my lip down my chin and into the front of my blouse. The pain ignited every nerve ending in my body, and it was all I could do not to cry out loud.

Crawford stood in front of the table, and handed me a napkin to blot the damage. His tie was off, and the top three buttons of his shirt were open. I could see a clean, white crew-neck undershirt peeking out. He was holding his jacket, his shirtsleeves rolled up into the neat cuffs that he had started when I was at the house. His demeanor said "off duty." He sat down across from me and stretched his legs out in front of him, laying his jacket across his thighs. "Are you OK?" he asked, taking in my red lip and chin. "Do you want some ice?"

I shook my head no, but he had already asked the girl at the counter for a cup of ice. He wrapped some in a napkin and handed it to me.

"How did you find me?" I asked, pressing the freezing napkin against my lip.

"I figured you'd be here," he said.

"There's really nowhere else to go in this town."

"They don't call you 'detective' for nothing," I said, and moaned slightly as I removed the napkin from my lip and threw an ice cube into the coffee cup. "Do you want anything?" I asked him.

He looked over at the girl behind the counter and something registered on his face — it looked suspiciously like disapproval to me — and shook his head. He leaned in and whispered to me. "I hope she doesn't have to bend over for anything."

"You find anything?" I asked.

He shrugged. "Not sure. We took some things out, but I don't think they were yours."

I wrapped my hands around the cup and jiggled my legs up and down. "Like what?"

"Can't say." Under the table, he put his hand on my legs to stop them from moving and left it on my knees.

"I hope you didn't take my vibrator. It's innocent, I tell you!"

He turned crimson and looked around. For an escape hatch probably.

"I'm kidding. I don't have a vibrator." I looked away. It had been so long that I didn't even know if I still had a vagina. Mental note: lay off the off-color sex jokes.

"When's the last time you slept?" I asked.

"A few days ago. Why?" he asked.

"You look like shit."

He laughed. "Thanks."

Something dawned on me. "Robert Edward, did you sleep in your cruiser outside my house last night?"

His body tensed, and I knew that I was right. It was his car that had pulled away this morning at six-fifteen. "It's not a cruiser," he said.

"Details."

"You've been under constant surveillance for the last week."

"I was the main suspect, wasn't I? That's what you were trying to tell me last night."

"I told Wyatt that the only thing you were guilty of was bad luck and a weak stomach, but he was still suspicious of you."

Weak stomach. Funny. I took a drink of the now-lukewarm coffee to prove him wrong. "Why?"

"He thought you were too nervous."

"I am. But not because I'm a murderer. I've got a million other things to be nervous about."

He chewed on a wooden stirrer and considered what I said. "He also didn't like the connection between you and the car that the body was dumped in."

Made sense.

"But you're a lot smarter than that. You wouldn't use your own car to dump a body." He took the stirrer out of his mouth and pointed it at me. "Would you?"

"No, I would steal a car from a total stranger and then dump the body in that," I said, going along with his train of thought. I must have answered too quickly because he looked at me closely. "Kidding!" I said. "I wouldn't know how to steal a car. I can barely program my dishwasher to 'pot scrubber.' "

Somewhat satisfied, he continued. "Once we found a connection between Kathy and Ray, it took the heat off you a bit. I'm trying to keep the heat off you altogether, so you have to tell me everything you know." He leaned back and caressed the gun on his hip, like I had seen Wyatt doing in the chapel. These guys loved their guns. "I think I'm right about you. I am, aren't I?" he asked, staring at me with red-rimmed eyes.

"You are right about me," I said. My coffee was approaching ice-cold but I finished it anyway. Weak stomach, my ass.

"Don't disappoint me."

"Well, don't set the bar too high," I said, thinking back to the old breaking-and-entering situation. "Why didn't you haul me to the station house and put me under the bright lights?" I asked, trying to sound more lighthearted than I felt. A suspect in a murder case. I guess it made sense. The cuckolded wife and all. Who's dumb enough to use her own car to stash a dead body. Believe me, I had thought about killing Ray and his paramours many times over the last several years, but none of my students or my car had figured into the scenario. Medieval torture devices maybe, but not my car.

"We didn't have enough to go on."

"The car wasn't enough?"

"No. And the deal was sealed for me when you passed out in your office and vomited on yourself. You didn't have the stomach to look at homicide photos, never mind be a coldhearted killer. Fred wasn't so sure." He saw the puzzled look on my face and responded, "Wyatt," by way of clarification.

"Oh. I call him something else." I picked up my debris from the table — countless sugar packets, wooden stirrers, and balled-up napkins — and pushed them down into my empty cup.

"And then there was all that crying and fainting," he said, looking at a spot over my head. He was either embarrassed or perturbed; I couldn't tell. "You cry an awful lot."

"Have *you* ever been a suspect in a murder case?" I asked defiantly. He shook his head. "So, so . . ." I couldn't come up with anything else. Being a suspect in a murder case was enough. "Anyway, I have very low blood pressure, which is why I faint more than your average murder suspect."

"You never seem to lose your appetite, though," he said, looking at the debris on the table.

I looked at him. What a freaking comedian.

"What happens now?" I asked.

He traced his finger along the design of the table. "We look at what we took from your house, see if we have enough evidence to charge Ray officially and take it from there."

"I called Mitch Klein. Ray wants out tonight," I confessed.

Crawford rolled his eyes. "I'll probably be on desk duty by morning if that guy gets involved. I'm sure somebody's civil rights have been violated or some kind of crap like that." He looked at me. "How do you know Mitch Klein? He's not the kind of guy you just call out of the blue."

"Remember Max?" I asked.

"Sexy, red-bottomed-shoe girl?" he asked.

I might have imagined it, but I thought I saw a hint of red flush his cheeks. It looked more like embarrassment than anything else, but I couldn't be sure. Max had that effect on certain men. The good ones, mostly.

"Oh, you noticed?" I asked. "Well, she and Klein used to date. Or something. Whatever you call it when two rich, successful people spend time together having sex."

"I think you still call it dating," he said, smiling. He straightened up in his chair. "I've got to go." He stood up. "Let me take you home."

I collected my garbage and threw it in the metal trash can by the door. He held the door open for me, and we walked onto the street. In the distance, I could see the river and a couple of boats swaying back and forth in the marina. It was early in the season for boats to be in the water, but a few optimistic sailors had taken a chance anyway. I thought about leaving the house after he dropped me off and going to the river to sleep on one of those boats. Maybe it would drift away in the middle of the night and deposit me in Bermuda. Or, maybe, with the way my luck was going, the police would be called, and I'd end up in jail for breaking and entering. An image of

160

me in the Bedford Correctional Facility wearing an orange jumpsuit and paper shoes popped into my head, and I shuddered.

I saw the Crown Victoria parked in front of the coffee shop. "Do I have to ride in the cruiser again?"

"It's not a cruiser, and yes, you have to ride in it again." He walked over to the car and opened my door, waving his hand ceremoniously for me to get in. I got in and closed the door.

The car sagged slightly as he threw his large frame into the driver's seat. He looked over at me and saw that I hadn't put my seat belt on, and like the night before, reached over and pulled the belt from its holder above the door. I was close enough to see the stubble on his cheeks and smell the slightest hint of the clean-laundry smell that I had detected before. Now it was mixed with something muskier, a pleasant smell nonetheless. We were nose to nose; his normally sad expression was replaced by one that either said, "I am in love with you," or "I'm going to fall asleep on you." I couldn't tell, but I suspected it was the latter. I found myself pushing my head as far back as I could into the headrest instead of leaning forward, as I probably should have, given our close proximity, my attraction to him, and the situation. I focused on his undershirt. "You were an altar boy, weren't you?" I blurted out as his left hand pulled the belt over my chest and his right hand dropped onto my upper thigh.

The moment gone, he clicked the belt into the slot and pulled back, a bemused look on his face.

"You knew the words to all of the hymns that were sung at the funeral."

He turned his body and faced the steering wheel, putting the key in the ignition. "You talk too much."

"So I've been told," I admitted, and looked out my window.

Before he backed out of the spot, he turned on the interior light and took my chin in his hand, turning my face to his. He stared at my lips. "I don't think you'll get a blister," he said. "Put some more ice on that when you get home." He pulled out of the spot, drove down Main Street, and hung a right onto my street.

"I'm off tomorrow," he said.

"OK," I said slowly, not sure why he needed me to know this.

"You have my card, though, so . . ."

". . . so, I'll call you if I remember any-thing." I finished the sentence for him. He seemed afraid to deviate from his cop script, and I didn't want to throw him off.

He pulled up in front of my house. It looked fine from the outside, but I didn't know what to expect when I got inside. "What does it look like in there?" I asked, my hand on the door handle.

"I made sure that everything was put back. We didn't do our usual ransack."

"That was nice of you." I took my seat belt off. "So, were you?"

He looked puzzled. "Was I what?"

"An altar boy."

"Six years," he said. "Trinity Church." He smiled. "Did I mention that I'm fluent in Latin?"

I'm a sucker for guys who speak dead languages. I cupped my hand to his cheek, surprising the both of us. "Get some sleep, would you?"

He grabbed my hand and put my knuckles to his lips. "I will."

I got out of the car, walked up the steps, and let myself in. He waited until I was inside and then drove away. I was sure of it this time.

Twelve

I woke up the next morning, later than I should have and having to rush to get ready. Only when I opened my underwear drawer and saw the tangled mess that it was did I remember that I had had a swarm of cops in my house the night before. When I had arrived home, my knuckles were tingling from where they had touched Crawford's lips, and I was in an oxymoronic state of exhaustion and caffeination. I stayed awake in bed until three, tossing, turning, and while I should have thinking about Ray in a holding cell, all I could think about was Crawford and his white undershirt.

I examined my face in the mirror in the bathroom, and I didn't look too bad. The spot on my lip hadn't blistered, just as Crawford had promised, but it was still a little tender. I put on some extra ChapStick as a precaution.

I threw on a printed rayon skirt that just

hit my knees, a T-shirt, and a pair of sandals that I knew would hold up well for my trek to the train. They were basically the sandal version of my clogs, but not as goofy-looking with a skirt. I pulled my hair back into a ponytail and ran downstairs to grab my briefcase.

I went into the kitchen and found my briefcase just where I had left it on the kitchen table. My wallet and cell phone were still in my jeans pocket upstairs. I cursed under my breath and turned to go back to my bedroom when there was a slight tap on the kitchen door. I looked up and saw Crawford standing there, holding up a bag and one of those slotted cardboard holders with coffee.

I opened the back door. "Don't you have a Mass to altar-serve?" I asked, not in the mood for questions, sexual tension, or unfulfilled fantasies. I was tired and cranky and not looking forward to my workday.

He laughed out loud, clearly a different man from the one whose only jewelry was a Glock fifteen-round gun. He was wearing jeans, a blue-linen shirt, untucked, and Teva sandals. He came in and put the coffee and the bag on the counter.

"What are you doing today?" he asked.

Obviously, he hadn't been getting enough

sleep. The answer to that question was obvious. "Going to work," I said.

"Call in sick," he commanded, taking the phone from the receiver and handing it to me.

I eyed the coffee on the counter, and he handed me a cup. "I can't just call in sick."

The sad face almost made a reappearance, but not quite. He had bags under his eyes, but he was clean-shaven and appeared pretty chipper. "Just trust me. Call in sick."

I took a sip of the coffee as carefully as I could. He watched me, a bemused smile on his lips. The coffee was some kind of café au lait or latte; I couldn't tell which, but it was different from what I usually drank — black and strong. I was still buzzing from the coffee consumption the night before, rotting insides and all. "What's going on?"

He leaned his frame against the counter. "We let Ray go last night. We didn't have enough to hold him. But the campus is a zoo. I don't think you should go in until things die down a little bit."

"And when will that be?" I asked. "I've got classes to teach and students who have to graduate. What are they supposed to do?"

He placed the phone squarely in my hand and spoke slowly. "Call Sister Mary and tell her you'll be back tomorrow." The way he stared at me convinced me that he was serious, and that this was a good idea.

I thought for a moment. I had two classes today. One was the senior seminar in which students chose an author and did a semester's worth of research on that author and his or her works. The seniors were mature and would do whatever assignment I left for them, or do their own thing. The other was freshman composition, which wouldn't be a loss either; those students could sit in class and diagram sentences for the day and be none the wiser. I dialed Dottie's number, told her I was sick, and told her what assignments to leave in each classroom and by what time.

She asked me to hold on and clicked off for a minute. "I'm back. One of the students was looking for you. That good-looking Costigan kid."

"Did he say what he wanted?" I asked.

"No. I told him that you were sick today and that you'd be back tomorrow. I hope that was OK."

"Yes, Dottie. That's fine. Thanks for helping out. If anyone else looks for me, tell them I'll be back tomorrow." I made a mental note to buy her flowers and to be nicer to her for a year. I hung up and looked at him. "Happy?"

"Drink your coffee." He pulled the lid off his and dumped a creamer into it. He proffered the bag of baked goods and I reached in and grabbed a chocolate-chip scone. "Can we sit down?" he asked.

I nodded and pulled a chair out. He sat next to me at the round table. "You did a good job of keeping my house neat." I waited a few seconds. "Thanks," I said begrudgingly, remembering my underwear drawer.

"You're welcome."

"Did you see my underwear?" I asked.

He shook his head. "I didn't go into your bedroom."

I breathed a mental sigh of relief.

"Did Ray tell you anything helpful?" I asked.

He shrugged.

"You wouldn't tell me anyway," I said.

He smiled and nodded. He reached back with a long arm and grabbed a muffin out of the bag. He held it up to me. "Split it?" he asked, pulling the paper from around the sides.

I shook my head and picked at my scone. "You must think I'm a real idiot."

"Why?" He looked down at his muffin, working intently on taking the paper off neatly.

"Because of Ray."

He kept his eyes down. "I don't make judgments like that."

I laughed. "Sure you do. Everyone does."

He finally looked up. "I really don't."

I took a slug of coffee.

"I don't know Ray; I only know you a little bit. You must have seen something in him to make you want to marry him, right?" He pulled the top off the muffin. "You seem levelheaded."

Levelheaded. Quite the compliment. Next, I'd have common sense.

"Do you like lobster?" he asked suddenly, breaking an uncomfortable silence.

I looked up from my scone. "Does that have something to do with the case?"

"I'm not working today," he reminded me.

"Then yes."

"Do you want to take a drive with me?" He crumpled the wrapper of his muffin into a tiny ball.

I was taken aback. "Uh, I guess so."

"Come on. I know a great place," he said, and took my hand.

I remembered my cell phone and wallet and told him that I needed to go back upstairs for a minute. As nice as it was to have his hand around mine, I extracted it and ran upstairs.

I came back with the phone and my wallet, grabbed my coffee and the rest of my scone, and followed him outside to a car that was thankfully not the it's-not-a-cruiser. It was a very nice Passat station wagon with an impeccably clean interior. I didn't peg him for the station-wagon type, but it was a nice change of pace from the SUVs I usually encountered on the roads. No gold chains or sports cars for this almost midlifer. I got into the passenger seat, put my coffee in the cup holder, and my head against the headrest. He got into the driver's seat of the car and started it. As usual, he reminded me to put on my seat belt, and I obliged.

He headed north on Route 9 toward the Tappan Zee Bridge. Once across the bridge, he went north on the Thruway to the exit for the Garden State Parkway going south. I stayed awake until we passed through the first toll plaza at Exit 168, but that was it. I awoke as we were exiting at Exit 98 and merging onto Route 34 south. I had only been down this way once but recognized that we were at the Jersey Shore.

I sat up and pushed my hair from my face. My scone was still in my lap, with the paper wrapped around it. I looked over at him. "Where are we?"

"The shore," he said. "Did you have a nice nap?"

I looked at my watch. Two hours had passed since he had arrived at my house. "Where are we going?"

"Ocean Beach," he said. "I know it's kind of a long way to go for lunch, but I wanted to give you a change of scenery for the day."

"This is different," I agreed. This stretch of 34 was home to window stores, a few restaurants, a large grocery superstore, and lots of advertisements for Realtors. I was hoping that if we had come this far, I would see the ocean, but judging from the landscape, I wasn't so sure.

We crossed over a drawbridge and pulled up to a red light. When the light turned green, we drove a few hundred feet to a small shack on the bay called Spike's Fish Market. It was on the other side of the street, so he pulled a quick U-turn and drove up to the front of the store.

"You can wait or come inside. Whatever you want to do," he said.

"I'll come," I said, and opened the door. We went inside. Directly in front of us was the fish display, and tables were to the left. Slabs of every kind of fish imaginable rested on chipped ice in a display case. The tables were planks of wood with sea salt, ketchup, and oyster crackers on each; there were long wooden benches on either side. As far as ambiance went, it had none, but judging from the fact that not one table was empty and it was still spring — technically off-season — I figured the food must be incredible.

The grizzled old guy behind the counter — Spike, I presumed — said hello to Crawford and gave me the once-over. He pulled a big sheet of butcher paper off a roll, and said to Crawford, "Shoot."

"Two lobsters, one pound of the tiger shrimp, a quart of jambalaya with rice on the bottom, a pound of coleslaw and a pound of potato salad." He looked at me. "Is there anything else that we should get?"

"That should cover it," I said. I hope he had plans to prepare whatever needed cooking, because I was off duty.

Spike put everything in a big plastic bag and waved Crawford off from paying. "I'll put it on your tab."

We got back into the car and headed south on 35, a new road, until we reached a small beach community in which the houses were about six hundred square feet each, very close together, and all within walking distance of the ocean. He made a left onto a street called Tarpon, and drove up to a house that was right on the beach. He pulled the car into a small apron of a drive-way.

I got out of the car and walked to the right side of the house. The ocean was steps from the house, and, from what I could see, the water was calm on this gorgeous day. There were a few people on the beach south of us, but in front of the house was an empty expanse of smooth white sand.

Inside, the house was one big room with two smaller bedrooms to the side, fronted by a giant picture window that faced the water. It was paneled in dark wood, with slipcovered furniture and hardwood floors. The galley kitchen was next to the large window, and contained a tiny, four-burner stove, a few cabinets above and below the counter, a small sink and a refrigerator.

I looked at the walls. They were covered with pictures of his family and it seemed that he had the brother he mentioned, plus a sister. All looked younger. The parents were your stock Irish characters: the little, gray-haired father with the ruddy complex-ion, and the redheaded mother with freckles. Judging from the rest of the family, Craw-ford must have been adopted. None of the people in the picture was over five-foot-seven. In every picture, he towered over the rest of the family like some kind of lanky interloper.

I focused on his father's face, much like Crawford's, but weathered. "What did your father do for a living?"

"Cop."

"Brother?"

"Assistant District Attorney. Brooklyn."

"Wow," I remarked. "You've got a one-family crime-fighting team going. It's like a bunch of Irish superheroes."

"I guess." He opened the refrigerator and assessed its contents. "We're Irish. If you're smart, you become a lawyer, if you're not so smart . . ." He grinned sheepishly and put his palms up.

"I think you're selling yourself short." I continued looking at the picture. "I've known my fair share of dumb lawyers, and I've met some really smart cops recently." There was a slight facial resemblance between him and the brother — around the eyes mostly — but that's where it ended. "Where do your brother and sister live?" I asked.

"My brother lives in Hawthorne — by you actually. And my sister lives in northern California."

"Is she a crime fighter, too?"

"If you call breaking up slugfests among

her four sons crime fighting, then yes." He rooted around in the upper cabinet and came out with a lobster pot and a lid. He filled it with water from the little sink and put it on the stove, placing the lid on top. He grabbed the lobsters from the bag, still squirming and fighting against their inevitable execution, and put them in the sink. One was on top of the other, their claws taped together. "You can't get water to boil down here unless you put the lid on. I don't know why that is." He opened the refrigerator. "Do you want something to drink? Beer? Soda? Bloody Mary?"

"The last," I said. I would begin the twelve-step program next week.

He pulled out a bunch of ingredients and whipped together my drink. Then he set about putting the shrimp on a plate and mixing up a cocktail sauce from ketchup, horseradish, and Tabasco. He got a beer from the refrigerator. It was Labatt's, just like my parents used to drink. He took the plate and a beer and kicked open the back door. "Come on outside," he said.

The back of the house sat on the sand with a deck stretching out onto the beach. A glass-topped table and some wrought-iron chairs looked like they hadn't been cleaned for the season yet, but I took a chance and sat down, hoping I wouldn't end up with some kind of rust print on my skirt. Crawford went back into the house and returned with a towel, asked me to get up, and spread it on the chair. "Thanks," I said.

He plopped into his chair, unconcerned about any dirt that might end up on his jeans. He threw his head back and took a deep breath of the ocean air.

I took a sip of my drink and felt white heat travel down my throat and into my stomach. I wasn't sure if it was the alcohol, the Tabasco, or the horseradish, but it tingled and was a pleasant feeling. He pushed the shrimp plate in front of me and sat next to me, his back to the ocean.

"Eat," he said.

I obliged and took a bite of shrimp.

"How often do you come down here?" I asked.

"In the summer, every weekend I can. Depends on the chart," he said and seeing my confused look, he clarified, ". . . work schedule. We call it a chart. It rotates, so sometimes I'm on days, sometimes on nights."

"Oh," I said. "Do you get overtime for sleeping in front of my house?"

He laughed a little. "Sure. We get overtime for surveillance." He leaned in toward me.

"So, how did you know?" A light breeze ruffled his hair.

I thought for a moment. "Contrary to appearances, philandering husband and all, I'm not a complete moron." I looked down at my hands. That sounded a little more caustic than I had intended. "I just wasn't sure it was you. What did you do to deserve that duty?" I looked up and saw that he was embarrassed. "What? Did you lose the cruiser? Use too many bullets? Wear a blue shirt when the memo called for red?"

"It's not a cruiser," he reminded me. "I volunteered."

"Ah," I said, for lack of a witty retort. "We're done with that now, though, right? You can sleep indoors if you want? I'm off the most-wanted list?"

"Back to my apartment," he said. He held up two fingers: Scout's honor. "Promise."

Darn. "And what the hell kind of surveillance is that anyway? Surveillance implies a state of consciousness," I said, giving him a small punch to the shoulder. "What if I had taken off in the middle of the night?"

He shook his head, remaining serious. "On foot? In clogs? You weren't going anywhere. I knew that. And you were never a real suspect in my mind."

"But Wyatt thought I was. And by the

way," I said, the Bloody Mary becoming the equivalent of truth serum, "what is with him? Why is he so nasty?"

He laughed. "He's really not. He's actually a very nice guy."

"I thought he was going to kill me the last time you were in my office."

"He might have if you had pulled out a gun instead of a water bottle."

So he had thought the same thing. I shook my head. "You'll never convince me that he's not a hard-ass."

"It's an act."

"Whatever," I said. "He was a real jerk-off the first time I met you both."

"It was his turn," he said.

"His turn?"

"We take turns. Next case, I'm the jerk-off," he said.

I shook my head again. "No way. I don't believe you."

"What if I told you that he's a Big Brother and spends one night a month at a homeless shelter?" he asked.

"I would think he's nice to little kids and people with nowhere to live."

He threw his hands up, defeated. "Your mind's made up. I can see I'm not going to change it." He seemed a little perturbed.

"All right, I believe you. I'd just like my

own evidence," I said. "You didn't seem entirely comfortable with the way he was acting, I have to tell you."

He didn't respond.

I cocked an eyebrow. "Am I right?"

"No, I didn't like it." He ran his hands through his hair. "You seemed so scared that I thought it was over the top."

Being right was enough for me.

"Is it true that partners fall in love with each other?"

He laughed. "Sometimes. But Fred's a Yankee fan. And a Gemini. It would never work."

"By the way, let's see your jerk-off act." I took a drink and noticed that I had finished almost all of it. No wonder I felt like my joints had oil between them.

"Didn't you already get a taste of it after our meeting on Broadway? Under the el?" He smiled.

"I was a little bit scared," I conceded. "But then you drove me to the train station and gave me your handkerchief. And gave me medical advice. I knew you weren't all bad." I waited a moment before asking my next question, not sure I wanted the answer. "How did I do?" I asked. "You know, as interrogatees go?"

He shook his head solemnly, implying

"not good." "Let's just say that I felt bad for you. And I don't usually feel sorry for people we're interrogating. I've been a cop for sixteen years, so I know that most of the people I get to meet are guilty."

"Except in my case," I emphasized.

He nodded. "Except in your case." He paused for a minute and ate some more shrimp. "Can I ask you something?"

I nodded. What the hell.

"How long have you known Ray?" he asked, his mouth full.

"I started at the college nine years ago. We started dating almost immediately and married two years later. You know the rest." I took another drink of my Bloody Mary.

"When did he start cheating?" he asked and then seemed to realize that he had crossed the line. "If that's not too personal . . ."

"No, it's one of those things that's almost become common knowledge. He basically never stopped. He admitted in counseling that he had started seeing someone the week before we got married and continued seeing her the first year we were married. Then, there was someone else, who I think may have been local, but I'm not sure. After that, someone from Manhattan he met at a convention, and I guess Kathy." He was looking intently at me, and I tried to hold his gaze, but the shame I always felt when talking about my marriage to Ray made me look away. When I thought about all that I had overlooked and how I had compromised myself in a sad effort to keep him, I knew that I had lost myself along the way.

"How did you know?"

"Ray's what I call a 'confessor.' "

He raised an eyebrow questioningly.

"You know, one of those people who can't keep their mouths shut. The minute the affair was over, he had to tell me. And then promise it wouldn't happen again. And then treat me really well until it did. It was his pattern." I looked out at the surf. "But I got some really nice jewelry out of it." I tried to laugh, but it sounded like I was being strangled.

He shook his head, disgusted.

I attempted a joke, my natural defense mechanism. "Does it surprise you that Ray wasn't an altar boy?" When he didn't laugh or respond in any way, I stood up. "That water must be boiling by now, don't you think?"

He jumped up. "Darn. I forgot." He opened the back door and let me go in first. The water was boiling, and the lobsters were still plotting their getaway in the kitchen sink, but he picked them up, dropped them quickly into the water, and put the lid back on. "Couple of minutes." He took the salads out of the refrigerator and dumped them into mismatched bowls that he took out of one of the upper cabinets.

"Can I help?" I asked.

He shook his head. "Remember? I'm controlling?"

I laughed, thinking back to our walk/drive in the rain only two nights ago. It seemed like a year ago. "And I'm stubborn, so I'll keep asking until you give in."

He stood with his hip resting against the counter, waiting for the lobsters to be done. "You want to take a look?" he asked, taking the lid off the pot.

I came into the kitchen and leaned over the pot. He leaned over me from behind, his hand resting on my hip. "What do you think?" he asked, a blast of the clean-laundry smell hitting me and making me more than a little weak. I had no idea whether or not the lobster was done; I was more adept at testing a Lean Cuisine fresh from the microwave. If you lost the top layer of skin from the roof of your mouth, it was done. Anything less was an extra minute or two in the heat. Seeing I'd be no help, he decided on his own that they needed a few more minutes.

I extricated myself from between him and stove. I went back outside and got the two drinks. I was in that nice state before I would begin slurring my words and falling down and feeling very clear of mind and mellow. I went back inside and handed him his beer. "Do I have to wear a bib?" I asked.

"You?" he asked. "Most definitely," he said, obviously referring to my penchant for vomiting at will. Realizing that he might have embarrassed me, he immediately retracted his statement. "You don't want to get your shirt dirty."

I held up a hand. "It's OK. I can take it. I was wondering when we were going to get to the point where we could joke about it."

He turned back to the stove. "You do owe me a pair of shoes," he mumbled, and looked up at me sideways, a grin spreading across his face.

"What size do you wear?" I asked.

"Fourteen."

Max would have fainted on the spot, her theory about big feet being related to other body parts having been scientifically tested (by her) and found to be true. I left it alone, flashing back to my vibrator comment and his reaction.

"If I give you a couple of plates, would

you set the table outside?" He rummaged around in the cabinets and came up with a couple of blue-tin plates with white speckles, forks, knives, and some paper napkins.

I went outside and put everything on the table. When I went back in, I gathered the salads, drinks, the butter, and some condiments. He put the lobsters in a big bowl and got some nutcrackers out of one of the drawers. Once outside, he surveyed the table. "What else do we need?"

"I think we're fine," I said, and sat down at the picnic table.

He sat down across from me. We were perpendicular to the ocean and both had a sideways view.

"Seriously, though," he said, and picked up a lobster, "do you want something to tie around your neck?" He waved the cooked lobster in front of my face.

I shook my head. "I'll take my chances." I took the lobster and put it on my plate. Actually, I had no idea what to do, so I fooled around with my drink until he put his lobster on his plate. As soon as he made his first crack with the nutcracker, I followed suit. He pulled a big piece out of one of the red tails, dunked it in the butter, and dropped it into his mouth.

He attacked the shell some more and

pulled out another giant piece of white lobster meat. He held it over to me. "Here."

I held my plate up and he dropped it in the middle of the potato salad. At this point in our suspect/cop/we're-just-friends part of our relationship, I didn't think opening my mouth and being fed was appropriate. I cut the chunk of lobster into smaller pieces and ate it. When I was done with that, he handed me more, seeing the trouble I was having with my own crustacean. While I ate, he asked me where I was from.

"My parents were from Montreal, but I was raised in Tarrytown."

"Do they still live there?" he asked.

I shook my head. "My father died when I was a senior in high school, and my mother died two months before I got married. She made me promise to go through with the wedding." I laughed, even though the thought of her last days was still a source of pain. "I guess it was her dying wish that I not spend the rest of my days alone." I looked away quickly so that he wouldn't see the pain, or tears, in my eyes.

"No pressure, though," he said, trying to lighten the mood.

"I think she had an inkling about Ray's shortcomings, but she would never say anything. She was old school — better to be married to a bum than not married at all."

"My mother wanted me to be a priest," he blurted out between mouthfuls of potato salad.

I held my hands up like a scale. "Homicide detective, priest. They're similar. You're still hearing confessions."

"The celibacy thing would have been a huge stumbling block for me." He handed me some more lobster without looking up.

For you and the faithful female flock, I thought. "Father What-a-Waste." It was out of my mouth before I realized that I had spoken.

He looked at me questioningly. "What?"

"Father What-a-Waste. I read that in a book somewhere. Handsome priests who turn on female parishioners are called Father What-a-Waste."

He let out a big laugh. I had to stop saying the first thing that came into my head. Now he knew that I thought he was attractive. I felt like I needed a complete refresher course in male/female interactions. I didn't think you were supposed to reveal the attractiveness factor until much later in a relationship, but my timing was off on everything now. I was relieved when I heard the insistent beeping of my cell phone go off in my bag, inside the house. Crawford looked down at his waistband and checked his beeper, but I knew it was mine. I jumped up, went in through the screen door, and grabbed it out of my briefcase, which was resting against the leg of the ship's-wheel coffee table. I answered it just before it went to voice mail and heard Ray's voice.

"Well, I'm out of jail," he said, obviously mad at me for not checking on him sooner.

I wanted to scream, "We're divorced, you asshole!" but I didn't. I wasn't sure how to react so I didn't say anything. I wouldn't have been that upset had he spent the night in lockup, or whatever the cops call it when you're thrown in a cell with a dozen un-washed men and given bologna sandwiches to eat.

"Are you there?" he asked.

"Uh, yes," I said. I still wasn't sure what this had to do with me. I had called Mitch Klein, which was my only participation in Ray's situation and all I was going to do to help him, philanderer and possible mur-derer.

"I thought you would want to know that I'm out," he said.

"That's great, Ray. Did you connect with Klein?"

"Yes. He got me released. The police don't have anything to go on except the fact that

I once had your keys in my possession and that I . . ." — he hesitated for a brief second — ". . . knew Kathy. From intro bio." Liar. He waited a moment and then changed the subject. "Where are you, by the way?"

"What?" I asked.

"Where are you? I called school and Dottie said that you called in sick. And you're not home, because I tried you there." His tone was proprietary and not concerned at all, and I didn't like it.

I looked through the picture window and saw Crawford spread out on the chaise, facing the ocean with his shoes off and his fingers laced across his stomach. The outdoor table was covered with the lunch debris. A mixture of guilt and awkwardness flooded over me. I couldn't tell Ray where I was exactly, but I wasn't sure why I had to lie entirely. "I'm at the beach. I needed a break."

"You don't have a car. How did you get there?"

I cleared my throat. "I'll call you later, Ray." I flipped the phone closed and put it back in my bag. Before I was outside, it began ringing again, but I ignored it.

In the two to three minutes it took for me to have my conversation with Ray, Crawford had fallen into a deep sleep on the chaise lounge, one foot touching the deck, and the other bent at the knee. His mouth was open, and his shirt had ridden up to expose the space between his ribs and his waistband. The top button on his jeans was open, I guess in an attempt to make room for more food. I averted my eyes quickly, feeling as if I had just walked in on him in the shower. At my age and under the constant tutelage of Max, I should have been able to deal with looking at the flat stomach of a very attractive man, but I felt like a Peeping Tom. I slipped off my shoes and headed out into the sand and toward the water, putting as much distance between myself and the snoring detective as I possibly could.

THIRTEEN

There were only two ways to go on the beach without either getting wet or hitting road — north or south. I chose south and started walking, enjoying the feel of the wet sand between my toes and the occasional splash of chilly ocean water on my legs. I looked at my watch and saw that it was almost three o'clock. I was in no rush to leave, but knew that I had to get home by ten or eleven in order to get ready for work the next day and get enough sleep in order to face my classes with a modicum of composure. I pushed the thought of the two-hour car ride out of my head and the probable traffic that we would face and enjoyed meandering down a deserted beach, destination unknown.

In the distance, I saw a hazy amusement park sticking out into the water, almost a mirage. I remembered from my teenage years that it was the boardwalk and amusement park at Seaside Heights, the after-prom destination of most high schoolers of my generation. I figured it was about five miles from where I was, going south. I wondered how long it would take me to walk that far in sand, barefoot.

I walked for about an hour and didn't feel any closer to Seaside, but I was so relaxed that I hadn't even thought about the last few weeks. In the distance, I saw a dune buggy approaching, its giant wheels carving huge tread marks in the damp sand. To my amazement, the driver pulled up next to me and stopped.

A young man wearing a tan police uniform with a badge on the sleeve that said LAVAL-LETTE POLICE DEPARTMENT looked right at me. "Afternoon, ma'am."

The ma'am thing. I hated that. "Hi."

"Are you" — he consulted a clipboard hanging from the dashboard — "Alison Bergeron?"

Great. Interrogated in two states. I nodded. Facing west, I had to shade my eyes from the sun, which was now low in the sky.

He picked up a cell phone, dialed a number, and handed it to me. It was Crawford. His voice crackled on the other end. "What is with you and walking? I woke up, and you were gone."

"I figured you were doing surveillance, and I didn't want to disturb you."

"Funny."

"You didn't have to call the police." I looked at the young cop, who was pretending not to listen but was hanging on every word. The side of the dune buggy said LPD. "You didn't have to call the LPD." How many cops could Lavallette have? Three? And now one was dispatched to look for a wandering English professor. Must have been an exciting day in the station house. "You've either greatly overreacted, or you're too lazy to go out and find me."

"Just get in the car and ask him to drop you off at the back of the house. I'll be outside," he said, and hung up.

"It's a dune buggy," I yelled into the phone, but he had hung up. "Would you mind driving me back down? It's north of here. I'm not exactly sure where the house is, but my friend will be outside." I hoisted myself into the dune buggy, and he gunned the engine.

A few minutes later, and after a nice conversation with Ted, the cop (who really wanted to teach surfing in Hawaii I learned), I was deposited at the back of the beach house. Crawford was standing on the deck with his arms folded over his chest and gave me a stern look. "You could have left me a note."

"I left my shoes. That's the beach equivalent of a note."

Officer Dune Buggy Ted stayed a moment longer than he should have, waiting to see if fisticuffs would erupt, I guess. When he was sure that all was well, he drove off. I waved at him, and called "Thanks for the ride, Ted!"

"You didn't have to call the LPD," I said, giggling. "I was actually going to see how long it would take me to walk to Seaside."

"A long time." He had cleared the table of the lunch dishes and lit a citronella candle. I pulled up the same chair that I had been in before and sat down. He sat down next to me. "We shouldn't leave for a while because the traffic on the Garden State will be horrendous. If you really have to get back, though, we can get started." He looked at me, it seemed, hoping that I would agree to stay. "Or, you could start walking, which you seem to like to do."

I didn't want to leave, truth be told. I told him that I didn't need to rush home.

"Great," he said, and jumped up from the chair. He returned a few minutes later with a bottle of chilled chardonnay and two wineglasses. The bottle had already been uncorked, and he put the glasses on the table and poured the wine. "If you want dinner, we still have some food from lunch. Or, we can go out."

"I promised Ted we'd go out later."

He looked at me.

"I'm fine," I said, and took a sip of the wine. It was delicious. I wondered if he had chosen it or if it was the family beach house stash. We sat quietly for a long time, watching the waves crash onto the beach, one after another. We finished the wine during that time and started on a second, even better one. "Do you collect wine?" I asked.

He looked surprised. "Me? No. I have a good friend who owns a restaurant in the city, and he buys my wine. My father and brother drink wine out of a box, so I bring a case down here every once in a while so they don't get cirrhosis of the liver."

"Good friend to have," I said.

"I should take you to his restaurant sometime," he said.

I took a sip of my wine. "Do you think we should do that?" I asked.

He looked back at me, obviously confused.

"We really shouldn't do this." I looked away from him. "We don't know what we are, really."

He shrugged. "We're friends. Like you and Ted."

"Really? Because you're still a cop, and I'm still the ex-wife of a murder suspect and the owner of the murder vehicle, or whatever you would call that. And we're alone at your beach house. Do you really think we should do this?"

He slumped in his chair. "No," he admitted. "But the case will end soon and our lives will go on and someone else will get murdered," he said, his voice trailing off. "Then, it will be all right." He looked away, almost like a kid caught in the middle of an act of disobedience. "You're right, though."

Being right in this case didn't make me feel any better. "So, nobody will know where I was today or who I was with. Except for Ted, of course."

"Ted. It's always Ted with you, isn't it?"

"You know, you and Ted may be working together if anyone finds out we spent the day here eating lobster and drinking wine. So, try to get along."

"The dune buggy is so much cooler than the Crown Vic," he mused, smiling. But I could tell that I had hit a nerve. We weren't supposed to be anywhere near each other. I returned to my thought that he might be the worst cop I had ever encountered, and the only ones that I had ever encountered were on television. They were usually very handsome, had great clothes, and broke all of the rules in the name of justice. Two out of three was pretty good.

He held his hand out to me. "Come here." He reached over and took the wine out of my hand, putting it on the edge of the table. I took his hand, thinking we were going to shake on our new friendship and his new career as a beach cop. Instead, I was shocked when he pulled me onto his lap. I thought about the fact that at my height and weight, I could render him a paraplegic if I stayed there for any length of time. Our faces were as close as they could be without touching. "As long as we'll never see each other again in a social capacity," he said, putting his massive hands on either side of my face to pull me closer, "I'm going to kiss you just once." And he did. And I didn't vomit, as I often did when he was around, but I did almost faint.

FOURTEEN

Crawford dropped me off around eight that night, having endured a car ride with me in which I never moved and remained completely silent. What he didn't know was that I was mentally berating myself for not moving and being completely silent. What was wrong with me? After so many years with Ray and having not a shred of self-esteem or self-respect left, I didn't know how to act around an attractive and obviously, *interested,* man anymore.

Sadly, I had lost my mojo. If indeed I had ever had any.

And, to add insult to injury, I had pissed Max off. After he kissed me, I heard my cell phone start chirping inside the house. When I saw that the number on the screen belonged to Max, any pleasure that I had gotten from having kissed a very attractive man was erased by the sound of her shrill voice screaming about the fact that I was late for dinner. I apologized profusely, hanging up somewhere between "you'll pay for this!" and "crappy house chardonnay."

I went to bed filled with a mixture of sexual desire and self-loathing, just like a good Catholic should, and woke up some time around seven in the morning. Despite the fact that I had had one of the most enjoyable days that I could remember in a long time, I had a bit of a headache. Maybe it was a kissing hangover. I hadn't been kissed like that in a long time; it must have had some kind of profound effect on my equilibrium. I stumbled into the bathroom and found a bottle of Excedrin headache medicine in the cabinet over the toilet. I shook two out of the bottle and put them in my mouth. Unable to find a cup, I put my mouth under the sink and tried to wash them down with the running water. I ended up with a bitter mush of aspirin and water in my mouth that made me gag.

After a shower, I went into the bedroom and sifted through the clothes in my closet. There was a yellow T-shirt and a pair of black pants in the mess that didn't look too wrinkled, so I shook them out and put them on after unearthing a bra and underpants in my underwear drawer. Today would be "casual day." My sandals were next to my bed, right where I had left them, and I slipped those on, too. After brushing my wet hair and putting on a bit of makeup, I felt like I could go to school and not look like the wreck of the *Hesperus,* as my mother used to say.

I found my briefcase in the hallway, right by the front door. I checked for my wallet and my phone, grabbed a couple of Devil Dogs and a bottle of coffee from the refrigerator, and left for school.

It was Friday. Two weeks since I had found out about Kathy's murder, since I had met Crawford. What was it they always said on cop shows? The longer a case goes, the colder the trail gets? Well, if they didn't step it up and soon, this case would be as dead as that dead young girl. I still had a hard time imagining Ray as a cold-blooded killer, but then again, I had had a hard time imagining him as anything less than my devoted husband. I guess I wasn't as perceptive as I thought.

I thought about Crawford. It just figured that I met a nice man who seemed to think I was nice, too, and it was in the middle of a murder investigation. I felt incredibly guilty, thinking about what Gianna and Peter and their family had to live with for the rest of their lives. They wanted the case to be over so they could find out who killed their daughter, and I wanted the case to be over so I could go on a date. Maybe I'd track down Kevin when I got to school and figure out how not to feel so guilty about that.

Crawford could always join the LPD. And drive the dune buggy. But maybe I was getting ahead of myself. Maybe I was putting the cart before the dune buggy.

I mulled all of this over as I stood on the platform of the train station. I looked northward up the tracks as everyone else did in the morning, willing the train to come so that we could begin our day of rushing and running through the tasks that would put us on another platform, looking for the same train to take home. I saw it, like a mirage down the tracks, moving through the morning mist and hazy sunshine, making its way toward all of the type-A commuters I was sandwiched between.

I sat in my usual seat, with the same pregnant businesswoman next to whom I sat every day. She acknowledged me with a nod. We never spoke, but she had started looking for me in the last two weeks, and I for her. I didn't know if it was against train etiquette to speak to her — it seemed there were some very ingrained rules regarding commuting, one of them mandating silence as far as I could tell — so we never spoke. I took out my Devil Dogs and began eating. I glanced at her out of the corner of my eye and caught her looking at me. By the way she was looking at me and the way I was stealing glances at her, it seemed that we both wanted what the other had — me, her swollen stomach and she, my Devil Dogs.

When the train arrived at the station, I began my laborious journey up the hill. To say that I literally dragged myself up the hill and down the avenue would not be an exaggeration. I continued my trek until I reached the front entrance of school. I thanked God silently as I saw Joe, in his golf cart, shooting the breeze with Franklin over a box of Dunkin' Donuts and two giant coffees.

I stumbled up to the guard booth. "Can I get a ride?" I managed to get out, nearly to the point of hyperventilation. "And a donut?"

Franklin held out the box of donuts and I took a chocolate glazed. Joe put his donut down on the guard booth shelf and motioned to the golf cart. "At your service," he said. I made a vow never to make another crack about Joe and his giant belly, either out loud or in my head.

He drove me to the back entrance of the building and after thanking him profusely and eating my donut, I went down the stairs, through the back door, and around to the door of the floor of offices. Dottie was in her usual spot, talking on the phone in that sotto voce way that you do when you're at work and you're talking with someone who really doesn't have anything to do with your profession. Although calling what Dottie did a "profession" was stretching it. She mumbled something to the person on the phone and hung up.

"Feeling better?" she asked.

"Yes. Thanks for helping out with class assignments." I turned around and went to the mailboxes behind her. There were various notices, papers, and messages, all of which I scrunched up into a stack and put in the outside pocket of my briefcase.

She swung around in her chair, blocking my exit. "The cute detective called," she said, and winked at me. Dottie is sixty, looks seventy, and can be coquettish with the best of them.

"Cute detective?" I asked in that ridiculously casual way you do when you know exactly to whom someone is referring but don't want to let on.

"You know. Crawford," she said. "The

202

Irish-looking one. Not the one that always looks like he's in a bad mood. Although he's kind of handsome, too, in a more rugged . . ."

I looked at her, waiting for the message. "And?"

She looked back at me, her eyes, heavy with mascara, blinking at me. "And what?"

"What did he want?" I enunciated.

"For you to call him," she enunciated back. She whipped back around in her chair and faced her desk, her back to me. Thank God this conversation was over.

I made my way across the expanse of the office floor, past the long, antique prefect's table and its mismatched chairs, and the closed doors of the offices belonging to my late-arriving colleagues. I stopped outside of my door, with its frosted glass insert, and saw Father Kevin emerge from the office of the French Department chair, Denis Marchant, whose office was to the right and down a short hallway from mine. Denis was a little younger than the rest of us and quite the bon vivant. Handsome, single, and French, he was a favorite among the female population on campus. French majors had increased by 20 percent when he joined the faculty. A cloud of smoke followed Kevin out of the office, and I knew immediately that the two of them had had their usual morning Gauloise smoke-a-thon, a no-no in a "nonsmoking" building. Kevin had on his black shirt, priest's collar, well-worn jeans and Birkenstock sandals. It looked like an outfit from the Stoner Priest collection.

"Later, Denis," Kevin said, and he came down the short hallway to the main area. He saw me and stopped. "Hey! Feeling better?" he asked. "I can do the intercession of St. Blaise thing if you have a sore throat."

My level of guilt rose with every query of concern I had to answer to. "It was my stomach." I lowered my eyes. "But thanks, Kevin." I made the process of looking for my keys into a long, drawn-out affair so I didn't have to make eye contact. He stood next to me, waiting for me to ask him in. I took the keys out of my briefcase and put the key into the lock, opening the door.

My office had been vandalized, ransacked, burgled, and turned upside down, basically. My file cabinet had been upended, and all of the files and papers were scattered all over the room. Books had been pulled out of the two large built-ins, and were strewn across my desk, the radiator, the floor, and every other clean spot. A large "X" had been carved into my desk, and my phone cord cut. Kevin came up behind me and none too delicately, shouted, "Holy crap!"

Dottie wheeled out from behind her desk and into the main area of the office area to get a better look. She called out to me. "Everything OK back there?"

I stood for a moment, taking in the destruction. Finally, having gleaned a bit about securing a crime scene from watching shows on Max's cable station, I slammed my door shut and locked it, running past the large table to Dottie's desk. "Give me the phone," I commanded, holding out my hand. Without a word, she handed it to me, and I rested it on the edge of the glass partition that separated her from the rest of the floor. I had memorized Crawford's cell number and punched it into the phone. He answered after three rings. The din in the background suggested to me that he was at work. "It's me," I said. Kevin came up beside me and stood there. "My office has been broken into."

He sighed. "I'll get some uniforms over. Don't go in, and don't let anyone in. Even campus security. Especially campus security."

We hung up, and I handed the phone back to Dottie. "Thanks, Dottie." She looked at me expectedly, like I was going to let her in on something. "My office was broken into."

She whistled through her teeth. "The cops coming?" she asked, hopefully.

I nodded. "Let's keep this as quiet as we can," I said. "As a matter of fact, Kevin, stand outside and run interference with the students coming in for office hours, if you would. I'll go outside and meet the police so I can bring them right in."

I left the building through the back way and trotted up the steps to the front entrance of the dorm behind my building. I turned around and saw that if I had paid any attention while entering the building, I would have noticed the destruction as I had descended the steps. But I hadn't, too busy eating my donut and making deals with God about Joe's belly.

As I reached the top of the steps and went into the dorm park-ing lot, a police car screeched to a stop almost at my feet. Two officers — a young black man named Simons and an older, ruddy-faced man with a flat top whom I immediately renamed "Officer Jarhead" — jumped out. The older one, whose real name was Moriarty, spoke. "Alison Bergeron?" he asked.

I nodded. "Follow me." A few students had gathered in the parking lot and begun to mumble among themselves.

Once inside, I sat down at the long table

to wait for Crawford. Simons stayed with Kevin on the landing outside of the main office area and kept the door shut. Dottie, Moriarty, and I sat in silence, looking at each other occasionally.

Crawford showed up within a half hour. Although his hair was damp, and he was clean-shaven, he was still wearing the jeans and Teva sandals that he had on the day before. His shirt was new, though: a blue T-shirt, with big, white NYPD letters stamped across the front and back. The gold shield was on its silver chain and hanging to the middle of his chest. He had the big gun on, and it was in the leather shoulder holster over the T-shirt. I looked over at Dottie, who was staring at him and fanning herself with a college catalog.

Simons entered behind him, followed by Kevin. They closed the door to the office area and walked toward my office, where Moriarty was standing guard. Crawford asked Kevin to sit with me at the table. "Anyone else here?" he asked.

"Just Denis Marchant, the French chair," I said, pointing to the alcove where Denis's office was.

Crawford took a pair of rubber gloves out of his pants pocket and put them on. He asked for my keys and opened the door to my office and stepped in, careful to avoid the debris. When he saw the deeply etched "X" in the middle of the desk, he turned to Moriarty, and said, "Call Crime Scene."

Moriarty, a little over five feet five and quite rotund, lumbered down toward Dottie's desk and asked for her phone. Before handing it to him, she murmured, "I'm Dottie."

I couldn't hear his response clearly, but it sounded like "I'm good," or "I'm food," or "I'm Mook." Whatever it was, these two were made for each other. They were the same size, same age, and had the same haircut.

Crawford looked at me. "I'm going to need a complete list of what was in here." He saw the alarmed look on my face, and said, "To the best of your knowledge."

"I've been here nine years. What wasn't in there?" I asked, out of patience, a little hysterical, and into full-blown snotty mode.

He remained impassive, either used to crime victims or the moods of women; he did have teenage daughters. "Why don't you start now? Do you have paper?" He turned his attention from me to Simons. "Simons, do you have a camera in the car?"

Simons nodded and left the floor to get it. His monotone was annoying. Was this our first fight? If it was, he didn't seem to know it. I sat down and pulled a blue exam book from the pile on the center of the table. I started jotting down what I thought might be the contents of my office. "Year one," I said aloud. "Midterms, essays, research papers . . ."

He looked over at me and gave me a pained smile. "That's not necessary." He looked up and saw Moriarty, deep in conversation with Dottie, leaning against her desk. "How we doing on Crime Scene, Charlie?" he called out.

Moriarty looked up in surprise. "They'll be here in twenty, Detective." He bid Dottie good-bye and came lumbering back toward my office.

Simons returned with a large, black camera with a big flash panel across the top. He handed it to Crawford and put the bag outside the office. "Here you go, Detective."

Crawford nodded and put the camera to his face, starting with the desk. He seemed particularly interested in the "X" on it. To my thinking, it was just the vandal being an even bigger asshole than he or she already was. But Crawford seemed to think it had some significance. He took several pictures of it from different angles. He then turned his attention to the bookshelves and took several pictures of them and the books on the floor. He moved around the small office, gingerly stepping over the contents, and snapped pictures. He turned around at one point, and asked, "How's that list coming?" more to be a pain in the ass than out of genuine concern.

I gave him a double thumbs-up. "Excellent!" I was on the third year and sure that I had missed a bunch of things already. I was beyond caring, though.

Wyatt arrived just as Crawford was reviewing some of the pictures he had taken with the camera. He was dressed as casually as Crawford in jeans, T-shirt, and giant basketball sneakers. He nodded at me in greeting when he arrived, but I still got the feeling that he didn't trust me completely. Or maybe he knew what was going on between me and Crawford and didn't approve. For the third time that day, I felt guilty. I was ahead of schedule in the daily guilt allotment. I returned to my blue book and the list of office contents.

Crawford brought Wyatt up to speed. Crawford's back was to me, and Wyatt faced me, looking at me over Crawford's shoulder while he recounted the events of the morning. I stared right back at him, my pen poised above the paper. When Crawford finished, Wyatt came over and sat down. "Tell me what happened."

"Didn't Crawford just tell you?" I asked. I saw Crawford wince a bit at my tone.

Wyatt let out a breath. "Tell me again."

I was getting tired of telling the same old stories again and again. "I got to work, opened my door, saw that the office was trashed, and closed the door."

"Was there anyone on the floor at the time?"

"Just Dottie, Denis, and Father Kevin," I said, hooking a thumb in Kevin's direction. Kevin, who was slumped in a chair playing with a paper clip, perked up a bit at the mention of his name.

"Padre," Wyatt said, acknowledging Kevin's presence.

"Detective," Kevin said, and held out his hand.

The phone rang at Dottie's desk, and she picked it up. "Professor? Sister Mary." She held the receiver out to me, even though I was too far away to reach it.

I rolled my eyes at Kevin and went over to Dottie's desk. "Yes, Sister?" She read me the riot act about closing the office floor, and when she took a breath, I was able to explain the situation to her. She asked me when they would open the floor again. "No idea," I said. "But as soon as I find out, I'll let you know."

We hung up. Moriarty had arrived back at Dottie's desk to take her statement. He pulled up a chair next to her desk and began questioning her. The way she described her job made it sound way more important and complex than it really was.

Wyatt was sitting across from Kevin, getting information from him. I walked over to Crawford, who put an arm across the opening of the office to keep me out. He looked down at me. "Fred?" he called. "I'm going to take Professor Bergeron's statement. Crime Scene should be here any minute."

Wyatt nodded and turned back to Kevin. Crawford looked at me. "Is there an empty office?" he asked.

I shook my head but led him to Denis's office, around the corner. I tapped on the glass of his office door slightly and heard one of the desk drawers slam shut. Probably hiding the contraband. "Denis? Can we borrow your office?" I asked in French.

The door opened and Denis appeared, the usual cloud of smoke hanging heavily in the air. He looked terrified when he saw Crawford, but he nodded and exited as quickly as he could.

Crawford and I went into the office; I sat

at Denis's desk, Crawford in the chair between the desk and the door. Denis's office was more long than wide, with the desk, visitor chair, and bookshelf all crammed against one wall. Unlike mine, the window opened onto a brick wall so nobody could see in. I looked at Crawford, and he looked back at me — not with the sad face, but with the really bad-news face. I fought the urge to burst into tears. "I'm sorry," I said.

He looked at me blankly.

"For being such a snot. I'm mentally and physically exhausted. It's all getting to me," I admitted.

"It's fine. You don't have to apologize."

"Why is this happening?" I asked.

He leaned in close, and whispered, "You've obviously got something that someone wants. Think. What could that be?" he asked, looking deep into my eyes.

I folded and unfolded my hands in my lap. "I don't know." I thought for a moment and shook my head. "I don't know."

He nodded, resigned. I wasn't going to be any help. "Think. What could you have that someone wants? Is it something of Ray's, maybe?" He pulled back a bit. "If you think of anything . . ."

"I know, I know. We've been through this a hundred times. Call you. Anytime. Day or night," I intoned.

He stood. "Let's go back out. I want to see if Crime Scene has come so we can finish this up and open the office again."

"That's a cool T-shirt," I said, as he opened the door. I fingered the sleeve. "Can I get one when this is over?"

He looked back at me and smirked. "You can have anything you want when this is over."

I had a feeling he wasn't referring to police-issue clothing, and my stomach fluttered slightly.

FIFTEEN

The investigation progressed for most of the day. I sat at the table, watching the Crime Scene detectives do what they do best: put stuff in little baggies. I watched seven pencils and four markers be bagged as evidence, along with my fake Rangers' hockey puck and my framed photograph of Mark Messier, the greatest Ranger of all time, in my opinion, which I hoped I would get back. I couldn't fantasize about being Mrs. Mark Messier if I couldn't stare at his picture for hours on end. At two-forty, I grabbed Crawford. "Can I go to class?" I asked. "I have Shakespeare in a few minutes."

He nodded. "I'll walk you."

Sister Mary ambushed Crawford on the landing outside the office floor. "This is very disruptive, Detective," she said. She stood six feet two inches in stocking feet and probably had twenty pounds on him. She had the bearing of an army drill sergeant and the monochromatic wardrobe to match. I might have imagined it, but he looked cowed.

"We'll be done shortly, Sister," he said. "I'll be back in a few minutes, so I'll give you an update." Crawford slunk away, with me at his side. We went up a flight of stairs to the fourth floor and down the hall to the class where I taught the Shakespeare course. The hallway was empty and the door was closed. We stood in front of the door, me clutching my briefcase like a football, and him with hands plunged deep into his jeans pockets.

"You haven't talked to Ray, have you?" he asked.

I shook my head. "Not since yesterday." I told him about our phone call at the beach while he was sleeping.

He looked at me intently. "Did you tell him where you were?"

"No."

"If you talk to him again, you need to call me. Or if he shows up at the house. Any contact at all."

I nodded to show him I understood.

"I would feel better if you spent the weekend with Max. I'll drive you if you want to go." He stood for a moment and thought, looking at me intently. "You're not going to go, are you?"

I shook my head.

"You are stubborn," he said. "I'll be over later," he said, and walked away before I had a chance to respond. "And I'm not sleeping in my car, so let's figure something out," he called back over his shoulder.

"I'll be grading papers!" I yelled. His rubber sandals made a squeaking noise as he walked down the hall; he didn't respond. "So, don't expect anything exciting!" He disappeared through the door; I heard it slam shut.

Several students made their way down the hall a few moments later. I opened the door to the classroom and let the five students out of eight who had shown up — John Costigan, Mercedes Rivas, Fiona Martin, Jake Carlyle, and Deb McCarthy — into the room. I went over to the desk and put my briefcase down and decided to answer the question before it was asked. "Before you ask, no, I have not graded your papers yet." I held my hand up as the groans, complaints, and accusations began. "However, I promise that I will have them back to you by Monday." I stopped and waited until they were silent. "Promise," I emphasized.

Fiona Martin raised her hand, and I nodded to her. The students were in two rows, Fiona at the front of the row to my left. "What's going on in the office area?" she asked.

Word gets around fast. I picked up a piece of chalk from the ledge on the blackboard behind me and rolled it between my fingers. I was still a bit off-kilter from what had happened this morning and was having a hard time focusing on the class and the lesson plan. "Just a little problem with one of the offices," I said, and turned to write on the board, trying to keep the focus on *Macbeth* and off the crime that had taken place in my office.

"What kind of problem?"

I stopped writing, the chalk in midair. I thought the subject was closed, but apparently she didn't agree. I turned around. "Fiona?"

She looked at me blankly. "What kind of problem?" she repeated.

I put the chalk down on the ledge. "Someone broke into my office."

A couple of the students gasped. Fiona looked down at her books and then up again at me. "Why?"

I shrugged. "Don't know," I said shortly, and turned back around to the board.

"Now, who can address this issue?" I asked, writing "Compare and contrast the ways that Macbeth and Lady Macbeth deal with their guilt."

There were some murmurs, but none of the students could come up with anything even vaguely resembling an answer. Mercedes Rivas, the star of our softball team and a decent student, finally raised her hand. "Macbeth continues to do other wrong things and goes insane and Lady Macbeth kind of goes crazy, too?" she said.

I resisted the urge to shudder at the lack of grammatical structure in her response and focused on what was correct. "That's a start. What else?"

Fiona raised her hand. "Lady Macbeth's guilt, even though she didn't physically commit the act, gets the best of her." She shot a look at her classmates to see if anybody would back her up, but there were no takers. It seemed they understood the concept of "aiding and abetting."

I nodded slowly. "But what about her complicity in helping Macbeth bring the plan to fruition?"

They stared at me blankly so I decided to rephrase. "Doesn't she really push Macbeth to kill Duncan, thereby making herself part of the plot and just as guilty?"

A few heads went up and down. They were finally getting it. John Costigan raised his hand, and I noticed that he had a bandage across the palm of his right hand. He quickly put it down when I pointed to him. "I'm not sure she's just as guilty, but she thinks she is."

I nodded. "Right." I turned back to the board and began writing some of their responses, creating a cluster map on the board with the word "guilt" in the middle. After discussing it until there were only five minutes to go, I felt that we had covered the topic of guilt in as much detail as we were going to, and I bid them a good weekend, sending them on their way. I figured letting them go early might make them forget that I still had their papers. When Fiona approached my desk after the others had left, I knew that I was wrong. I looked up from my position behind the desk and waited for her question.

"Are we really getting the papers back on Monday?" she asked, her gaze steely and unwavering.

I held up two fingers like I had seen Crawford do. "Scout's honor," I said, laughing slightly.

She stood for a few more minutes, staring at me in silence. Finally, she picked up her backpack, which rested at her feet, and left the classroom without saying good-bye.

To her back, I called, "Have a good weekend!" but in my head, I said something else about her which didn't make me proud. I packed my briefcase, making sure I had the papers, and closed the door to the classroom behind me.

There was a small lounge outside the classroom and a crowd of students — Fiona and Vince among them — were lounging in the overstuffed chairs, chatting and laughing. I took a good look at Vince, thinking that he had recovered very well from his girlfriend's murder. He stared back at me, holding my gaze, almost as if he knew what I was thinking. After a few minutes of the staring match, I turned and walked down the hall, noticing that the group behind me had fallen silent.

Sixteen

Rather than return to my office, which was now a crime scene, I left the campus immediately upon the completion of my last class and went to the train station. It was a gorgeous day — sunny, mild, with a few fluffy clouds in the sky. I had no idea what time the next train happened by, but I thought I would take my chances and wait on the platform. If I had a long wait, I would stare at the river until the train came. After the day that I had had, I thought that might be a nice thing to do.

As I descended the hill, I heard the train approaching the station. I took off running. Who was I kidding? I didn't want to stare at the river. I wanted to go home. I reached the parking lot as the train pulled into the station. I saw the conductor hanging out the window of the engine car and yelled to get his attention. He acknowledged me and yelled that I should hurry if I wanted to make the train.

Once on board, I rested my head against the headrest of my seat and closed my eyes. I dreamed of sand, waves, the ocean, and Seaside Heights. Thoughts of my senior prom and my seafoam-green-polyester dress floated into my head. Had it only been a day since I walked along the sand with not a thought in my head? So much had happened. Seconds later, or so it seemed, the conductor screamed out "Dobbs Ferry" and I awoke with a start. I exited the train and began my walk up the hill.

I arrived at the house and headed up the driveway to the back door. My neighbor, Terri, peeked out from the row of hedges that separated our two driveways. She called out to me.

"Alison! Hi!" she called.

I stopped in the middle of the driveway. "Oh, hi, Terri."

She was a petite blonde who was often in either workout or tennis attire. Today, she had on a little sundress and looked perfect. I felt like a giant, sweaty behemoth standing across from her. She seemed to want to chat.

She ran a hand over her blond ponytail. Her pink scrunchie matched her sundress, which, for some reason, really annoyed me. Maybe because I was wearing black and yellow and looked like an oversized bumblebee. "I heard about what happened with your . . . with your car and all." She paused. "It was terrible." Another pause, this one of the pregnant variety. "The dead girl went to your school, didn't she?"

I nodded.

"That was terrible."

I thought we had already established that.

"Did they find out who killed her?" she asked.

"I don't think so."

"Did you know her?"

I nodded again.

She looked at me questioningly. "There was something in the paper today that said the police had Ray in for questioning. Is that true?"

I was surprised. I had stopped reading the paper, so I had no idea that Ray's name had been mentioned in connection with this. It made sense. "Yes, it's true. But they let him go. They didn't have enough to keep him."

"Does he have good representation?" she asked.

I was sick of talking about Ray already. "I think so. I think Mitch Klein has taken the case."

She gasped. "The lawyer who . . ."

I knew it by heart. ". . . defended the guy

who shot the kid on the subway," I repeated in a monotone.

"Well that makes me feel better," she said, a little too concerned with Ray's well-being for my comfort. She wrapped her arms around her little body. "Is Ray OK?"

"I guess," I said, trying not to let on how little I actually cared. Why did she care so much?

"If you talk to him, tell him that I was asking about him," she said, not able to look at me.

That's when it hit me. I took a step back. "You . . ."

She looked at me, all doe-eyed and perky. "What?"

I shook my head. "Nothing." But I knew. Terri had been one of Ray's affairs. I was surer of it than I had ever been of anything. And I was furious, all over again. "Good . . . then . . ." I said, picking up my briefcase. "I'll see you later. Say hi to Jackson. Your husband," I said pointedly as I went inside. That was mature, I thought as I stood in the hallway. I closed the door and closed my eyes, banging my head against the door-frame, murmuring "stupid, stupid, stupid . . ."

When the shock of this new revelation wore off, I took my shoes off and left them inside the front door, along with my briefcase. I padded up the stairs and sat on the edge of my bed, looking around. Magda wasn't coming for another four days, and my house needed a cleaning desperately, and not just because there was fingerprint dust everywhere; there was your regular garden-variety dust as well. I guess I knew what I'd be doing over the weekend. I didn't know if Crawford had been serious about coming over, but if he was, I figured I had a few hours before he showed up, so I decided to take a nap before I broke out the vacuum and the rubber gloves.

The room was dark when I awoke. A soft wind was blowing through the window of the bedroom, and I heard rain hitting the pavement outside. I sat up with a start and squinted to see the clock next to my bed. It was seven, three hours after I had arrived home. I threw my legs over the side of the bed and rested a moment before getting up.

I heard footsteps on the stairs, the person coming up treading so lightly that they hardly made any noise. I tensed. The room was pitch-dark, except for the glow of the clock-radio numbers. I heard my name being whispered and before I could find anything to defend myself against the intruder besides a paperback copy of the latest Harry Potter book that was on my nightstand, the doorframe was filled with an outline of a body. I grabbed the book and hurled it with every ounce of strength that I had.

As my eyes adjusted, I could see that the shape was unmistakably Crawford's, but the book was already out of my hands and flying through the air. Tall and lanky, yet broad-shouldered, the detective stood in the doorway. He was dressed as he had been earlier, sans the gun and shield. He let out a shout as the book hit him in the gut. "What the hell?" he yelled.

"Sorry."

He kicked the book back into the room but stayed in the doorway.

"You can come in, you know. It's not the inner sanctum or anything."

He came in and walked over to the bed, bending over me.

"No kissing," I reminded him as his face got close. Had my teeth been brushed, I might have broken the rules, but the taste in my mouth told me that this kiss might be my last.

He stood up. "I was going to take your pulse," he lied.

"I wasn't sure you were coming," I said, not fully awake. "If I knew you were coming, I would have baked a Bundt," I said, referencing a commercial from my childhood.

"I wasn't sure I was coming either," he admitted. "What's a Bundt?"

I stifled a yawn. "You're going to get in trouble."

"I'm off duty," he said. "Besides, I've already run the Sister Mary gauntlet today. What else could happen?"

"How did you get in?" I asked.

His tone got serious. "Through the front door. Don't you think it would be a good idea to lock it, considering the events of the last few weeks?"

He had a point. "You smell like garlic," I said, getting a whiff.

"There's pizza downstairs. I'm just glad you'll be alive to enjoy it," he said, and turned to go downstairs.

" 'I'm just glad you'll be alive to enjoy it,' " I mimicked, and got up off the bed.

My jeans and a clean shirt were hanging on a hook on the back of the bathroom door. I pulled off the khakis and put on the jeans, which were noticeably looser than they had been a few weeks earlier. I tried to recall when I ate last and flashed on the Devil Dogs, bottled coffee, and chocolate donut. Hours ago. My brush was still on the dresser, along with a thin sheen of fingerprint powder; I brushed my hair, flipping my head over and giving myself an instant head rush. I stood up straight, let the dizziness pass, and pulled my hair into a ponytail. I slipped on my trusty clogs.

I washed my face and brushed my teeth. There was nothing I could do about the dark circles under my eyes, so I went with clean over glamorous and left off the makeup. Crawford had seen me in all states, and clean would be an improvement over many of them. I went downstairs.

"What did you come up with from my office?" I asked, not really in the mood for small talk.

He really didn't have too much to tell although he was still fixated on the "X" that had been etched in my desk. "Someone with an unoriginal Zorro complex is looking for something and leaving their mark," he said, pausing for a moment. "It was on the dash of the car, too, but nobody's supposed to know that."

I guess he really did trust me. "That's one of those things you keep from the public, right?"

"Yeah, we don't want that getting out because every lunatic in the Bronx will come out of the woodwork to confess." He opened a box of pizza — there were two on my countertop — and the smell hit me in the nose, making my mouth water. "I'm off duty, though. Remember? No shop talk." Next to the pizza boxes was a bag from the store around the corner, from which he pulled out paper plates, napkins, forks and knives, and a bottle of wine. He had found two wineglasses in my cupboards and had taken those out as well. "I've got one plain and one extra garlic and sausage. You looked like an extra-garlic woman." He looked at me, waiting for my answer.

"You were right," I said, and got up to get a piece of pizza. He pulled a slice from the pie and handed it to me on a paper plate.

He also gave me a stack of napkins. "You also look like an extra-napkins woman," he said, a twinkle in his eye. I shot him a look, but took the stack of napkins anyway. He was right about that, too.

He pulled a Swiss army knife from his pants pocket and got out the corkscrew to uncork the wine. "Do you want a glass of wine or a big can of Foster's?" he asked.

"Funny," I said.

He had the bottle open in a few seconds and poured two glasses, one of which he handed to me. He took his glass and tipped it toward me. "A toast?"

I thought for a moment. "To solving this case?"

"You can do better than that," he said, his glass raised and still tipped toward me, a smile on his lips.

"I don't think I can," I said.

He thought for a moment. "Then I'll try," he said. "To you," he said softly, and clinked his glass against mine. I averted his gaze and took a sip, my face flushing. "You blush a lot," he remarked.

I blushed a deeper red. "It's kind of like your sad face. It only comes out sometimes."

"Sad face?"

I pulled my mouth down into my imitation of his face, drawing my lips thin. He laughed heartily, spraying wine into a napkin. On a roll, I continued, "Then, you've got the really bad-news face," I said, and did my impression of that expression.

His laugh was a deep bellow, punctuated by snorts. I generally wasn't a fan of the snort — the only component of Max's belly laugh and one that I was accustomed to — but because it was him, I accepted it. I actually found it attractive.

"Do they teach you that in cop school?" I asked.

"It's called the Academy, and no, they don't teach us to make faces," he said.

231

"Do they teach you how to deal with suspects who vomit?"

"I'm down one pair of shoes, remember?"

"What do they teach you, then?"

"Oh, I don't know. How to deal with criminals, shoot guns, how to drive a *cruiser*," he said pointedly and looked at me, ". . . eat donuts . . . you know, the regular stuff."

"I think they should add Vomit 101."

"I'll mention that at the next cop-school meeting."

I sat at the table and he joined me with his wine. I dove into my pizza like it was my last meal. I don't know where he got it, but it was better than any pizza that I had tasted in my life. Or I was just starving, and it was just the same crappy pizza from the crappy pizza place around the corner. He watched me for a minute. "You were hungry. When was the last time you had a meal?"

"If you count three Devil Dogs, a bottle of coffee, and a chocolate donut as a meal, this morning around eight." I finished my pizza in three more bites and got up to get another slice. "You ready?" I asked, opening the box.

He was still on his first piece and shook his head. I found it hard to believe that you could be as big as he was and eat pizza as slowly as he did, but apparently, it was true.

I returned to the table with another slice. I chewed on my thumb for a minute. "I thought we weren't going to see each other in a social capacity anymore."

"This isn't a social call. I'm guarding you," he said, unconvincingly.

"I don't think that's going to hold up in front of a police review board."

He focused on a piece of sausage on his pizza and didn't respond.

"Besides, if you have me under surveillance, shouldn't you be asleep?" I asked.

"There is a difference between guarding and surveillance." He ate the sausage. "We cover that in cop school, too."

I ate my pizza in silence. When I was done, I got up and got another slice and the bottle of wine. "One more?" I asked. He handed me his plate, and I gave him another slice; I poured more wine in both of our glasses. "How's your stomach?"

He rubbed his midsection. "Harry Potter?"

I bowed my head solemnly. "There are many life lessons to be learned from Master Potter."

"Like?"

"Like love thy neighbor." I paused. "Something my ex-husband apparently took to heart." He looked at me, puzzled. "I'm pretty sure that Ray had an affair with Terri, next door."

The look on his face told me that he wasn't going to comment. I didn't feel the need to elaborate, either.

He changed the subject. "Save some room," he said. "I brought cannolis from Arthur Avenue." He motioned to a box on the counter and when I opened it, there were four beautiful cannolis wrapped in wax paper; the ends were sprinkled with chocolate chips. Arthur Avenue was a street in the Bronx noted for its spectacular Italian restaurants and decades-old bakeries, which specialized in pastries like cannolis, napoleons, and éclairs. I stopped myself from falling instantly in love with him; my love of the cannoli was greater than even my love of God and country. "I hope you like cannolis," he said.

"Just a little bit," I said, putting my index finger and thumb together. I was disappointed that he brought only four; I had been known to eat at least that many by myself. I sat down again and got to work on the third piece of pizza, confident that I would have room for dessert. When I finished that slice, I drank the rest of my wine, and poured more into my glass. I was feeling pretty good now, full and more than a little drunk.

"How did you get to Arthur Avenue to get cannolis? You're a pretty busy guy." I stared at him closely. "Do you have a clone?"

"Honestly?" He looked away, a little bashful.

I nodded.

"I radioed a cop from Motorcycle One to pick them up and meet me at the Van Cortlandt Park entrance to the Deegan."

"You did a moving-vehicle cannoli handoff?" I asked, incredulous. "You are a crime-fighting Irish superhero."

"No, we pulled over." He ate his pizza. "He owed me. I got his kid out of a jam."

"Wow," I remarked. "That's love." He looked at me. "Of cannolis," I amended quickly. I drank some more wine.

Something dawned on him, and he jumped up from the table. "I almost forgot! I brought you a T-shirt." He pulled it out of the grocery bag and held it up proudly. "You can't get these in any store."

I looked it over. "What size is that?"

He looked inside at the tag. "Triple extra large. I took it out of Fred's locker."

I stared at it, horrified. I could have covered my dining-room table with it. "Are you suggesting that I need a shirt that big?"

"No, I took it out of Fred's locker. I just told you that." He looked disappointed that I wasn't more excited.

I imagined getting one that was close to my size, not one for the both of us to live in. "Thanks," I said.

"It's not like you can wear it out in public. It's police-issue. It's from the Fred Wyatt Law Enforcement collection." He folded it and put it back on the counter. He sat back down at the table.

"Thanks. Whenever I wear it, I'll think of Fred." I made a face and got up to finger the T-shirt. I held it up to my face, taking a deep whiff. "Does it have the eau de cranky cop smell?"

He pretended to laugh, but it looked more like a wince. "Such a funny lady." He gave me a sly smile. "Maybe you could wear it when you're performing your Joyce-reading lap dances."

The phone rang. I jumped up and answered it, and when I heard his voice, I covered the mouthpiece and whispered to Crawford, "Ray."

Ray was annoyed again. I wanted to scream into the phone, "Listen, buddy, if anyone should be annoyed, it's me!" but of course, I didn't. I listened patiently. "Hello, Ray."

Crawford stood and mouthed, "Where's your other phone?" I pointed above my head. There was an extension in the guest room; he left the kitchen and went up the stairs. I could hear the floorboards creak over my head and an almost-inaudible "click" as he picked up the extension. He was listening to our conversation, and I didn't feel any need to tell Ray. Ray kept nattering on.

". . . so, I spent the day with Klein and do you know what he bills per hour?" I didn't answer, so he told me. "Five hundred dollars! Can you believe it? But if it keeps me out of jail, it will be worth it. You have to believe me, Alison . . . I didn't do it. I knew Kathy, but I didn't kill her. I bet it was that crazy boyfriend of hers, that Vince hoodlum. Do you know him?" I remained silent, and he continued with his rant. "He's crazy. She always felt threatened. She told me several times."

I imagined that I heard Crawford breathing on the other end of the phone, and that made listening to Ray almost tolerable. "And you called because?" I asked.

Ray paused for a second before starting up again. "I need to tell you something, Alison, before you hear it from someone else."

And then I knew where this was headed.

Crawford must have changed position above me, because the floorboards creaked a little more. I was embarrassed now that he was on the extension; now he had to hear the lies and half-truths that I had heard for so many years. He would think I was a giant ass. I held my breath for a minute while Ray got up the courage to reveal his indiscretion. Although it would be humiliating for me to hear it with Crawford listening, I couldn't pass up the opportunity to make Ray confess.

"Kathy and I had a relationship, Al. We were in love," he said, sounding almost sincere.

I couldn't even respond. This was worse than what I normally heard from Ray. Usually, it was "she didn't mean a thing to me." Now, he was telling me that he was in love with a girl half his age. And she was dead. I leaned over and tried not to puke.

"Thanks, Ray. I'm glad I heard it from you and not from someone else," I said, as graciously as I could.

He let out a breath, relieved by my reaction, I suppose. "You're a class act, Al. You always have been."

My tongue loosened by the wine, I remarked, "No, Ray, I'm a fucking idiot, and I always have been." And with that, I put the phone back on the receiver. I couldn't stand his complimenting me on my graciousness and class. I was an idiot, and now Crawford knew it, too. I held on to my stomach for a few more seconds, a wave of nausea flowing over me. Ray and Kathy? It was too much for me to comprehend, especially after my epiphany about Terri. If he was capable of an affair with a girl — a teenager, really — what else was he capable of? When I thought about it, I really didn't want to know.

I strode toward the front door, catching a glimpse of Crawford at the top of the stairs. I ignored him and walked out the front door, down the front steps, and out into the night, the soft rain mixing with the tears running down my face.

Seventeen

Crawford was wise and didn't follow me.

I walked down the street, feeling sad, woozy, and overly full from the dinner of wine and pizza. I reached the end of my block and was about to turn onto Broadway, thinking about the cannolis I had left behind, when a car screeched to a stop next to me. It was a Lincoln Navigator, black, with tinted windows. Loud, insistent rap music could be heard before the owner rolled down the back passenger-side window. I stood under the streetlight and leaned in to see who was in the car, assuming it was one of my neighbors inquiring as to why I was walking in the rain. Before I could get a good look, the back passenger-side door opened, and just like in my dream, two strong arms reached out and attempted to pull me into the car. Only this time, I didn't get kissed. And the arms didn't belong to a cop.

When I realized what was happening, I pulled my body away and went into a full sprint. I stumbled in my clogs — sorry now that I had put them on my still-sore feet — and started running back toward the house, which was at least an eighth of a mile away. The rain was heavy, and I was drenched. The gravel crunched under my feet and made traversing the wet street in the clogs even more difficult.

The car screeched to a halt behind me, and I ran as fast as I could toward the house.

I could see it in the distance; the front door opened. I heard footsteps gaining on me as I watched Crawford amble down the front walk, umbrella in hand. God, he's slow, I thought, watching him take a leisurely stroll in the rain.

I screamed as loud as I could, but I knew the loud music would drown my voice out. "Crawford!"

Two hands grabbed me from behind and dragged me backwards. I screamed again and Crawford looked up the street, grabbing his gun off his ankle and getting into a crouch. But he didn't shoot. I was in the way, an arm around my neck, being dragged toward the SUV. The hand at the end of the arm had a bandage across the palm. I struggled and fell to the ground, taking my assailant down, too. I got up and attempted to take off again, but whoever it was that wanted me grabbed me by the ankle, making me fall flat on my face on the pavement.

I struggled to get up again but was dragged down. I heard, "Get her!" as we went down again. I rolled away from him and into a sewer grate, hitting the curb hard with my right knee. I was pulled up again and dragged backwards, this time, a little closer to the stopped car. My feet were off the ground and I clawed at the thick forearm around my neck.

Crawford was running toward the car, his gun out in front of him; he had it in a two-handed clasp. I was almost to the car as I heard the music get louder and my attacker scream, "He's a fucking cop!" obviously noticing the gun and the NYPD shirt. Those white letters against an inky blue background were hard to miss; I guess that was the point.

"Police! Let her go!" Crawford screamed.

The arm around my neck tightened, and the air to my windpipe was cut off. I'm going to die out here, I thought to myself as my eyes watered. "Shoot him!" I croaked with the air that remained in my lungs.

But he wouldn't, and I knew it. I was a shield.

We continued moving backwards until I felt the seat beneath my legs.

The arm loosened around my neck. "Crawford! Help me!" I cried as I was pulled in and thrown into the backseat.

I hit my forehead on the way in as the door swung closed. I immediately put my hand to my head and felt a giant goose egg grow under my hand, but I didn't feel any blood. I righted myself on the seat and attempted to get my bearings, but the speeding car and the loud music, coupled with what was probably my second concussion in as many weeks, made control of my limbs almost impossible.

I turned and looked out the back window but could only see Crawford's back as he ran down the street and back to the house.

Vince was driving. Not being familiar with pharmacology (where was Ray when you needed him?), I didn't know what he was on, but it was obvious that he was on something. My guess was his drug of choice, Ecstasy, but I couldn't be sure. He was tense, high-strung, and agitated. He turned around and screamed something at me which sounded like "Where are those papers?" but I didn't have a clue as to what he meant. I attempted to put my seat belt on so that if we had an accident, I would at least be strapped in. It took me a few minutes, but I did it. And then I noticed the guy sitting next to me, the one who had succeeded in dragging me into the car.

It was John Costigan from my Shakespeare class. He was a star athlete on a full athletic scholarship who played basketball, baseball, and lacrosse. He was big — Crawford's height — but had thirty or forty pounds on him. Since I was bigger than Vince, they probably figured John was the one who could manhandle me successfully. I had always imagined John to be the all-American boy; he was blond, handsome, and polite. He did well in my class and his other classes and was on the honor roll every semester. I couldn't imagine how he had gotten mixed up with Vince and in this kind of situation. I looked over at him in disbelief. "John?" I asked, still holding my head.

He didn't answer me and stared straight ahead. He didn't look high like Vince, but he looked agitated. I tried Vince.

"Vince, what is this all about?" I asked, feeling nauseous and dizzy. As Vince took the corner to merge onto the exit for the Saw Mill, a sea of red swam before my eyes, and I struggled to stay conscious. Vince, seeing the stop sign at the entrance to the parkway too late, jammed on the brakes; the car skidded forward on the wet pavement and my head hit the seat in front of me.

"Vince, where are we going?" I screamed.

He kept driving, careening down the winding Saw Mill River Parkway and changing lanes every time a slower car got in the way.

We were going ninety miles an hour; the illuminated speedometer was visible from the backseat. I grabbed Costigan by the shirtsleeve and begged him to get Vince to slow down. He turned and looked out his window and didn't respond.

We sped past the Yonkers exits and the exit for the Cross County Parkway. As we approached the entrance for Moshulu Parkway and the Major Deegan Expressway and entered New York City proper, Vince stayed to the right toward the Henry Hudson Parkway. Three police cars came out of nowhere, two staying on either side of us and one behind us.

"Tell me what you want, and I'll give it to you. Just stop!" I screamed. I found the button to roll down the window and did. I turned and looked out the window; the police car was a blue-and-white NYPD cruiser. Or not. I'd have to ask Crawford, if

I lived, if that constituted a cruiser.

Vince rolled the window up from the control panel on the front seat. "Just give me the fucking papers!" he screamed again.

"What papers?" I asked, and turned to Costigan. The music was so loud that I wasn't even sure I heard Vince correctly.

The police stayed to our sides and behind us. Costigan screamed at Vince to pull over, but Vince ignored him. Vince reached behind him and tried to grab me, but I ducked out of the way. I had once encountered a rabid raccoon going through my garbage; the look in his eyes was similar to Vince's: beady, red, and filled with anger. He kept one hand on the wheel and continued to search for something on me to grab. I pulled my legs up and kicked him hard in the back of the head. He screamed in pain and anger as two pounds of solid Swedish clog construction hit him above the ear on the right side of his head. Costigan looked surprised but didn't do anything; I got the sense that he was a reluctant participant in this caper.

Vince pulled a gun out of his waistband and pointed it at me. "If you tell anyone, I'll blow your fucking head off," he said calmly, keeping one eye on the road while turning to look at me. He rested his gun hand on the back of the front passenger seat; it was centimeters from my face.

I burst into tears. "What are you talking about?" I asked. I tried to slouch down and make myself small, but the gun hung above me.

We were at the merge onto the Henry Hudson Parkway southbound, the oldest, most winding highway in New York City. On a good night, it was treacherous, and all New Yorkers who took the road knew it; on a rainy night and at high speeds, it was instant death. Vince apparently wanted to get us all killed.

Vince crashed through the toll plaza, taking out an EZ-Pass lane and breaking the glass of the booth itself. I saw the raincoated toll collector in the next lane dive for cover and a New York City cop run out of the office area on the northbound side of the highway into the last lane. He had his gun drawn but didn't get off any shots, as far as I could tell. The car bounced back and forth as we entered the lane of traffic and I saw three police cars about a half mile down the road, parked across both lanes and blocking our way. In the distance, the lights of the George Washington Bridge twinkled.

I don't know if it was from shock, fear, or a heart attack, but I passed out.

When I awoke, we were still on the southbound side of the parkway, facing in the wrong direction. We had apparently skidded across the highway and into the cement embankment that led to Fort Tryon Park. I saw the sign for the park but I didn't want to think about how we got there or why we were facing in the wrong direction. Vince was half-in and half-out of the car, the windshield bisecting him and the airbag supporting his dangling legs. Blood covered the windshield, front seat, and dashboard. He was dead. Costigan was next to the car, on the ground, a state trooper standing over him. His hands were laced behind his head and he was flat on his stomach, crying. I was still strapped in, surrounded by deployed air bags, and with the exception of the goose egg, relatively unharmed. The door opened, and the second trooper looked in.

"You OK, ma'am?" he asked, a fresh-faced baby in a uniform with a baggie covering his hat.

"I hate the 'ma'am' thing," I said, and vomited out the door of the car, a projectile stream of pizza and red wine. The trooper stepped back and averted his eyes from the carnage. I unbuckled my seat belt and said a silent thank-you to Crawford for always reminding me to buckle up; it had probably saved my life. I eased myself out of the car and attempted to stand, but went to my knees in a puddle of mud, oil, and the contents of my stomach. The jeans and the clogs were done for good.

The trooper handed me a tissue, which was like putting a cork in the Hoover Dam. I blotted my mouth as best I could and used the bottom of my T-shirt to take care of the rest. He stood a good distance away, eyeing me. When he was sure I wasn't going to hurl again, he asked me if I wanted to sit in his car. I took his hand, and he placed me in the back seat, my legs sticking out of the car. I lay there and heard various vehicles approach — an ambulance, more police cars, the coroner's station wagon, and a tow truck. It was about twenty minutes later that Crawford appeared.

He peered into the car through the back driver-side window where my head was; to me, he was upside down. The window was open slightly. I could tell that he was wearing a combination of the sad face and the really bad-news face, but was trying hard to look impassive.

"Don't make me look at you upside down," I said from my prone position.

His smile looked like a frown from my angle. He moved around the car to the side where my feet were. He crouched between my knees in the open doorway, his hands hanging down between his legs. "I heard you threw up." He took stock of my clogs and jeans.

"It's become kind of like my calling card," I said, and put my arm over my forehead.

"The trooper put in for retirement." Cop humor.

I sat up and waited while a wave of dizziness came and went. "Is *this* a cruiser?"

He took a look at the car. "No."

I sighed.

"You put up a hell of a fight," he said quietly.

"Thank you."

"I think I'll ask the head of cop school if we could start wearing clogs."

"Such a funny man," I said, and touched my head.

"You should get looked at," he said.

"You know, this time I have to agree with you," I said, a gag rising in my throat. His face went white, and I put my hand to my mouth until the feeling passed. "False alarm," I said. He put his hand out to me and helped me from the car. Another ambulance had pulled up, and an EMT raced over and took me to the back of the vehicle. I stepped up into the brightness of the ambulance and sat on a stretcher in the back. The EMT stayed outside to talk with one of the policemen at the site, who looked like he was itching to get into the ambulance with me.

Crawford flashed his badge and held a finger up to indicate "in a minute." I guess I had to be questioned again.

Crawford sat next to me on the stretcher and took my hand. "I'm staying with you."

I nodded.

"I don't want you to end up with a Bic pen in your throat."

I looked at him, not sure I had heard him correctly. Maybe I was hallucinating now.

He lowered his voice. "EMTs are a little overzealous. No matter what's wrong with you, they'll want to cut you open. Got a concussion? They'll give you a tracheotomy. If I don't stay, you'll end up breathing through a Bic pen sticking out of your throat. Or worse." He sounded like he had experience with this. He got up and opened one of the metal cabinets. Medical supplies were stacked neatly inside.

I wasn't sure what was worse than a Bic pen sticking out of one's throat and didn't want to venture a guess. "Any Bic pens in there?" I asked.

He shook his head and pulled out a big,

soft ice pack, which he put on the counter and smashed with his fist. After he worked it back and forth, it was ice-cold. He put it to my head and told me to hold it there. "They're also big on cutting your pants off."

My eyes got big. I'd rather have a tracheotomy.

He pressed the ice bag to my head, holding his hand over mine. "I fell down a flight of stairs once and broke my arm. The next thing I know, I'm on a stretcher in my underwear."

"Any pictures of that?" I asked.

He shook his head. "I was out of there before Crime Scene and their cameras showed up." He laughed. "Thank God."

He told me what happened after he saw the SUV pull up and Costigan dragged me into the car. He got one shot off at the car, but Vince was going too fast for it to have any effect. He had run back to the house and called in the Navigator's license plate and general direction. Although I thought the police had been chasing us because of Vince's speeding, it was actually because of Crawford's all points bulletin. Now I could tell Max that I had been part of an APB. She would love that.

"Did Vince say anything to you?" he asked.

"The only thing I remember is him

screaming at me about 'papers.' I don't know what that means. John didn't say anything." I closed my eyes. "Vince kept trying to grab at me, but I kicked him in the head."

"Vince is dead," he said.

Thank God it wasn't because I kicked him in the head. "I know," I replied. "Is Costigan all right?"

His face turned cold and angry. "He's fine. Until he gets to lockup in Rikers."

"He didn't hurt me, Crawford."

"You could have been killed," he protested. "And that's *before* you got into the car." He looked away.

The activity outside was starting to subside. Costigan left in a state trooper's car, and the ME's car drove away, presumably with Vince's body. I peered outside and saw flares on the highway, a cop directing traffic around the wreckage. The rain was falling steadily and hitting the already slick roadway. The rubberneckers were out in force.

The fact that I still had my life hit me like a ton of bricks; I closed my eyes, and a faint image of my mother's beautiful face was imprinted on the insides of my eyelids.

EIGHTEEN

The medical technician pronounced me fit to leave. I had escaped the examination without a tracheotomy. And I still had my pants on. Remarkably, I had a contusion on my forehead but no concussion. He told me that I would probably have some neck pain and asked if I wanted a neck brace, but I declined. Although my status as queen of the nerds was never really in question, wearing a neck brace would certainly cement my reign. While I was being examined, Wyatt had arrived on the scene and taken copious notes on the incident, based on what Crawford and I told him. He was much nicer to me than normal. Maybe it had finally dawned on him that I had nothing to do with the murder. Or maybe he had just played basketball with an orphan and was feeling magnanimous.

He and Crawford conferred outside while I stayed inside the ambulance. When they were done, Wyatt poked his head inside the ambulance, his hands supporting him on either side of the opening. His glasses were covered with a thin sheen of rain, and he took them off and wiped them on his shirt. "I may need to talk with you again," he said.

I nodded that I understood. "Can I go home?"

"Detective Crawford will take you home," he said. "Get some rest, Professor," he said, respectfully and without any condescension.

I stood and went to the back of the ambulance. Crawford offered me a hand, and I took it as I went down the slick metal steps. The Navigator was on the flatbed portion of the tow truck; it was remarkably intact. The shattered windshield, splattered with blood, and the inflated air bags were the only evidence of what had happened. I thanked God that if Vince was going to try to kill all of us, he did so in an SUV the size of a tank and not a Hyundai.

Crawford's Passat wagon was parked north of the scene, facing in the right direction. We went to the car and he opened the passenger-side door for me, helping me in. He got in on his side, and satisfied that I was strapped in, he started the car, took the first exit, and got us onto the northbound side in moments. We went through the toll plaza. The southbound tolls were closed; the damaged one was already being repaired. We went across the Hudson River, through Riverdale, and merged onto the Saw Mill, in silence.

We passed the Cross County Parkway merge and went under the underpass. "Don't say anything about Ray," I said, thinking back to the phone call.

"I wasn't going to," he said, shaking his head. "You were almost killed, but the only thing you're worried about is that I'll say something about Ray." He turned and looked at me. "Sometimes, you're priceless," he said, with a bit of wonder in his voice. He pulled up at the red light at Executive Boulevard.

"He's an asshole . . ."

". . . but he's harmless. So I've heard."

Actually, I was going to stop at "he's an asshole." I was no longer sure about the rest. I swallowed and looked out the window. Although I would have been justified in falling apart, I didn't want to do it in front of him. Again.

We continued in silence. We arrived at the house in fifteen minutes, and he pulled up the driveway, parking as close to the front door as possible. All of the lights were still on, but he had closed and locked the front door. As we approached the door on the slick bluestone pavers, he reached into his jeans pocket and produced my house keys. "You're good," I said. "Not only did you remember to lock the front door, but you remembered to bring the keys."

We went in and he closed the door. I started up the stairs to the bedroom, but he remained rooted to the floor in the hallway. I turned, halfway up the stairs. "Come with me."

He hesitated for a short moment and then started up behind me. Once in the bedroom, we stood looking at each other. He stared down at me. "What now?" he asked.

I looked back at him. "Surveillance." I kicked off my clogs and found a pair of pajama pants and a tank top in one of my drawers. I went into the bathroom and changed. I looked at my head and whistled to myself. The bruise on my head was large, blue, and veiny-looking. No clever hairstyle was going to cover that up unless I got bangs. I washed my hands and face and brushed my teeth; the taste of vomit was a lingering reminder of the evening's events. I rinsed and held on to the sink, letting a few tears fall into the porcelain basin. I ran the hand towel that was hanging on a hook next to the sink over my face, careful of the lump on my head.

When I emerged, he was coming back up the stairs, having washed up in the powder room downstairs. He waited until I climbed into the king-size bed and sat down on the edge next to me, taking off his Tevas. He reached under his pant leg and pulled off the small gun, placing it on my nightstand. "Are you sure?"

"We've been through a lot tonight. Just stay and don't make it hard." I turned crimson from head to toe. "No pun intended." I pulled the comforter up and let him in. He sat up and stripped off his shirt, leaving his pants on. I nearly lost consciousness again as I took in nice pecs, a sprinkling of chest hair, and a flat, hard stomach. I reached over him and turned off the light next to the bed.

"What's six times eight?" he whispered in the dark, thinking I had another concussion.

"Twelve," I said.

"Good. Seven times four?" he whispered again.

"Six," I said, and giggled. "Shut up."

We moved closer. His hand rested lightly on my hip. "Who was the first president?"

"George Clooney."

"Excellent. Who's our current president?"

I thought for a moment. "Leopold Bloom."

"Who?" he asked, his hand reaching around and slipping under the back of my tank top.

"Never mind," I said, and leaned in to find his face in the dark. A steady rain fell outside the window as we lay in the pitch-black, our lips touching. His hands became entwined in my hair, and he pulled me closer.

I stretched out along the length of his body and buried my head into his neck. He wrapped his arms around me, and whispered, "I'm so glad you're alive."

"In what sense? Like 'I'm glad you were born,' or 'I'm glad you survived tonight'?" I asked, always literal.

He laughed in the darkness, the deep chortle with the snort. "Do you ever shut up?" he asked, and kissed me again. His hands traveled up my back and then back down. They found their way to the waistband of my pajamas. I wasn't sure if it was the head injury or just being with him, but I felt like I was leaving my body. I felt flushed and overly hot. Those old familiar feelings — longing, desire, a tingling deep in my gut — were replaced by something else: fear. Understandable? Maybe. Well timed? Probably not. I pulled away.

"I need a minute," I said, and lay on my back. He took my hand and laced his fingers into mine.

He leaned over and kissed me lightly on the forehead. "You need more than a minute."

I put my back to him and nestled in close, his arms around me. In minutes, we were both asleep.

I don't know how long I slept, but a nightmare in which I was crashing into the wall again and again made me wake with a start. I looked around the room, my heart racing, not exactly sure of where I was. I put my hand to my chest and felt my heart thumping erratically inside. I put my other hand down on the bed next to me, and while it was warm, it was also empty. I went back to sleep.

NINETEEN

I woke up at ten, bruised, sore, and alone in bed. The smell of frying bacon hit my nose, and I sat up, a little woozy, still tired, and starving. I gingerly put my legs over the side of the bed and my feet on the floor, sitting for a minute while the cobwebs cleared. I stood up and tested my legs; everything seemed to work.

I pulled on a St. Thomas sweatshirt that had a few paint stains on it but was fairly clean. I didn't think the sight of my naked breasts behind the thin material of the tank top was any way to greet Crawford first thing in the morning. I went into the bathroom and brushed my teeth, trying not to look at myself in the mirror. There was too much damage and not enough time to fix it before I greeted him. I left on my flannel pajama pants and padded down the stairs, barefoot, to the kitchen.

I passed the living room and looked in; I could tell that Crawford had spent the night on the couch. The indentation from his body was evident in the soft cushions, and a pillow and blanket from the guest bedroom had been neatly folded and placed at the end of the couch.

He was standing at the stove, frying a pound of bacon and reading the directions on the back of a muffin box intently. He held the box far enough away for me to tell that he needed glasses. He was wearing the big T-shirt from the Fred Wyatt collection and on his thin frame it was huge. He had the phone in the crook of his neck and was listening as the person on the other end spoke.

"Will she do the ID?" he asked. He waited a second. "Thanks for handling this, Fred." He hung up.

"You need bifocals," I said. I stood in the doorway, a vision in an old sweatshirt, pajama pants, and with hair that made Albert Einstein look well-groomed.

He turned around, surprised. "Good morning!" he said. "You had a pound of bacon in the freezer, and I found this muffin mix. I hope it's all right that I started cooking."

"You cook?" I asked.

"Well, I can cook bacon and follow directions."

He had made coffee. He poured a cup and handed it to me. "How do you feel?"

"I'm sore."

He looked at me with the sad face. "Anything else?"

I wasn't sure what he was looking for. "Sad?" I offered.

He shook his head; that wasn't what he meant. "Do you have any pain?"

"Nothing that a few Advil won't take care of." I took a sip of the coffee. It was horrible. He must have learned how to make coffee at cop school. "Mmmm . . . delicious," I lied. Bad as it was, it cleared the dust bunnies in my head, and I started to think. "Was that Fred?" I asked.

"Yeah. He's taking the mother down to the morgue to ID the body."

The mother. Vince's mother. I remember seeing her at the funeral. "So, is this whole thing done now that Vince is dead?"

He had his own cup of coffee next to the stove; he picked it up and took a drink. He shook his head. "We never had anything to link Vince to the murder. A lot of other things, but not this."

"Other things?"

"Vince had his hand in a few things, drugs

and cars specifically." The bacon crackled and popped behind him, and he turned around to lower the flame under the pan. "Vince liked to sell cars that he didn't actually own. He was also the Joliet Ecstasy connection. He was a hood, but probably not a murderer." He paused. "Not yet, anyway."

I wrapped my hands around my mug. "Do you think he broke into my office?"

"Seems likely. There's not a new print anywhere. And your office lock was picked. But I'm sure Vince would know how to do a break-in and would know to wear gloves."

"Did Fred say anything about Costigan? Did he say anything about why they kidnapped me?" I asked.

Crawford frowned. "He lawyered up. They got nowhere with him. The minute they got him to the station house, the lawyer was there. An uncle."

I chewed on that for a moment until my silent encounter with Vince and Fiona popped into my head, and I exclaimed. Crawford jumped slightly. "I forgot to tell you!" I said. "I saw Vince and Fiona together yesterday after I taught my last class. They looked kind of cozy."

Crawford narrowed his eyes. "Cozy how?"

"I'm not sure exactly. I just got the feeling that Vince was back to normal pretty quickly after Kathy's death."

He leaned back against the counter and folded his arms across his chest. "I'll file that away. Maybe we need to chat with Fiona again."

I continued drinking my coffee, and we stared across the kitchen at each other. "What now?"

He looked at me sadly. "I'm thinking it's Ray, Alison. I'm sorry."

I shrugged, casual and nonchalant. "No skin off my nose." But it was skin off my nose. And the nine years that I had spent with him.

He turned back to the bacon.

"Are you working today?" I asked.

He shook his head again. "No. You?"

"I have some correcting to do. As a matter of fact, I always have correcting to do," I said, "but I was thinking of something else."

He cocked an eyebrow suggestively. I guess celibacy *would* have been a huge stumbling block for Father Crawford.

"Not that," I said. "I want to get to the bottom of this. Would you take me to school and go through my office with me?"

He focused intently on the bacon, using a spatula to flip it in the pan, ignoring my question.

"Well?"

He turned around to face me, more than a little perturbed. "What do you think we're going to find that I didn't already bag?" He got a plate out of the cabinet and put two paper towels on it to soak up some of the grease. He loaded some bacon onto the plate and walked over to hand it to me. "You didn't answer my question."

"This is not an indictment of your investigative skills," I said, pushing a greasy bite of bacon into my mouth. "But Vince kept screaming about 'papers.' What was he talking about?" I took a slug of awful coffee, resisting the urge to gag. He seemed to be enjoying his just fine. "If I think long enough, I might be able to come up with something."

He picked up a piece of bacon and chewed it thoughtfully. "I'll take you to school," he said finally, but held up his hand. "But we do it my way."

"What? Naked?" I asked.

He blushed. "No," he said slowly. "We do it so that we don't compromise any possible additional evidence. We wear gloves, we take more pictures, and you follow my lead. I don't want you going in there willy-nilly."

I burst out laughing, a piece of bacon flying from my mouth. " 'Willy-nilly'? Is that the technical term?"

He was embarrassed. "Oh, shut up. You know what I mean."

I covered my mouth. "I'm sorry." I ate a few more slices of bacon. I stood. "Give me your clothes, and I'll wash them before we go. I don't have anything clean, so I have to do laundry anyway. And you've been in those jeans longer than hygienically acceptable."

He turned off the burner and put the rest of the cooked bacon onto the plate. "And what am I going to wear while you're doing laundry?" he asked.

"I'll find you something. You could spend an hour or so in my sweatpants, right?" I laughed when I thought about what I had said. "What I meant was you could spend an hour wearing a pair of my sweatpants. That didn't come out right."

He thought it over but I knew what the answer would be. "I don't think so. Is there a store in town where I could buy some pants?"

"Crawford, that's just stupid. Give me your freaking clothes and let me wash them." I stood up. "Come with me, and I'll get you those sweatpants."

He continued to lean against the counter, his arms crossed.

"Crawford," I said, cajoling. "Come on."

We went up to my room and I took my wicker laundry basket from the closet and put a couple of pairs of underpants, a bra, a few T-shirts, and two pairs of jeans into it. Crawford stood in the middle of the floor, watching me.

I went into the guest room and opened the closet in there. I knew that Ray had left a couple of items of clothing, and I found them on the top shelf. There was a pair of St. Thomas sweatpants and a couple of T-shirts. I pulled down the sweatpants and went down the short hallway and back into my bedroom.

Crawford was still standing there in uncomfortable silence. I handed him the sweatpants. "These are Ray's, so they should fit better than mine would."

He went into the bathroom and closed the door. He emerged a few seconds later in the sweatpants, which were loose but a little short, and Fred's shirt, his jeans, NYPD T-shirt, and boxer shorts in hand. The boxers were a blue-and-white check. He threw them into the wicker basket. "I'll do the laundry," he said.

"I've seen men's underwear before," I reminded him. "I've even touched a few pairs."

"I'll do the laundry," he repeated, and

picked up the basket. "I'll be right back."

I lay back down on the bed. Fine. Do the laundry, you big baby. "The washer is in the basement!" I called after him.

My house is small — twelve hundred square feet — and old enough that wherever water is running, it can be heard throughout the house. The water rushing through the pipes told me that he found the washer and even figured out how to turn it on. That was more than Ray had accomplished in seven years of marriage. It was nice to be involved with a grown-up bachelor; he could take care of himself, and most of his daily functions wouldn't involve me. How refreshing.

He came back up and sat at the bottom of the bed, one leg dangling over the side. I asked him why he slept on the couch, and he shrugged. "It seemed like the right thing to do."

If you've just gotten out of the seminary, I thought. "You look tired."

"So do you." He yawned. "I haven't gotten a lot of sleep in the past few weeks. Not enough surveillance, I guess." He grinned sheepishly.

I patted the pillow beside me. "Come on up here." He rearranged himself and came up beside me, putting his head on the pillow. I faced him and brushed his hair off his forehead. "You smell like bacon."

"So do you."

I kissed him, and he kissed me back. "I love bacon," I said. He wrapped his long arms around me, and I threw a leg over his body. "Where's your gun?" I asked.

He pulled back. "Why?"

"I'm still a little nervous after last night. I like for you to have it handy."

He reached around to his back and pulled it out of the waistband of the sweatpants. He held it a safe distance from me, on display, and then put it on the nightstand behind his head. "Better?" he asked.

"Better," I confirmed. I drifted off to sleep in his arms and didn't wake up until I heard the water drain through the pipes, signaling that the wash was done. I looked at him; he was in a deep sleep, his mouth open slightly. I didn't know too many men who would choose sleep over the more romantic alternative; he must have been exhausted. I took myself gently out of his arms and got off the bed.

I went down to the basement and opened the lid of the washing machine, pulling out the wet and twisted clothes. Crawford's jeans took up most of the washing machine, and were heavy when wet; I shook them out before throwing them in the dryer. I thought about the night before. The kidnapping, the ride in Vince's car, his screaming about the papers, and the crash. Crawford was right: I could have been killed. I shuddered, thinking about waking up in the back of the SUV, surrounded by deployed air bags, and said a silent prayer of thanks for being able to do a simple thing like laundry.

What did I have that could possibly make Vince, and his seemingly innocent sidekick, John, risk life and limb to get? It didn't make any sense. I turned the dial on the dryer to the timed setting — one hour — and went back upstairs.

Crawford was still asleep on the bed, but had turned onto his back and was emitting loud snores. His hands were folded over his stomach. I gently pushed him onto his side, and he stopped snoring but didn't awaken. I went into the bathroom, stripped off my clothes, and turned on the shower. While I waited for it to get hot, I looked at myself in the mirror. The bruise was a little deeper in color today, and my eyes were bloodshot. What the hell did he see in me? I was a mess. I puked all the time and cried a lot. I am sure that he had gleaned that I wasn't easy, so it couldn't be that. It had to be pity. I quickly pushed that thought out of my mind and got into the shower.

I showered quickly, wrapping both my hair and body in towels when I was done. I opened the bathroom door and let the steam flood the room. I looked over at Crawford and almost became concerned that he had slipped into a coma, but he groaned and changed positions, and I felt relief. I thought about our trip to campus; I didn't want to do it his way. I wanted to do it my way. I wanted to empty folders, go through my books, search my desk, and think. If I had him there, we'd be wearing rubber gloves, cataloging everything, and sniping at each other. "Go without him" flashed in front of my eyes, and I breathed in sharply. The plot germinated in my brain and while I was a little nervous at how mad he would be, I pushed that thought aside and promised myself I would do everything as quickly as possible so he wouldn't be that inconvenienced.

I ran as quickly and as quietly as I could down to the basement and put all of the almost-dry clothes into the wicker hamper, including Crawford's jeans and boxer shorts. I grabbed a pair of underpants, a bra, a shirt, and my jeans and hastily threw them on, realizing that I didn't have shoes. I looked around the basement, which was packed with detritus — rakes, hoes, a lawn mower that hadn't worked since the mid-nineties, and assorted half-filled paint cans — my eyes finally landing on a pair of rubber gardening clogs. I wasn't a big gardener, but I thought the clogs were cute and had ordered them from L.L.Bean. I grabbed them and dusted them off, sliding them onto my feet. They were roomy and comfortable. I put the basket on my hip and made my way up the stairs. I looked around the kitchen and spied Crawford's car keys on the counter, along with his badge, phone, beeper, and wallet.

Laundry basket in hand, I quietly exited the house and tiptoed down the walk to the Passat, which was next to the house. I pushed the keypad like I had seen him do and the car chirped, scaring the hell out of me. I looked up at the bedroom window, but he didn't appear. I opened the hatchback door to the trunk, threw the laundry basket into it, and went to the driver's side. I climbed in and backed the car down the driveway.

I was at school in twenty minutes, and in my office in another five. I thought about Crawford waking up in my bed and realizing I had his clothes — particularly his underwear — and his car. He would be furious, but hopefully he would get over it. I had left the gun, hadn't I? I wasn't a complete idiot. Maybe he would focus on that and not turn it on me when I came back home.

I sat behind my desk. I let out a strangled scream as the phone rang unexpectedly; apparently the custodial staff had replaced the cut phone cord. I knew who it was. "Hi," I said casually.

"Where's my underwear? My jeans? My car?" he growled. Interesting order, I thought. I would have thought my stealing his car would have upset him the most.

"I'll be back in an hour. I promise," I said.

"Now you can add grand theft auto to your résumé along with the breaking and entering." He let out a loud, exasperated sigh. "You are a royal pain in the ass. Why did you leave without me?"

"Because I didn't want to do it your way." I looked around at the mess. "And I'm not in here 'willy-nilly.' "

His voice dropped an octave. It sounded like the voice he had when he gave me the speech on breaking and entering. "Alison, your office is a crime scene."

"I get it," I said, kicking around a couple of files on the floor, the phone between my shoulder and my cheek. "I won't compromise anything."

"Just being there is compromising. Get out of there as soon as possible."

"Hey, I've got your car, so I can go shopping. What do you want for lunch?" I asked. I figured if I kept the conversation light and happy, his anger would dissipate. I was wrong.

"I'm not hungry." He hung up.

" 'I'm not hungry,' " I repeated in an imitation of his low growl. I picked up a stack of files from the floor and began going through them, one by one. It only took me five minutes to figure out what was missing: All of the files for my current courses were gone. I went through everything a second time to make sure and confirmed that not a file from the current semester resided in the mess.

I opened my desk and rummaged through the middle junk drawer with its pens, pencils, and folder labels, and then through the drawers to my right. Everything seemed to be there, even though the drawers were a mess. I started sneezing as the fingerprint powder that dusted every inch of every surface in the office started to fly around the air with my movements.

I leaned back in my chair. Did the "papers" that Vince was screaming about have something to do with something I was teaching this semester? I grabbed my grade book from the top right-hand drawer and Crawford's car keys and left, locking the door behind me.

When I was back in his car, I looked at the clock on the dash. It was noon. I didn't have any cops at my disposal to pick up lunch and hand off to me on the Deegan, so I decided to take a little detour myself on the way home and stop on Arthur Avenue. I knew he was really mad at me; if the way to a man's heart was through his stomach, I had a lot of shopping to do.

I drove across the Bronx, past the Botanical Gardens and the Bronx Zoo on the way to Arthur Avenue. Parking was a nightmare, so I drove around the block a few times, finally finding a small space in front of an Italian deli and bakery. I said a silent prayer as I pulled the Passat up a full car length next to the car in front of the spot, and gently eased it into the spot, only hitting the bumper of the car in back of me twice. I got out and looked at the back bumper of the Passat, and everything looked fine.

The deli had a few tables and chairs outside on the sidewalk, and a few old men were sitting, drinking espressos and enjoying the weather. The rain had passed through and it was now bright and sunny. I walked past them, into the shop and took in the large, glassed-in display, full of lasagna, ziti, chicken cutlets, and salads. Above the counter hung several hundred dried and cured meats: pepperoni, salami, soppressata.

"Help you?" The young guy behind the counter wore a white tank top and a large gold Jesus head on a chain around his neck. Furry black hair peeked out of the top of the tank top. He took a paper bag from a stack next to the cash register and a pencil to write down my order.

"Yes, thanks," I said. "I'll have a salami," I said, pointing to the one directly in front of my face, "four of those cutlets, two pieces of lasagna, a pound of macaroni and a pound of potato salad, and . . ." I reached behind me to the wire rack that held bread and grabbed a seeded Italian loaf, ". . . this, and two containers of the tiramisu."

He looked at me and smiled. "Anything else?"

I looked into the case. "Oh, and four pieces of that eggplant rollatine." I took a salted homemade mozzarella from a tray on top of the counter. "And this." Who doesn't love mozzarella?

"Hungry?" he asked as he set about getting all of my food.

"Starving," I said. And in huge trouble. "Hey, what does tiramisu mean?" I had always wondered about that.

He turned around from his position in front of the refrigerator which held meats and cheeses and gave me a sly smile. "Hold me closer."

"Oh," I said slowly, thinking, *not against that chest hair.*

After parting with thirty-five dollars, I had a large bag of food. I put it in the trunk, next to the clean laundry, and set off for home thinking about Italian translations, missing files, and the amount of trouble I would be in if I couldn't fast-talk my way back into Crawford's good graces.

I thought I'd lead with salami and see where that got me.

TWENTY

I went through the front door, calling Crawford's name. The bag of food was on top of the laundry in the basket as was my grade book; I set them both down on the floor. He wasn't downstairs, so I went up to my bedroom, balancing the basket on my hip. He was in my bathroom, shirtless and in the sweatpants, shaving with my pink Lady Schick and the shave gel I used on my legs. His hair was wet and his back was damp. He had one hand on the sink, and he leaned in toward the mirror to get a good look at his face as he shaved. Half of it was covered with green gel. I stood in the bathroom door and took in his half-naked form.

"I've got salami," I said. Not exactly an olive branch, but close enough.

He kept shaving, not responding.

"And chicken cutlets, lasagna, eggplant rollatine, and bread." I went into the bathroom and stood behind him, wrapping my arms around his waist. I leaned my head against his back. "And mozzarella. And tiramisu." I pulled him a bit closer. "I heard that tiramisu means 'hold me closer' in Italian."

"Funny. I heard it meant 'you just did a really stupid thing.' " He rinsed the razor in the basin, which was full of water, shave gel, and whiskers. He took a towel from the ring hanging next to the sink, rinsed his face, and dried it with the towel. He let the water out of the sink and then turned around to face me. "I'm still mad at you."

I hung my head in mock shame.

"This isn't funny, Alison. What if I had gotten beeped or called? What was I supposed to say? That nutty professor has my clothes and my car? I can't do my job because I'm trapped in her house without any underwear?"

I hadn't thought of that. "Actually, I'm a nutty doctor of literature."

He didn't think that was very funny, either.

I tried to give him some good news. "I know what's missing from my office," I said brightly.

He looked down at me.

"My files from all of my current spring courses."

He thawed a little bit. "Why would anyone

want those?" he asked, dubious. "With all due respect, Dr. Bergeron."

I went into the bedroom and sat on the bed. "I don't know. But I thought we could eat some of the food that I bought and hash it out. What do you think?"

He walked into the bedroom. "I'd be able to think better if I had my clothes." He leaned down and took his jeans, underwear, and T-shirt from the basket. "If you'll excuse me?" he asked, and closed the bathroom door. He came out a few minutes later, dressed, his hair combed. "I used your toothbrush," he stated. He looked at me for my reaction, but I had none. "To brush my hair. Payback's a bitch, huh?"

I grimaced. "Are you still mad at me?" I got up from the bed and walked over to him, putting my arms around his neck and kissing him. His arms hung at his sides for a few minutes, but he finally relented and put his hands around me and up the back of my shirt.

"You have tiramisu?" he asked, kissing my neck.

"And salami." I put my hands into his toothbrush-styled hair.

He let me go after one last kiss. "If you've got salami, I'm fine. Let's go downstairs so we can go over what's missing. I want to

know who's in each one of those classes."
He went over to the nightstand and put the
gun in the back of his waistband.

We went downstairs, and I picked up the
bag of food from the hallway floor. All of
the food was in microwaveable containers,
so everything was hot in no time. I put the
salami and cheese on a plate, cut up the
bread, and asked him what he wanted to
drink. Then I remembered I didn't have
anything to drink besides a frozen bottle of
vodka and the leftover wine from the night
before. "How's water?"

"Fine," he said.

I handed him a couple of plates, forks,
knives, and two bottles of water. We sat at
the table and dove into the smorgasbord.
"Cut me off a piece of that salami," I said.

He took his knife and cut off a big chunk,
holding it out to me. I opened my mouth
and he dropped it in. I chewed on the tough
piece of meat and opened my grade book.
"I'm teaching Creative Writing II, Freshman Comp, Intro to Shakespeare, Literature
of the Hudson River, and Senior Seminar."

He told me to start with Creative Writing.
I ran down the list of students. "Any of
those names ring a bell?"

He plowed into the lasagna and shook his
head. "Do Hudson River." He forked a big

hunk into his mouth, sauce on his lips. I now had proof that he wasn't the dainty eater that had sat at the same table the night before.

I read off the names from that class; three of those students were also in the creative writing class. I went on to Shakespeare: Costigan, Martin, Carlyle, Rivas, McCarthy, Dumont, and Franklin. He perked up at the name Martin. "She was the roommate."

"Right." I said.

He wiped his mouth with a paper napkin. "Freshman and sophomore years."

"You questioned her, right?" I asked.

He nodded. "First thing. All she did was cry and carry on. She didn't have anything to give us, and we haven't spoken with her since." He took a piece of eggplant and put it on his plate. "How's she been in class?"

"The same. A pain in the ass. She's on my back about returning her *Macbeth* report, but normal." I ripped a piece of bread in two and layered a piece of mozzarella onto it. I looked at the Senior Seminar and read those names off: Troy, Manning, Slater, O'Toole, and Davis. He shook his head; he didn't know any of them.

We ate some more and made a big dent in

the food. "Ready for dessert?" I asked.

He stretched his arms over his head. "Give me a few minutes. I ate a lot."

I closed my grade book and pushed it to the side. The doorbell rang just as I was polishing off the remains of my lasagna. He looked at me. "Expecting anyone?" he asked, getting up and putting his hand to his back, drawing his gun out of his waist-band and holding it close to his leg.

"No." I got up and padded down the hallway to the door and looked through the frosted glass panel on the side of the door. It was Ray. Crawford stayed in the doorway of the kitchen, his hands in his pocket.

I opened the door and let him in.

"I was hoping I would catch you at home," he said, coming into the doorway. He stopped short when he saw Crawford. "What is he doing here?" he asked, eyeing Crawford nervously. He shifted from one foot to the other.

Crawford took a few steps forward; the gun was nowhere in sight. "We were just discussing the case, Dr. Stark."

Ray sized him up. "Can we have a moment, please? I need to talk with my wife alone."

I looked at Ray and wanted to remind him that I was not his wife. Now we were in an alpha male pissing match. I half expected Ray to undo his pants and pee in the corner to mark his territory.

Crawford stood and stared at Ray a few more minutes, the air in the hall becoming charged with pheromones, testosterone, and every other male hormone. Crawford looked at me. "I'll be outside."

I led Ray into the kitchen and told him to sit down. "Are you hungry?"

He looked at the leftovers on the table, the two plates, and the two water bottles. "You fed him?"

"Yeah. That's the trouble with cops. Once you feed them, they keep coming back," I said. "Do you want a plate or what?"

He shook his head and took a long breath. "I just wanted to come by and thank you for helping me out the other night. With Klein."

A little overdue, but nice, nonetheless.

He pushed Crawford's plate out of the way and put his hands down on the table. "Alison, I had nothing to do with this," he said, his tone pleading. "You have to believe me."

I still wasn't sure if I could believe him considering our history, and I wasn't sure I could give him the benefit of the doubt anymore. "I guess I have to take your word for it," I said, but it came out almost as a question.

"Thank you," he said immediately, and then thought back on what I had said. "I guess." He cocked his thumb toward the front door. "Did he give you any idea as to who the other suspects are?"

He thinks you did it, Ray, I wanted to say, but didn't. "No."

"Klein's a great lawyer, but I don't know if he can keep me out of jail." He paused. "Or get me my job back at St. Thomas when I'm exonerated."

"What have they got on you, Ray?"

"My fingerprints were all over your car, for one."

"Of course they were. You used to drive it all the time."

"And Kathy's fingerprints were all over my car." He looked down at the table when he said this.

That was a discomforting thought but one that made sense. When he looked up again, I studied his face, but if there was one thing I knew about Ray, it was that he was the best liar in the world as well as the worst husband. I didn't know if that combination equaled his being a murderer, though.

"And there are a bunch of e-mails between me and Kathy." He paused. "In one of them, I said I would kill her if she told her parents about us."

I sighed. "That was bright."

"But I meant it in a funny way, like I'll kill you," he said, shaking his fist. "Too bad that didn't translate in the e-mail."

What an idiot. "You should have taken my class on 'Tone.'" I picked up my fork and started pushing pasta around on the plate. "*Did* you kill her, Ray?" I asked quietly.

"No," he said emphatically. He stood up. "Anyway, thank you for helping me out. I'm sorry I called you the other day and yelled at you about not getting in touch. That was immature."

The counseling must have had some effect on him.

He pointed to the door again. "Is something going on there?"

I assumed he meant to ask if Crawford and I were involved, but he couldn't bring himself to say the words. "We're friends, Ray."

"Is he nice to you?" Implicit in that was "nicer than I was to you?"

I nodded. "He's very nice to me." I knocked my knuckles against the wooden table. "So far." I don't know why I said it, but just being in Ray's duplicitous presence cast a cloud of doubt over everyone.

He looked a little forlorn. "That's good." He started for the door. "I can't say that he and I are on great terms, but that doesn't really matter, does it?" he asked, and laughed.

I walked him to the door.

"I'm sorry, Al. About everything," he said, putting his hand on the knob. "I really am." I used to cry when he said things like that, but this time I just stood there. I had become impervious to his penitence.

He stood there a few more minutes, looking as if he wanted to say something else. Finally, he spoke. "I'm thinking about leaving St. Thomas next semester. Regardless of what happens." He let out a rueful laugh. "Well, I guess that's obvious. If I go to jail, I'll really have to leave. But if I get out of this, I'm think I'm going to go out West for the fall semester. I need to think. Then I'll decide whether or not to come back."

I couldn't disagree with that. It was on the tip of my tongue to say, "If you need anything, just call," but I didn't. I didn't want him calling. Or asking for anything.

Ray hooked a finger toward the door, motioning to Crawford. "Your friend there is a bit intimidating in the interrogation room."

"So I've heard."

Crawford was sitting on the front steps and stood up when the door opened. He put his hand out. "Dr. Stark."

They shook, and Ray went down the sidewalk to his car. We stood on the stoop and watched him as he drove away.

Crawford came back inside and went into the kitchen. "I'm not going to ask you what you talked about."

"Good. Because all he wanted to do was apologize."

He looked at me, eyebrows raised.

"For calling and yelling at me the other day. At the beach."

"Oh."

"He also wanted to know about us. If you're nice to me."

He continued looking at me. "And what did you say?"

"I said that despite your erectile dysfunction, we were trying to make it work."

He blanched, and his mouth hung open. When he figured out that I was kidding, he chuckled slightly. "What did you really say?"

"I said that you were nice to me." I left out the "so far" part; I didn't want to seem insecure and paranoid. Even though I was.

He looked at his watch. "I'll help you clean all of this up and then I have to go. I'm taking my girls to dinner tonight."

I picked up a couple of dishes. "I'll take care of it." I walked over to the sink and put the dishes in, running water over them. I handed him his wallet, keys, badge, phone, and beeper. He had a lot of equipment. "Is that it? You didn't forget anything?"

He looked around. "That's it." He put his hand to his head. "Wait. There is one thing. When I see you tomorrow, I'm going to bag all of the papers in your office. It's been bugging me since last night that Vince was asking for 'the papers.' Have you ever had him in class?"

I shook my head. "I only knew him from around campus, but I never had him in class."

Crawford thought for another minute. "Where are those papers you were supposed to correct last night?"

I continued washing the dishes. "What are you thinking?"

He chewed on the inside of his mouth, lost in thought. "The only thing I can come up with has to do with Ecstasy. Ecstasy is huge with Vince's demographic and at Joliet, in particular. He was a small-time dealer, but Narcotics had been watching him for months." He explained to me how Ecstasy could be printed on a special paper that someone like me couldn't recognize, but that someone who was acquainted with drugs could. "It's possible that one of the papers that you have was printed on Ecstasy paper, meaning that Vince was out thousands of dollars and maybe, in deep with the dealer above him. That would be one explanation as to why Vince — if he was the break in — left an 'X' here and in your office." He looked at me, and I stared back at blankly; he had lost me at "Ecstasy papers."

"I know. It's crazy. But it's all I've got. I think I should take the papers and have them tested."

My briefcase was still inside the front door, so I dried my hands and went down the hall to get it. I pulled out the Shakespeare papers and brought them back into the kitchen. I handed them to him. "Do me a favor, though."

He took them and riffled through them. "What?"

"Test these first. These are the only ones that need to be corrected and handed back."

He nodded. "OK. I'll get them back to you as soon as I can."

I looked up at him and paused for a minute. "Are we OK?"

He sighed. "Yes." He put his arms around me. "Just don't pull a stunt like that ever again. I'll have to take you to the precinct in the cruiser." His voice was serious, but his eyes twinkled.

"It's not a cruiser," I intoned solemnly.

He put one hand behind my head and bent down to kiss me. Things got out of control quickly, and I ended up sitting on the counter, my legs wrapped around him and him half on top of me. I pulled away, a little flushed and a lot disheveled. "Is that a gun in your pocket or are you just happy to see me?" I asked.

He laughed out loud. "You have been dying to say that, haven't you?"

I pulled a dirty fork out from under my ass and waved it at him. "You've got to go. Right now."

He looked at his watch. "You're right. I do." He walked down the hallway and stopped, halfway to the door. "I've been thinking."

"Uh-oh. More thinking. Where's my fire extinguisher?"

He smirked. "I think we should have dinner. Out. In a restaurant. Without my questioning you. What do you think?"

"But the case isn't over yet," I reminded him.

"So, we'll do it around here. I don't know anyone in Dobbs Ferry."

I thought it over. "When did you have in mind?"

"Tomorrow?" he asked. "I'm driving my girls home at five and then I'll head down here. Pick you up at seven?"

I had an honor society awards ceremony from five to seven. "I can do seven. But you'll have to pick me up at my office or in the Blue Room. If you get there early, you can have a drink and listen to my scintillating speech on the history of Lambda Iota Tau."

He smiled. "Mmmm . . . Greek . . . sexy." He thought for a moment. "The timing sounds good. I'll go straight to school on my way back." He opened the door. "I'll see you then." He gave me a peck on the forehead and started down the sidewalk. I heard him mutter, "Erectile dysfunction, my ass."

Despite being full of good Italian food, my stomach rumbled and did a little flip.

TWENTY-ONE

After an eventful and exciting start to the day, I now had many hours of solitude facing me. I still wasn't completely comfortable on my own, but the last few weeks had been so action-packed that it hadn't seemed to matter. I had plenty of things going on and a lot to think about. Now, after spending the night (sort of) with Crawford and feeling those initial tinglings of hope that someone would be in my life again, I was back to square one — alone in my house with nothing to do. The relationship that seemed to be beginning was a little strange to me; he seemed perfect. What was the catch? After being with Ray for so long, I couldn't help but look for the catch. I had had a great-looking, smart husband, but he had a fatal flaw — he didn't really love me, and he liked to have sex with other women. But I tried to push the thought of Crawford's potential fatal flaw from my mind and continued cleaning up the kitchen.

After I had put all the food away and tidied up the room, I went into the living room and lay down on the couch; I was still exhausted from the night before and the aching in my bones was getting more acute as the day wore on. I stretched out, putting my feet up on the pillows and blanket that Crawford had neatly folded and left at the end of the couch.

I put an arm behind my head and thought about Vince. If he didn't kill Kathy, what had him so spooked that he felt like he had to kidnap me? What was my connection to all of this besides the fact that my car was Kathy's final resting place? What was the feeling that I had about Vince that had gripped me at the funeral? Was his connection to the drug world the connection to the papers? None of it made sense to me.

I must have fallen asleep. About an hour into my snooze the phone rang, disturbing a very peaceful, dreamless nap. I jumped up from the couch and picked up the phone on the end table. I winced as I rolled over to get the phone and felt a sharp twinge in my shoulder, a painful reminder of what had happened the night before. It was Max. She started talking before I could even manage to get a "hello" out.

"So, I find myself with a free night, thanks to being stood up by my date. What are you doing tonight?" she asked. As usual, it sounded like she was doing a million other things while she was talking to me, the sound of drawers being opened and slammed shut in the background.

It took me a minute to focus and get my head around what she was asking. "I have no plans."

"Come into the City," she commanded. "I have reservations at Nobu and I'm not giving them up because some schmuck got Knicks tickets at the last minute and canceled on me." She paused for a second. "Good in bed or not."

"What time?" I asked, looking at the clock hanging in the dining room. It was four-thirty.

"Do you think you can get yourself together and into Manhattan by seven?" She paused for a moment. "You sound like you're sleeping."

"I was taking a nap. I had a rough night." I thought for a moment, trying to rid my mind of the many cobwebs encasing it. "I think I can make it by seven."

"Rough in a good way or rough in a bad way?" When I didn't respond, she kept going. "Never mind. I know you. You probably had one martini too many and have been spending the entire day chastising yourself for it."

"Not quite, Max."

"Then what?"

I recounted my story about being kidnapped by Vince and the subsequent car wreck but left out the part about Crawford. Nothing says "loser" than being in the same bed with an attractive man and just *sleeping.* I would never live it down. I continued with my story. "And then Ray, the philanderer, showed up." If I thought of him as part of a Dickens tale and gave him a stupid name, I could almost think about him without becoming nauseous.

"He's collecting stamps now?" she asked, completely serious.

It took me a minute before I figured out what she was talking about. "That's a philatelist, Max. A philanderer is someone who is unfaithful."

"Oh, right," she said, the light dawning. "What did he want?"

"To apologize. For being a jerk the other day." I recounted our phone conversation after he got out of jail. "I think we have finally reached détente."

Max has always been onto me and knew

that there was more to the story. "What else? You're holding back."

"No, I'm not." I think I doth protest too much.

"Forget it," she said. "I'll get it out of you tonight. Seven o'clock. Don't be late." I thought she was done, but I heard her whisper, "I'm glad you're all right," before she hung up.

I got up and went up to my bedroom. I went through my closet and found a sleeveless black turtleneck sweater and a pair of black pants that could be ironed and made presentable. I would be walking to the train, so I dug out a pair of black boots with a heel that wasn't too high.

It took me about an hour to get my pants ironed, my hair combed, and my makeup on. After waking from the nap, it seemed like every muscle in my body had seized up; everything ached. I went downstairs and took the things that I needed out of my briefcase: my phone, wallet, keys, and train schedule. I almost knew the schedule by heart now, but since it was the weekend, it would be different and I wanted the schedule with me so that I didn't have to stand around Grand Central Station at midnight or later waiting for the last train out.

I went out the front door and down the

walk. Jackson was at the end of his driveway with Trixie, his golden retriever, helping a young boy ride a bike. He looked up when Trixie pulled on the leash and attempted to come my way. He let go of the leash and the dog bounded over to me. She immediately planted her nose in my crotch, and I pushed her snout away, grabbing her leash so that I could return her to her owner.

I said hello to Jackson, handing him the end of the leash. I tried not to look as uncomfortable as I felt, now that I knew what Terri and Ray had been up to. Try as I might, I also couldn't come up with the kid's name. "Learning to ride a bike?" I said, leaving out any proper names.

"He's doing great, isn't he?" Jackson asked, looking at the child proudly as he did figure eights on his tricycle. "This is our nephew, Hayden. We're babysitting. Learning the ropes, so to speak, before taking the plunge ourselves," he said, giving me a little wink.

Holy multiple metaphors, Batman. "His parents better start saving for a Harley Davidson."

Jackson laughed. "Don't even say that." He continued watching the boy, a cute little blond who looked a lot like Jackson's wife, whom I now thought of as "that slut Terri." Must be her side of the family, I thought. "Terri said that she saw you yesterday."

I nodded and immediately felt embarrassment for both of us, the cuckolded spouses. "Yes."

"She told me about this whole business with Ray," he said, shaking his head. "Shame."

"It certainly is," I agreed, sure that she hadn't told him the "whole business"; she might have left out the part where they spent hours screwing.

"Terri always liked Ray a lot," he said, oozing pity for me as the poor wife. He crossed his arms over his chest.

"Hmmm," I said. More than you know, you pompous ass.

He hesitated a moment, starting the sentence, stopping, and then starting again. "What do you think, Alison? Is Ray capable of what they . . . of murder?"

I could see his mind working overtime: if Ray did it, then he's a murderer, and he lived next door to us. His property values would plummet. I answered his question with a shrug. Ray was capable of a lot, but murder? It was anyone's guess.

He fixed me a look mixed with pity, sympathy, and sadness. "I'm sorry, Alison.

You deserve a lot better than that."

And so do you, I thought. I got a little annoyed. I deserve a lot better than a murderer? Yes, most women do. And you don't have a clue about what's going on in your house, buddy, so save the pity for someone else. But instead of saying what I really thought, I stood with a smile plastered on my face. I watched the kid on the tricycle for another second before saying good-bye to Jackson and giving Trixie a pat on the head. Trixie was fast becoming my favorite next-door neighbor.

The street was more deserted farther away from my house. I supposed that most people with kids ate early, and everyone was safely tucked inside, serving chicken nuggets and french fries to hungry young ones. I started down the street, glad that I had grabbed my black-leather blazer out of the front-hall closet; the day, once sunny and bright, had turned dark, windy, and cold. I stopped at the corner at the intersection that united my street and the street down to the station and buttoned the three buttons on my jacket.

A black Mercedes sedan, shiny and with tinted windows, pulled up alongside me. The passenger-side window disappeared and I looked in at Peter Miceli's round face.

"Hi, Alison!" he said, as if running into me was the most normal thing that could happen. Staten Island was a ninety-minute drive from my house; this wasn't an accident. Or a social call.

I froze in place, a terrified smile on my face. "Peter, I have a train to catch."

He stayed in the car but kept talking. "Where are you going? I'll drive you."

I backed away from the car. "The City." I thought short answers might be better under these circumstances.

He slowly maneuvered the car so that it was as close to me as it could get without running me down. His tone changed. "Get in."

I looked in the window at him and saw a gun on his lap.

"Get in," he repeated. He reached across the seat and opened the passenger door.

I got in and pulled the door shut, staying as close to the door as possible. The door locks went down with an ominous "thunk," and Peter started driving, away from the train, my street, and the town.

After five minutes of silence, he looked over at me. "Put your seat belt on." He waited until I did so before continuing. We were now on the Saw Mill River Parkway, heading south. "So, I understand you've

been spending time with Detective Crawford."

I stared straight ahead and kept silent. My
right leg went up and down, shaking uncon-
trollably, and I put my hands and my purse
on top of it to stop the trembling.

"He's good-looking. Seems like a catch,"
he said, as if he approved of my taste in
men. He should have met my ex-husband.

"I guess," I said, morphing into a seventh
grader.

"He tell you anything about who slaugh-
tered my Kathy?" Instead of heading toward
Manhattan on the Henry Hudson, he
merged left and got onto the Major Deegan
Expressway going south, which would take
us through the Bronx. I felt a sob rise in my
throat but kept it there; I'm sure he knew I
was scared, but I wasn't going to let him
know it by crying.

"We don't talk about the case," I said, my
voice steady and calm.

"What do you talk about?"

I shrugged. "Nothing much."

He grinned. "Oh, it's one of those kinds
of relationships. Not a lot of talking. Before
I met Gianna, I had a few of those kinds of
relationships." He looked over at me. "Are
you scared of me, Alison?"

"A little."

He put the gun into a leather-lined pocket on his car door. "I'm sorry. I didn't mean to scare you." He continued driving on the Deegan, weaving in and out of traffic. "I heard what happened with you and that idiot, Vince. Did he hurt you?"

"No."

"Shame about that kid. But that's what happens when you don't have a father growing up," he said. He clucked sympathetically and looked over at me again. "Funny thing is, he was just like his father even though he never knew him. Loose cannon." He switched lanes again. "You know what they say: the apple doesn't fall far from the tree."

I didn't say anything and let him talk.

"We weren't crazy about it when Kathy started dating him. She's just like her mother, though. Bad taste in men," he said, and then caught himself. "Before she ended up with me, that is." He let out a throaty laugh. "Do you remember the guys Gianna used to date before she met me?"

I shook my head.

"Crazy guys. Nuts," he said, taking his index finger and rotating it around by his head. "Her parents were so happy when she started dating me. You could say that they had picked me out for her."

I looked at the speedometer; he was going the speed limit, so there was no chance that we would be stopped for speeding. He turned off an exit that I wasn't familiar with and headed east on a dark road.

He continued with his stream-of-consciousness monologue. "The only thing I can't figure out — besides who killed Kathy, that is — is why they left her in your car. Why your car, Alison?"

I had asked myself that a thousand times and had come to the same conclusion as Max. "My car was shitty. It was easy to steal."

He had a look on his face that told me he had never considered that explanation. "Shitty? In what way?"

"It was old, the locks didn't work, and it's the kind of car most people wouldn't miss." I looked out the window and tried to figure out where we were, but couldn't. The area became more desolate, with old, dilapidated houses dotting either side of the street but becoming fewer in number the farther east we got. I tightened my grip on my bag and almost gave in to the urge to cry.

"That's a shame. You really should have invested in better transportation."

Thanks for the advice, asshole, I thought to myself. I'll be dead soon, and the only transportation I'll need is a hearse.

He slowed the car down and crept along a side street. "I want you to do something for me, Alison. I want you to find out everything your detective boyfriend knows about this case. Everything. Got it?"

"He's not my boyfriend, Peter, and he won't tell me anything." Although I should have agreed with him, I knew it was fruitless to try to pry anything out of Crawford. So, what happened when Peter came back, and I still didn't know anything? I was starting to suspect that the things that I had heard about Peter were true, and that made me fish food any way you looked at it.

"He'll tell you. Just keep asking," he said, and pulled the car over. I saw a series of large warehouses, but nothing else. "Maybe you can take another trip to the beach. The long car ride might give you the opportunity to chat a little more."

I froze. So, he knew about Crawford's beach house and our trip there. I looked out the window of the car to hide the fact that tears were rolling down my cheeks. The street outside was dark and deserted. So, this is where I'll die, I thought.

"Let's just say it would behoove you to find out anything you can and let me know." He patted my knee.

It would also behoove me to stay alive, but that didn't seem likely, given my driving companion, the gun in the side pocket of the driver's side door, and the location — a dark, deserted area of the southeast Bronx.

"By the way, I understand they had your ex in custody. What's that about? The paper says he's the main suspect," he said.

I inched closer to the door; I was practically sitting on the door handle. That wouldn't help me if he pulled out the gun and shot me in the head, but it made me feel better. "They questioned him. Just like they questioned all of Kathy's teachers."

He turned toward me. "They didn't bring you into the station house. Or Sister Mary. Why'd they bring Ray in?"

"I don't know, Peter."

"He did it, didn't he?"

"I don't know, Peter," I repeated. I was glad that it was dark in the car; I didn't want Peter to see the fear on my face.

He began muttering, almost to himself, like I wasn't in the car. "It's not like the old days. There was honor! Respect!" His voice rose. "You left the families alone. They had nothing to do with business!"

I had nothing to add. So this was about who killed Kathy, and a potential turf war to boot. I didn't know which situation was better — if Ray killed her, he would end up dead. If one of Peter's rivals killed her, that person — and maybe others — would end up dead. It was going to be ugly any way you looked at it.

He pulled the car over to the side of the road and put it in park. In an instant, he turned menacing, grabbing me roughly by the neck and pulling me close to him. The change in him was so quick that I didn't have time to react. I heard a squeak emanate from my throat as his hand, the size of a bear claw, wrapped around my throat. We were nose to nose, and his breath was hot on my face. "Find out who did this, Alison."

I squeezed my eyes shut so I wouldn't have to look at him.

"Let's put it this way: if you find out, I'll owe you big-time. And if you don't — well, let's just say I'll continue to owe you." He calmed down slightly, but retained his hold on my throat. "You might not be too crazy about the ex, Alison, but I'm sure you don't want him dead, either." His fat, stubby fingers tightened around my throat, and I began to choke. "Find out, Alison. Find out who did this. Because if you don't, after I'm done with Ray, I'm gonna start looking for your friend, Max."

There was no more air left in my lungs, and dots danced in front of my eyes. Tears rolled down my cheeks. There was nothing I could say. Peter finally let go of my throat and I gulped in air. He hit the button that opened the locks on the doors. "Get out, Alison."

I looked at him, unbelieving, but I took off my seat belt. We were in the middle of nowhere. Worse than that, we were in the middle of a crime-filled nowhere. I'd be dead in an hour if I didn't get out, but I'd also be dead if I stayed in the car.

He gripped the steering wheel. "Get out of the car!" he shouted.

Before I had a chance to act, Peter opened the car door and shoved me with a force that stunned me more than anything else. He reached over and closed the door, giving me one last furious look before driving away.

Twenty-Two

I watched in disbelief from my position on the ground as the car sped away, the taillights getting smaller until the car was out of sight. I got up and looked around, putting a hand to my hip, feeling my bloody leg through a gaping hole in my pants. The blood seeped through my fingers, and I rooted around in my purse for a tissue to blot some of it, coming up empty-handed. I hobbled over to the sidewalk and stood under the one streetlight that was working and looked around. There was nothing and nobody around who could assist me in getting from this point to a safer haven. As I stood there and took in the broken concrete of the sidewalks and the huge warehouses in the distance, instead of getting scared, I became angry. I started walking toward the Major Deegan Expressway, which I could see in the distance, elevated above the street I was on.

My next thought was to call Max. Although I seemed to have a little grace period until Peter killed both of us, my thoughts turned to her sitting at the bar at Nobu, waiting for me, and possibly being tailed by some Mafia hood with a name like "Tony Two Legs" or something like that. I pulled my phone out and dialed her number, in shock when her cell phone went directly to voice mail; Max's phone is always on, and she always answers it. I tried to figure out what kind of message to leave. "Max, you're probably going to get killed tonight . . . get out of Nobu and find a safe house" didn't seem like an option. I was clearly out of familiar territory. After listening to dead air for a few moments, I settled on the old standby: "Max, please call me when you get this message."

How in God's name had I gotten mixed up in this? And how was I going to get myself out of it? I guess I was lucky that Peter hadn't killed me. At the same time, I was angry that he thought he had so much power and was in such command of his intimidation skills that he could kidnap me right on my own street, drive me into the Bronx, and hurl me out of his car, warning me that he would probably kill my best friend if I didn't do what he wanted. I limped along the deserted street, angry, confused, and alone, thinking that if I could get to civilization, I could get out of here and get back home and put the whole evening behind me.

As I got closer to what I was hoping was civilization, it became apparent that "civilization" might not be an apt term for what I would encounter. I had watched enough nightly news shows to know where most crimes took place and where in the City to avoid. Where I was ranked highly on the list of places that a solo, female college professor should avoid. As much as I wanted to get out of this situation by myself, I realized that I couldn't go to the nearest inhabited block; nor could I climb up to the Major Deegan Expressway and hail a cab or a good Samaritan. Which left me no choice but to call the one person I knew could help me.

"For fuck's sake," I muttered, and opened my cell phone again. With shaking hands, I dialed Crawford's cell-phone number, which I had committed to memory. He picked up after a few rings. "Hi," he said warmly. He seemed happy to hear from me, which was a good sign. I was sure his mood would change once he heard my predicament. Even if we stayed casual friends, I was becoming a giant pain in the ass.

I tried to steady my voice but it was tight after Peter had cut off the air to my larynx. "I'm sorry that I called you because I know you're out to dinner with the girls, but I don't know what to do and I don't know where I am," I babbled. I looked around and saw a rat scurry out from under a sewer grate.

"What's going on?" he said, sounding alarmed.

"Crawford, I'm somewhere in the Bronx. I don't know where I am," I said, giving a little laugh and trying to convey a calmness that I clearly didn't feel.

"Why are you in the Bronx?" he asked.

Good question. "Peter Miceli dropped me off here. How do I get out of here?"

"Peter Miceli?" he said, confused. He must have decided to come back to that later, because he said, "Just stay calm for a minute." I guess I wasn't as good an actress as I thought. "Do you see any street signs?" he asked.

"I'm sorry that I interrupted dinner with your girls," I said, looking around.

"Stop apologizing and just tell me where you are."

I didn't see any street signs, but in the distance, on one of the large warehouses, I saw a sign that read BRONX TERMINAL

MARKET. "I'm about two blocks away from the Bronx Terminal Market. Do you know where that is?"

"Are you north or south of the market?"

I told him I was south of it. "I can see Yankee Stadium, and the Deegan Expressway over me," I said, and focused on a street sign down from me a bit. "I think I'm on 151st Street. Do you know where that is?"

"Stay put," he said. "Don't move unless you have to."

Unless I had to? I didn't like the sound of that but I kept listening.

"I'll send someone from the four-one over. Keep an eye out. I'll call you back as soon as I know a car is on the way. Keep the phone on," he said, and hung up.

I stood under the streetlight and waited for what seemed like a lifetime for the sound of a siren breaking through the menacing still of the night. I crossed my arms over my chest, nearly jumping out of my skin at the trill of the phone. In the distance, I could see revolving lights atop a cruiser, coming my way. "Hello?"

"They're on their way," he said.

"I can see them."

"They're going to take you to the station house. Wait until I get there before you talk to anyone. I've already told them that I want to question you."

"But what about the girls?" I asked.

"We're just finishing up. I'll rent some movies and set them up at home. They'll be fine." He paused. "They're kind of used to this."

The cruiser sped down the street toward me and skidded to a stop right in front of me. I wasn't hard to spot, a lone woman with ripped pants standing under the one streetlight that worked. "They're here. I'll wait for you at the precinct. Thank you, Crawford." I put the phone back in my bag and ran over to the police car, jumping into the back before the officers could even speak to me.

There were two of them: a Hispanic man and a black woman, who was driving. She turned around. "Are you OK, ma'am?"

It was the nicest "ma'am" I had ever heard. "I'm fine. Thanks for coming to get me."

The male officer turned around. "We're taking you back to the four-one. Detective Crawford from the fiftieth is coming to get you."

I took a deep breath. "You guys don't by any chance have a barf bag, do you?" I asked, as my stomach roiled. The adrenaline rush of being picked up by Peter, tossed from his car, and discovering the gaping wound on my leg had left me a little queasy.

The female officer took a hard right and drove the car straight up onto the curb. "Open the door!" she yelled as she looked in the rearview mirror and saw my face go from bright red to white in an instant. I opened the back door and hung my head out over the sidewalk and waited a moment while everything went upside down and then right side up.

"False alarm," I said, and pulled myself back in the car. I rested my head against the back of the seat, thinking of how many skanky prisoners had been in this car and wondering what percentage of them had head lice. I sat up straight, moved to the edge of the seat, and tried not to touch anything.

We arrived at the station house a few minutes later. The male officer opened the back door for me and led me into the building, through a door flanked by two green lights. The interior was lit by the harsh fluorescent lighting that makes everyone look green and terminally ill. There was a huge desk, behind which a senior officer was perched. He looked down at me and smiled.

"Got a little lost, huh?" He had a chestful of colorful bars, which I guess made him the head cop comedian for the evening.

I managed a weak smile. "Where can I wait for Detective Crawford?" I asked as my escorts, the two cops who had driven me here, drifted off to parts unknown. Maybe they had some kind of bullpen where they told idiot civilian stories. Mine was sure to be a hit. "So, then, she gets in the car . . ." they'd be saying, having a good laugh at my expense.

The cop behind the desk pointed to a long wooden bench against the wall. I sat between an elderly Asian woman and a large white woman with a headful of cotton-candy hair who was painted into a purple spandex dress. What separated me from my bench mates was that I was the only one not handcuffed to the bench. I looked down at my purse and tried to remember how to mentally recite a decade of the rosary; Kevin had told me that it was a good meditation and would relax me in times of stress. This was about as stressful as you could get. I started saying Hail Marys.

The purple-spandex lady trained a heavily made-up eye on me. "What did they get you for?"

I looked over at her. "Get me for?"

She sighed. "Yeah. What are you in here for?"

It slowly dawned on me that she thought I had been arrested. "Oh, I'm not in for anything. I'm just waiting for someone."

She chortled. "OK," she said, not believing that explanation. "Me, too."

"No, really. I'm just waiting for a detective." Against my better judgment, I asked her, "What are you in for?"

She rolled her eyes. "Stabbing my man. The way he treats me, they should be giving me a fucking medal, not throwing me in jail." She held up her handcuffed hands and screamed at the desk sergeant. "I told you that these are too tight!"

He looked at her. "If you don't shut your freaking mouth, I'm sticking you in a cell."

"I haven't gotten my phone call!" she screamed. "Anyway, I told you that he fell on the knife!"

The sergeant pantomimed playing the violin.

She kept screaming. "I have rights! I've been here all fucking day!"

He came down from around the desk and stood in front of her, a short, sausage-shaped man who looked better behind the high desk than in front of it. "I have rights, too! I have the right to do my job and not get a freaking headache! That's it! Vasquez!" he shouted toward a cluster of cops standing in front of the men's room. "Get her out of here! And give her her freaking phone call!"

The Asian lady started babbling in what sounded like Chinese and let out a big laugh as Vasquez — the cop who had picked me up — came over and hoisted the spandex lady off the bench. "You should have kept your mouth shut. Now I gotta take you downstairs," he said, shaking his head sadly. I held my breath for a minute while Vasquez dragged her off. The woman was nearly twice his size and was flailing about like a giant grouper on the deck of a fishing boat. A couple of cops watched Vasquez struggle for a few minutes before taking pity on him and helping him pull her down to the floor. One of them sat on her midsection and the other held her arms down. I watched this car wreck of police activity for a few minutes and finally had to look away when it became apparent the woman wasn't wearing any underwear. My cell phone began to ring a minute later, and I nearly wet my pants, the sound of it jolting me back to reality. I reached into my pocketbook, grabbing it before it rang again and flipping it open. Max was screaming into my ear before I even managed to get out a greeting.

"We're going to lose our table!" she hollered into the phone. "You promised me you were going to be on time!"

"I can't talk to you right now," I hissed into the phone. "You're going to have to cut me some slack. I was just kidnapped by Peter Miceli and left in the middle of nowhere. I'm waiting for Crawford at some precinct that apparently has been fashioned after Dante's seventh ring of hell, and I will not be coming to dinner. Got that?"

She continued yelling at me, even though I could hear her perfectly well. "What do you mean you were kidnapped by Peter Miceli?"

"What part of that do you not understand?" I hollered back at her. I was out of patience. As far as I was concerned, if someone tells you they were kidnapped, there shouldn't be any additional explanation necessary. I was so angry that I forgot to tell her that she might be in danger, too, before I hung up. I looked over at the Asian woman, who was staring at me. "What are you looking at?" I asked, and she turned away. I guess she spoke English after all.

Crawford arrived almost an hour later, during which time I came close to having a nervous breakdown. He walked into the station house, glad-handed a couple of uniformed cops, and greeted the desk sergeant by name. When he was done with his "return the conquering hero" routine, he turned to me, a little smile playing on his lips. I had crossed my arms and legs in an attempt at making myself as small as possible while sitting on the bench and waiting for him. He knew me well enough to know that this was the worst possible place I could be: it was loud, dirty, filled with criminals, and not the place you would usually find someone like me. I don't even like going to the Port Authority Bus Terminal for precisely the same reasons. He had on a white oxford shirt and jeans, the gold shield hanging over the pocket of the shirt. He came over to the bench, and I stood.

He asked me if I was hurt, and I told him that I was fine except for the scrape on my upper thigh. He looked at the scrape and told me that he would get me some Band-Aids. He smiled. "Let's go over this again. If someone pulls up next to you on the street and says 'get in the car,' what do you do?" he asked in a patronizing tone, I guess for the benefit of all of the other cops who were watching the two of us. Out of the corner of my eye, I saw a couple of the uniformed cops chuckle. I resisted the urge to give the whole lot of them the finger as he took my arm and led me to a staircase next to the high desk.

We walked up a flight of stairs to the detectives' area and went through a swinging door. "He had a gun, Crawford."

"Did he point it at you?" he asked, concerned.

I thought for a minute. "Well, no, but he had one. And it was big."

"As big as mine?" he asked.

"I don't know," I said, out of patience with him, too. "I haven't seen yours up close."

He looked down at me and couldn't control the urge to laugh out loud. We went down a short hallway, passing a couple of detectives, who fortunately did not have prisoners angry about the fit of their handcuffs or otherwise. He asked one of them as they passed if they could bring a first-aid kit to Interrogation Room Number One.

He knocked on the door of the interrogation room and, satisfied that it was empty, brought me inside and closed the door. Once we were alone, he wrapped his arms around me, and I let out a couple of the sobs that I had been holding in.

He took a handkerchief out of his pocket and handed it to me. "Here."

I sat down at a chair next to the table. "Thanks. You bought a new package of handkerchiefs, huh?" I wiped my eyes with the new, pressed handkerchief.

"Do you want a cup of coffee? Water? A Coke?" he asked, pulling out the chair next to mine. He took a yellow legal pad and a pen from the center of the table and began to write — the date, time, and our names.

I shook my head. "I just want to go home." I noticed two black marks on his clean white shirt and knew that they were from my supposedly waterproof mascara. I blew my nose again. "I'm sorry I had to call you. I didn't know what else to do."

He grabbed both of my hands in his; his were warm and mine were like ice. He rubbed my fingers. "You did the right thing. Tell me what happened."

I started with the walk down the street toward the train and ended with being dumped out of the car in the Bronx. I told him how Peter said that whether I helped him or not, he "owed" me. I told him that Peter knew that we had gone to the beach, and his sharp intake of breath told me that that wasn't good news. I managed to get the story out without crying until I got to the part where he threatened first Ray, and then Max.

I had never seen him look alarmed, so the fear and concern on his face now made me nervous. "Where's Max now?"

"I suppose she's eating at Nobu on Hudson Street. I was supposed to have dinner with her, but I got kidnapped instead."

"You get kidnapped a lot." He stood and went over to a metal credenza against the wall. There was a phone; he picked up the receiver and punched in some numbers, mouthing "Fred" to me. "Hey, it's me. Yeah." He laughed at Fred's apparent witty repartee and then turned serious. "Listen, we've got a situation." He explained where he was and why. "Miceli kidnapped Alison and has made a threat against the ex and Max Rayfield." He listened for a few minutes and then turned to me. "Where does Ray live?" he asked me, his hand over the mouthpiece.

"Twenty-two-thirty Kappock Street. Apartment five," I said.

He repeated Ray's address into the phone. "And Max is probably at Nobu . . . One-oh-five Hudson Street," he said, as I recited that address and then her home address, which he also gave to Fred. "Send a patrol car," he said. He listened for a minute, "You want to go?" He seemed confused. "OK. Just make sure someone picks her up outside the restaurant. You can tail her or let her know what's happening. Whatever you think is best under the circumstances." He hung up. "Fred's going to get Max. He says he's not too far from downtown and that it won't take him long to get down there."

I felt better. At least I knew that if she got mowed down, gangland-style, in front of the restaurant, she would have spent her last moments with her new crush.

"Do you want Miceli picked up?"

"No!" I screamed, startling him. "Don't pick him up. I don't want him to know that you know what he did. He'll kill me for sure then."

He thought about that for a moment. "I think you'll be safe for a little while. I'm thinking that you are more valuable to Miceli alive than dead. But I'm going to stick a detail on you anyway. I'm sure Miceli will have one on you, too."

Oh, good.

He put a few more notes on the pad. He continued looking down. "I'm your detail for tonight."

I shook my head. "Oh, no, you're not. You've got your daughters for the weekend, and I don't want to ruin that."

"My aunt Bea lives in the apartment below me, so she'll take care of them." He ripped a few pages off the legal pad and put them in his pocket.

I could only focus on one thing, having grown up watching *The Andy Griffith Show.* "You have an aunt Bea?"

He nodded. "And she's already up in the apartment, engaged in her favorite activity: torturing the girls about why they don't go to weekly confession." He stood. "See? Everyone wins."

There was a knock at the door and a detective walked in with a first-aid kit. Crawford thanked him and closed the door again, putting the kit on the table. "Let me see that cut."

I stood and turned to the side. My right pant leg, which was in tatters, was stuck to the wound, the blood acting as an adhesive. I winced as he knelt and pulled the flap of my pants away from it and took a good look. "I think you have to take your pants off." Sad face. That was a new reaction to my being pantless.

"Nice try. You going to invite me up to your apartment next to see your etchings, too?"

He shook his head. He was serious.

"I'm not taking my pants off in front of you in a police station. You do get an A for effort, though." I left out the small detail that I hadn't shaved my legs in a few days and that the lower half of my body was beginning to resemble that of a woolly mammoth. I opened the first-aid kit and took out a piece of gauze. I stuck it to the cut and tried to wipe off some of the dried blood, but I could see that, in fact, I would eventually have to take my pants off. I gave up and just pressed the gauze to the wound, holding it there until I was sure the bleeding had stopped.

He stood in front of me, his arms crossed, watching me try to take care of the scrape. "You might be the most stubborn person I have ever met."

"Shut up and take me home," I said. I looked at my watch; it was only eight-thirty, but I was exhausted and wanted to go to bed.

Crawford picked up the phone again and dialed out. "Erin? It's Dad. I've got to work tonight. Did Aunt Bea come up?" He waited, smiling as she kept talking. "If I'm not back, take Bea out for breakfast in the morning." He looked over at me. "I'll see you tomorrow. I love you."

I felt terrible that he wasn't with them. "I'm sorry, Crawford."

"It's fine. I was getting on their nerves anyway. They say I'm too strict. And they claim that I interrogate them," he said, and laughed. "Can you believe that? Me? Ask questions? I don't know where they come up with some of this stuff." He laughed, but I could tell that he was only half-joking. I could only imagine what he put them through during their day and a half together every week. He took his keys out of his pocket. "We're done here. I'll follow up with the desk sergeant tomorrow and do a formal report. Let's get you home."

We drove back to Dobbs Ferry, a half hour or so from the police station. As he pulled the car up the driveway, I asked him if his station house was like the one that I had just spent time in.

"The four-one is a special place," he admitted. "Why do you want to know?"

"It's hell. How do you go to a place like that every day?" I asked. I thought about the woman in the spandex dress and the fact that she had stabbed her "man" but didn't feel a bit of remorse. And the fact that she went out in public without underwear.

"You get used to it," he said dismissively. It sounded like the subject was closed.

I didn't believe him, but I let it go. Although he attempted a tough-guy act, I suspected that he was more sensitive than he let on. I had a hard time imagining him being unaffected by what he saw at work every day if the two women I had sat between were any indication of the human flotsam and jetsam that floated in.

I opened the car door and got out, feeling a cool mist cover my face. I saw Jackson in his backyard, calling for Trixie, but he either didn't see me or didn't want to talk to me. He never looked up but continued searching around and calling the dog's name.

Crawford waited until I came around to his side of the car and put his arm around my shoulders. My arm encircled his waist. "You have a neighbor named Trixie?" He pulled me closer. "She's someone I have to meet. Sounds like the kind of girl who spikes the punch at the prom."

"Trixie's a dog. A very beautiful and voluptuous dog, but a dog, nonetheless." We went in through the front door. I looked into the living room and saw that the bedclothes on the couch were still there. "I'll sleep down here tonight," I said.

"No, you won't," he said. "I was fine down here last night and will be fine down here again." He took off his badge and put it in his pants pocket. "Why don't you get cleaned up? Are you hungry?"

I couldn't tell. My stomach was still a little upset. "I don't think I'm hungry, but I could use a drink. Can you make a martini?" I took off my coat and put it in the closet.

"I think so. Even though the Irish usually stick to things they can drink directly from a can or bottle, we know our way around the back of a bar, too."

I started up the stairs, my bones achy and my muscles tired. My sense of humor was gone. "Find the biggest glass you can, chill it, and then fill it to the brim with frozen vodka. Can you handle that?"

He gave me a salute. "Got it." He called up after me. "Is there any tiramisu left?"

I told him there was.

"Can I eat it?"

I told him he could. I got upstairs and closed the bedroom door. I gingerly took my pants and shirt off and sat down on the bed in my underwear. I was in shock; it was almost as if Peter had scared the life out of me. After a few minutes, I heard a soft knock at the door.

"Can I come in?" he asked.

The knock shook me out of my fugue state. "Just a second," I called. I got off the bed and pulled on the pajama pants I had worn the night before, which I had left hanging on the bedpost. I called to him that he could come in.

He opened the door and peeked in. "Are you decent?" When he saw that I was clothed, he came all the way in. He had a big martini in one hand and a piece of tiramisu in the other, which he put on my dresser. "I'm serious about that scrape. We really need to disinfect it. I saw some gravel in there." Sad face. "You might need stitches."

I thought about my options. I could go to the emergency room and sit there all night, not do anything, and die of infection, or let him look at the wound and my hairy legs. I went into the bathroom. "Fine. Get in here." I opened the cabinet under the sink and took out a bottle of hydrogen peroxide, some Band-Aids, and a washcloth, and handed them to him. "Do your thing. Just make it fast."

He laughed. "That's not the first time I've heard that," he said. When I didn't laugh, he became serious again. He put the supplies on the counter, along with the martini, which he had carried into the bathroom. "Do you have a tweezer?"

I felt the blood drain from my face. This was going to be worse than I thought. "We need a tweezer?"

I got the sad face and a nod. I opened the medicine cabinet and took out the tweezer and handed it to him. He, in turn, handed me the martini. "Take a big drink," he said.

He washed the tweezer in the sink and dumped some hydrogen peroxide on it.

I finished half of the martini and the warmth spread from my throat down to the pit of my stomach. I rolled the waistband of my pants down, sat on one cheek on the closed toilet-seat cover, and looked away, my eyes closed. I winced as I felt his hand on my upper thigh.

"I haven't done anything yet," he said. He put a washcloth in my hand. "Squeeze this. I'll try to be fast." He knelt down and put the tweezer into the wound to start extracting gravel. After a few minutes, he seemed to have gotten all of it, and he took the washcloth from me. Tears were rolling down my cheeks. "I'm sorry," he said, and put his arms around me. "We're almost done." He soaked the washcloth in hydrogen peroxide, washed the scrape, and put a few Band-Aids over it. "Done," he said, and stood. "Do you want me to make you some dinner?"

I wasn't hungry. "I'm really tired, Crawford. I think I'm just going to go to bed."

We walked back into the bedroom; he carried my drink and the plate of tiramisu over as I got under the quilt. "At least finish your drink first," he said, and handed me the martini. He sat down at the end of the bed and took a bite of dessert.

I took another drink. "How many guns do you have with you tonight?" I asked.

He held up two fingers. "And one of them is really big." He gave me his most lascivious smile and held his hands two feet apart.

I still wasn't in a joking mood. "That should be enough." I took another long drink of the martini and finished it off. I closed my eyes because I couldn't look at him. "Please stay up here with me tonight."

He put the tiramisu on the bed, unbuttoned his shirt, and got under the quilt. He grabbed the plate. "Only if I can hold you closer," he said, and fed me a piece of tiramisu.

TWENTY-THREE

My daytime detail consisted of a large female police officer who made Crawford look like a ninety-eight-pound weakling. She spent the day in a car outside my house until I asked her in for a cup of coffee around three. She told me that her name was Sally Hiney, and being the four-year-old that I am, I couldn't look her in the eye without choking back a guffaw.

She must have sensed the hilarity bubbling beneath my calm exterior because she mentioned that the last person who had made fun of her name ended up with a black eye, eying me over the top of her coffee mug.

Crawford and Hiney had met up at the precinct earlier that morning and he had given her the Shakespeare papers. She returned them to me that afternoon; I put them in their permanent resting place in my briefcase. He had had them tested by a drug analyst in the police department and had come up empty. No drugs were found on this set, but they still had all of the papers from my prior classes to test. He and Wyatt couldn't get anywhere with Costigan to find out why they had kidnapped me besides the fact that they wanted papers that I had in my possession; his lawyer had advised him to remain tight-lipped, and he was obeying. So, they were back at square one.

I had to go to the awards ceremony that night, and Officer Hiney told me that she would drive me to school whenever I needed to leave. She dropped me off behind the building and parked the car next to the dorm, letting me know that she was there and would keep an eye out for anything out of the ordinary.

The entire office area was empty, as I suspected it would be late on a Sunday afternoon. It was dark and dreary, the large windows illuminating the rain and fog, and nothing else. The door to my office was closed and locked. I put my things onto the prefect's table.

I had a little time to kill until Max arrived — Sister Mary had invited her to attend the ceremony as well — so I pulled out the Shakespeare papers and thumbed through them, trying to assess just how much work I had to do in order to get them back to their respective owners.

Max arrived a few minutes later. She looked beautiful in black, hip-hugging pants and a cobalt blue silk shirt with a wide collar and French cuffs. She carried a bag the size, color, and shape of a pork chop. I must have missed this month's *Vogue* because I didn't know pork had become hot.

She didn't make eye contact with me right away. "Are we still talking?"

I hugged her. "Of course we are."

She gave me a kiss on the cheek in which her lips actually touched my face; she hadn't kissed me like that since my mother's wake. She must have been feeling contrite. "So, what happened to you?" she asked.

I told her the entire story of my night with Peter Miceli, leaving out the part where he said that he was probably going to kill her.

"I have something to tell you!" she exclaimed before I could continue.

"Yes?" I said, waiting.

She suddenly broke into a huge smile, and the conversation turned to her favorite subject — herself. "You'll never guess who I ran into last night," she said, obviously excited.

I played dumb.

"Fred Wyatt," she said. "I ate at Nobu

anyway, which was great, by the way, and as I was leaving the restaurant, he was standing right in front of the door. How weird is that? He was just standing right there, in front of the restaurant. It was almost like he was waiting for me."

He *was* waiting for you, you idiot, I thought, but I kept it to myself.

"And then he walked me home. All the way up to my apartment door," she said, a flush in her usually pallid cheeks.

"Did he come in?" I asked, flashing back on Crawford's conversation with him.

She shook her head. "Sadly, no." She chewed her lower lip. "But something tells me I'm going to see him again." She picked up the papers on the table and began thumbing through them. She read the title of one aloud: "The Role of Guilt in *Macbeth:* 'Tis Safer To Be That Which We Destroy." "Wow," she said. "Heavy."

"Actually, that's not bad."

"It's not? I would have just called it 'Max's *Macbeth* paper' and left it at that."

I took the paper from her hand. "And, that, my dear Max, is why you were a math major."

The paper was a muck-covered mess. "Where was that written? A sewer?" she asked.

I flushed, thinking back to my dream on the train about who I now knew was Crawford. I kept my head down as I shoved the papers back into my briefcase, unlocked and opened my office door, closed my eyes, and tossed the briefcase in. I didn't want to see the destruction again. I took my purse from the table and asked her if she was ready to leave. We exited onto the little landing and went up one level to the chapel floor. We arrived at the Blue Room and were greeted by Sister Mary, who was the only one in the room, besides the food-services people.

"Alison. Maxine." She gave a few orders to the food-services people and dismissed them with an imperious wave of her hand. "Alison, I thought that we'd wait until about six-fifteen to give out awards. Let the guests have a bite to eat and a drink before the ceremony starts."

I knew she wasn't looking for my input, so I just nodded.

"You look lovely, dear, except for that huge bump on your forehead," she said, and swept off in her queen-sized panty hose, a cloud of Jean Naté, Aqua Net hair spray, and general pissiness.

Max rolled her eyes at me. "She hasn't changed since we went here. There's a woman who really needs to get laid."

I put my hand over Max's mouth and went over to the bar area, where Marcus, the head chef of the commuter cafeteria, was tending bar. Since I usually ate there, we had become quite friendly. He leaned in conspiratorially when I approached the bar and whispered in my ear. "You'd better get a drink now. Sister Wicked Witch will be back before you know it."

I introduced Max to Marcus. He took her hand and kissed her knuckles lightly. "Enchanté." Although he was sixty-five if he was a day, he was all Jamaican cool and charm, with a head of white hair atop a face the color of teak. Max gave him a thousand-watt smile and asked for a couple of Cosmopolitans. She looked at me. "They're so out they're in again." Marcus whipped up a batch of the pink drink and handed them to us with a flourish. "Ladies." They had even broken out the martini glasses for tonight's festivities.

People began filing in, and I greeted a few parents who I had met before. I looked and saw Max at the bar, flirting with Marcus and starting her second Cosmopolitan. I had a nagging sense of dread as I saw her hoist the drink to her lips; the last thing I wanted to do tonight was peel Max off the floor of the Blue Room before my date with

Crawford. That would certainly be a mood killer.

She caught my eye, and I drew a flat palm across my throat to signal "Enough." She smiled back at me and turned back to Marcus, who was now completely in her thrall.

A couple approached me — he, short and bespectacled, and she, a grown-up version of her daughter: redheaded, petite, and attractive. The Martins, I suspected. Mr. Martin held a glass of scotch, his wife a glass of white wine. He held out his hand but I could see his eyes travel to the bump on my forehead. "Frank Martin. Are you Professor Bergeron?" I nodded. "Our daughter raves about her Shakespeare class with you. This is my wife, Genevieve Martin."

With my "date shoes" on, I towered over both of them by a good four inches. I shook hands with both of them. "Nice to meet you. Fiona's had a wonderful year in my classes."

"We're very proud that she's in this honor society. She tells us that you were one of its first members on campus," he said.

"I was." I looked around. "Where is Fiona?" I asked.

Mrs. Martin answered. "She actually went to find you. She wanted to talk with you about the last paper she wrote for the Shakespeare class."

I decided to play it casual, an immense wave of guilt flooding over me at the thought of the papers in my briefcase. "Oh, she did? We'll have to chat before the night's out." I picked my drink up. "Would you excuse me?" I headed over to the bar, where Max was picking peanuts out of a silver bowl and sipping her Cosmopolitan.

"Who are they?" she asked, draining her drink and motioning to Marcus to fix her another one.

"Parents of one of my students," I said.

"It's kind of depressing when the parents start to look the same age as you, huh?" she mused. "And we didn't even get pregnant in college like some people we know," she said, referring to Gianna. Marcus set our drinks down in front of us, and Max continued picking peanuts out of the bowl. A waiter floated by with a trayful of canapés, and she picked two off the tray and popped them in her mouth one after the other. "I'm starving," she said, her cheeks bulging.

"I got that impression." I took a sip of my Cosmopolitan and watched a few more sets of parents float into the room. Sister Mary returned and began greeting everyone with her usual mixture of officiousness and graciousness. Whatever she had, the parents ate it up. Maybe her bluster was part of her charm, or maybe it lent the school and our department some credibility. I had given up trying to figure it out.

She led a group of parents over to me just as I was hoisting my drink. I didn't know whether to take a sip or put the drink down, so I fumbled and spilled a little down the front of my dress and into my décolletage. I grabbed a napkin from the bar and mopped up as much as I could before shaking hands with the parents of several of my students. Sister Mary introduced everyone to each other.

"And, this is Maxine Rayfield, one of our illustrious alumnae," she said, her Latin conjugation impeccable. If Latin hadn't been a dead language, I'm sure Sister Mary would insist we speak it within the walls of the school. "Maxine and Dr. Bergeron graduated in . . ." She looked to us for confirmation.

"Another decade," Max chimed in, breaking up the group.

We stood and made idle chitchat for about fifteen minutes. The large windows were open facing the river, and as the rain began to fall in heavy, torrential drops, Sister Mary rushed over to close them. When she was done, she came over to me. "I count fourteen students, and we have fifteen awards. Who's missing?"

I looked around the room and scanned the faces. "Fiona Martin," I said. "I think she's looking for me to discuss a paper."

Sister Mary's face turned grim. "We need to start the awards ceremony in thirty minutes, latest. Find her," she commanded.

I whispered to Max that I had to go back to my office for a minute. She was deep in conversation with Desiree Franklin's parents about her Tribeca neighborhood and property values. Apparently, they were looking for real estate. I felt comfortable leaving her side, knowing that a conversation about Manhattan real estate values would have Max talking for at least an hour. Besides sex, that was one of her favorite topics, so I was glad that they had chosen real estate to chat about.

I entered the office floor and saw Fiona sitting at the prefect's table, alone. Her hands were folded in front of her, and she almost looked like she was sleeping. She must have heard my heels hit the hardwood floors, because she looked up and then over at me, her reverie interrupted. The office floor was almost completely dark, and I switched on the light that hung over the table.

"Hi, Fiona," I said. "We're going to start the ceremony soon, and Sister Mary would like you to come to the Blue Room."

She pushed her chair back, stood up, and faced me. She was more cute than she was beautiful, with wavy red hair, beautiful skin, and big blue eyes. She was smart and did well in school; she was on the dean's list each of the three previous semesters and she was just finishing her sophomore year. She was wearing a lovely blue-linen suit with beige pumps, a grown-up outfit for an almost-woman who looked like a little girl. She smiled at me. "I really wanted to talk with you about my Shakespeare paper."

I walked toward her. I felt guilty that I had to be tracked down by a student to discuss a paper. "I'm so sorry, Fiona. With everything that's been going on here and at home, I've really let the ball drop on those papers."

She smiled again. "Well, I'd really like to know my grade, but at this point, it's not a big deal. Can I just have my paper back?"

I was confused. "I still have to grade them, Fiona, even if they are a bit late getting back to you. If I give you the paper back, you'll have a missing grade for my class."

"I think I'd still do fine in the class. I'll take that chance." She pushed her chair in with her hip and moved closer to me.

I thought for a moment. "Listen, I'll move you to the top of the pile and grade your paper tonight. You'll have an answer Monday. Just like I promised the other day in class," I reminded her.

She shifted from one foot to another and took another step. "Just give me my paper back, Dr. Bergeron."

"I can't do that."

She continued to stare at me.

I thought for a moment and looked at my watch. "Why don't I read it now quickly and give you an idea of what I think?" I thought that that might pacify her. She obviously wasn't going with my plan of getting the paper back on Monday, and I didn't want her to jeopardize her place on the dean's list just because of her impatience.

She stared back at me. "I just want the paper back."

I walked to my office; the briefcase was just where I tossed it and on its side, papers spilling out. I picked it up and brought it back out into the main area, pushing the papers back in until I could put the briefcase onto the table and sort everything out.

I sat down at the table and she took her

seat across from me. I opened my briefcase and pulled all of the papers out, trying to neaten them while searching for hers. I pulled it from the pile; it still had a fair amount of gunk on it from the time I dropped it on the train floor. I looked up, and said, "Sorry. I dropped my briefcase on the train one night."

She stared back at me, impassively.

There was a coffee can in the middle of the table that held pens, tape, scissors, and pencils; I grabbed a red pen so I could mark anything that I saw on the paper that needed highlighting. I also grabbed a large pair of scissors; the top of the paper was as hard as parchment from the dried muck that covered it. I remembered the paper floating to the ground on the train and watching it soak up mud, water, and spilled beer that pooled under my feet on the train a few weeks earlier. "Do you mind if I cut off the top of the paper?" I asked her. She didn't, so I cut off the hardest parts, and put the scissors down on the table. I held her paper up in front of my face and began to read her paper: "The Role of Guilt in *Macbeth:* 'Tis Safer To Be That Which We Destroy."

"Good title, Fiona," I remarked. "Nice allusion to Act III, Scene 2."

She sat across from me, fidgeting in her chair and sighing loudly as I read the first couple of paragraphs.

This had been a short assignment, so I got to the conclusion with a quick scan of all of her major points in less than five minutes.

So, it stands to reason that there was truly no blood on Lady Macbeth's hands — just the guilt that she had conspired in committing a murder.

I took a pen from my briefcase and made a note on the paper: *"Guilt cannot be on her hands. How about 'It stands to reason that there was no blood on Lady Macbeth's hands, but that she now has to live with the guilt that she conspired with Macbeth in committing a murder.' Need to develop this thought more."*

Macbeth commits the murder, but ultimately, Lady Macbeth feels responsible for the crime against Duncan, the king of Scotland. Once his best friend and confidant, he has turned against him in a way that no friend should turn against another.

Her grammar stank and I didn't agree with the statement, but I thought I would leave it alone until I could do a closer reading. I read on. She referenced Act V, Scene 1, which is Lady Macbeth's penultimate scene displaying her guilt and insanity.

When Lady Macbeth says, "Yet who would have thought the girl to have had so much blood in her?" it illustrates the fact that although she didn't see the crime being committed, she knew that the crime against the king was bloody and indeed, violent. In today's world, her only hope would be the insanity defense. Because she didn't mean to do it.

I reread the line. "Girl" was an obvious mistake. Duncan is an old man when Macbeth kills him. I drew a circle around the two words and inserted a question mark, thinking that she may be mistaking the line for that from another play. *Hamlet,* maybe?

I looked up at Fiona from over the top of her paper, my eyes landing on the necklace resting on her throat: a diamond-encrusted "X" on a short gold chain.

Twenty-Four

I put the paper down slowly and stared across at Fiona, who stared back at me.

"Nice work, Fiona," I said, my voice shaking slightly. I pushed my chair back from the table a bit, but hit an uneven floorboard and couldn't go any farther.

"Thank you," she said, coldly. "May I have my paper back now?"

I shook my head. "I don't think so." I folded it in two and pushed it back into my briefcase. I pushed the chair back hard over the floorboard and stood up.

She stood up as well. The table separated us.

Even though it was getting dark, I could see a familiar shape bounding down the back steps of the building through the glass of my office windows. Crawford. I didn't know whether to be relieved or frightened. Moments later, I heard the back door of the building open and his footsteps on the stairs. I prayed that he would come to the office before going to the Blue Room so that I had some company. I heard him call my name as he opened the door. He was dressed in a white-cotton oxford and black pants. No sign of the big gun, but I mentally flashed on the one he wore on his ankle.

Fiona looked at him coming through the door. She turned back around, her face cold and hard. "Give me back my paper," she snarled.

Crawford made his way into the room and stood at the far end of the table. "Ladies," he said, a question in his greeting.

"Detective, this is Fiona Martin. She's in my Shakespeare class," I said, motioning to her. "Fiona, this is Detective Crawford."

He walked over and shook her hand. The look on her face was a mixture of confusion and anxiety. She looked to him and then back to me.

"Detective Crawford is a friend of mine," I said.

He looked at me for some clue as to what was happening. I looked down at the table and the paper in front of me.

"Detective Crawford is working on Kathy's murder."

Fiona glared at me. "Why is he here? Did you already know?"

350

"Know what, Fiona?" I asked, wanting to hear her say it.

"Is that why you wouldn't give me my paper back?"

Crawford perched on the edge of the table and crossed one leg over the other, his hands wrapped around his right ankle. "Why don't you both sit down so we can talk?" he suggested, his posture casual and nonthreatening.

Fiona's eyes filled with tears. "You know, my father's here, and I can ask him to come in and make you give it back." She continued to stand and stare at me.

I sat down. "I don't think you want to do that, Fiona. Tell me what you were writing about in the paper."

I saw her mind working as she decided what to do.

"Please."

Crawford stayed silent, watching Fiona as she sat down and buried her head in her hands and sobbed. His hands wrapped the bottom of his pant leg tight around his ankle.

"Did you kill her?" I asked.

She nodded. "But it was an accident!" she cried.

"I'm sure it was," I said, trying to keep my voice even and soothing. "What happened?"

"She caught me with Vince," she said. "And she freaked out."

I would have freaked out, too, I thought. But then again, she had been with Ray. Would she really care if Fiona was involved with Vince? I didn't say anything and let Fiona keep talking.

She narrowed her eyes and looked at me. "You know she was sleeping with your ex-husband, don't you?" She fingered the "x" around her neck with her free hand.

I nodded.

"She wasn't as nice as everyone is saying she was."

"I didn't really know her well." I looked at Crawford.

"She didn't want Vince with anyone else. She was really mad that he took up with her roommate, of all people. She was like that. Jealous."

Crawford waited a minute before asking, "How did she die?"

She crossed her arms over her chest and leaned back in the chair, taking a deep breath. "We were in a bar on Broadway when she found us. Vince left like the big chicken that he is . . . was," she said, "and it was just the two of us. I knew that she was sleeping with Ray, and I told her that, but she was still pissed off that I had hooked up with Vince. She said it wasn't right. We left the bar and started walking home."

"Along Broadway?" Crawford asked.

"Yeah." She shot a look at him, but he didn't respond in any way. "We went through the woods between the apartment buildings and our dorm, and that's when she told me that Vince was only using me to get back at her." Tears started falling down her face. "That just wasn't true," she protested.

"I'm sure it wasn't true," I said, thinking that that was what I was supposed to say.

"Right!" she said, agreeing with me. She cried for a few more minutes. "Vince always told me he loved me. And he gave me this," she said, rolling the diamond necklace between her fingers. "He was really hurt when she broke up with him."

"The breakup wasn't his idea?" I asked.

She shook her head. "No. It was all her idea." She looked down. She looked like she had something else to say, but she kept silent. Something unspoken hung in the air.

Crawford looked over at me questioningly.

"What else, Fiona?" I prodded her.

She wouldn't look at me.

"Fiona, if there's more, we have to know. Anything you tell us could help you," Crawford lied.

"Did you know that Vince is dead?" she asked, changing the subject.

I nodded. I heard Crawford take a deep breath and exhale slowly. I didn't feel the need to go into any more detail.

"And Johnny's in jail."

I was surprised that she knew that. "How did you know that?"

"He's my cousin. My mother's sister's son. They called my dad to get him out." She fiddled with the edge of her skirt. "But he couldn't."

Her parents apparently hadn't told her the whole story. Crawford led her along with her story. "So, what happened in the woods?"

"I pushed her," she said, matter-of-factly. "And she fell backwards and gashed her head open on a stump sticking out of the ground. I think she died then." She wiped her nose with the back of her hand. "There was a lot of blood."

"How did you get the body to my car?" I asked.

"Kathy told me that Ray let her drive his car every once in a while and that he kept a spare set of keys in his desk drawer in his office. I went into his office and took them. I knew he had a BMW, but there was an old Volvo key on the key ring, marked 'Al.' I figured that was your car key. I also figured you wouldn't miss that junker too much, so I asked Vince and Johnny to help me get the body and dump it." She paused for a minute. "I wasn't trying to frame you. I thought you'd be happy to be rid of that wreck. I told Vince and Johnny to take the car and get rid of it. I didn't think that they'd only go a few miles. How stupid was that?"

I didn't say anything. Vince and John were certainly not criminal masterminds, that was for sure.

I tried to keep her talking. "Why did you break into my office?" I asked. "Were you just trying to get the paper back?"

She looked at me quizzically and then a mental light went on in her head. "Oh, that was Vince. I told him that I thought I might have given away something in the paper, and he freaked out." She smiled slightly. "How weird was it that we were doing *Macbeth*?"

"Yeah, weird," I agreed. "When did Vince give you the necklace?" I asked.

She touched it to make sure that it was still there. "A few weeks ago."

"What does the X mean?" I asked.

"It's my birthday. October tenth. The

tenth day of the tenth month."

"And X is ten in Roman numerals," I said. "Clever."

"Well, it's a heck of a lot nicer than wearing a ten around your neck. That would look cheesy." She shifted again. We sat in silence, looking at each other for what seemed like hours, but what was really only a few minutes.

"So, what do you think I should do?" she finally asked, breaking the silence.

"I think you should give yourself up," I said.

"What's going to happen to me?" she asked.

I looked at Crawford to provide some kind of explanation. "If you explain everything to the judge just like you explained it to us, I'm sure you'll be able to work things out," he said. I knew that he was lying, but looking at her, I could tell that she was buying whatever he was selling.

She stood up and smoothed her skirt down and wiped her nose on the back of her hand. "Well, that's good. I feel much better."

Crawford stood as well. "So, let's take a ride to the precinct, and we can get everything down in writing and on video."

She looked at him in shock. "I've got an

awards ceremony tonight."

"I'm afraid you're going to have to miss it, Fiona," he said gently, taking her arm. It was the first time I had seen him use the sad face with anyone but me.

Fiona shook loose from his grasp and lunged across the table, grabbing the large pair of scissors that I had used on her paper. She turned and stabbed him once in the shoulder, and another time right above his heart, stunning herself and the two of us. She looked at me, dropped the scissors and ran for the door.

Crawford put his hand over the shoulder wound and doubled over at the same time. Blood seeped between his fingers, and his white shirt bloomed crimson in seconds. He grabbed the gun from his ankle and pointed it at her back. "Fiona! Stop or I'll shoot you dead," he said, loudly but calmly.

She skidded to a stop, inches from the door to the stairway. She slowly put her hands up over her head, but kept her back to us. Crawford got up, holding the wound closest to his heart closed with his left hand, aiming the gun with his right. I watched as he walked over to her, grabbed her roughly by the collar of her silk blouse, and dragged her back to the table. He threw her into the same chair in which she had been sitting during our conversation. The chair moved back several inches when her body hit it, and she let out a yelp. She rubbed her left elbow with the palm of her right hand.

"Alison, call nine-one-one," he said, pressing on his shoulder with the palm of his hand. "Tell them it's a ten-thirteen. My badge number is one-seven-four-three-oh."

Wyatt told me later that a 10-13 meant "officer needs assistance," and that it would bring every available squad car in a twenty-mile radius to the scene. He held the gun on Fiona, inches from her face. She stared into the barrel, perhaps finally understanding the severity of the situation.

Crawford cursed under his breath, and winced. He was furious with her, and I think it took every ounce of control for him not to blow her head off. The blood was pooling on the floor around him, and I watched him as I made the call. The color was draining from his face, and he was getting weak. After I hung up, I ran back to where they were sitting and stripped off my half slip.

I bent to pick up the scissors. "Leave them. They're evidence," he commanded, but his voice was small.

I ripped the black nylon slip in two and wrapped it around his shoulder and tried to stop the bleeding. It was only minutes later that I heard the wail of several police cars and the steady bleat of an ambulance siren. I stood behind him and put my arms under his armpits as he slid down in the chair, losing consciousness. His head fell straight back and I could see the thick layer of sweat covering his face. The gun slipped out of his hand and fell to the floor, dropping beside him but inching closer to Fiona.

Fiona and I looked at it. I had Crawford and her chair in my path. She reached down and grabbed the gun.

"It was an accident!" she screamed, the gun waving wildly in her trembling hand.

I took my hands out from under Crawford's armpits and positioned him so that he wouldn't fall out of the chair, his head and upper torso resting on the table. If I was going to get killed, I didn't want it to appear that I had been using his body as a shield. I looked over Fiona's shoulder and saw through the windows of my office that a virtual phalanx of police officers were running down the stairs behind the building, but I kept my eyes on her and the gun.

"Give me the gun, Fiona," I said, starting toward her slowly.

She was sobbing. "I didn't mean to do that," she said, pointing the gun at Crawford.

I nodded like I understood. I held my hand out to her. "The police are here."

Her face crumpled, and she let out a gut-wrenching sob. She put the gun to her head.

"No, Fiona!"

The window in my office exploded as three officers, dressed in head-to-toe black and wearing riot gear, burst through the glass. They were through the windows and by Fiona's side in seconds. They all screamed simultaneously for Fiona to drop the gun and for me to hit the floor. We both obliged.

Fiona began sobbing as two of the officers surrounded her and pointed large automatic weapons at her. The other officer, a woman, checked all of the offices and called out "All clear!" The main office door opened and Wyatt ran in, his gun pointed into the room. He ran to Crawford's side and checked his neck for a pulse. "Get the EMTs in here!" he shouted to the door, and, immediately, three EMTs entered with a stretcher. Within seconds, they had Crawford on a stretcher, his shirt off, and an IV in his arm. One of the EMTs set about cutting Crawford's pants off and I looked away, knowing that he would want me to. After they covered him with a sheet, I took one last look: he was still unconscious and looked about as close to a corpse as someone with a pulse can get.

"Multiple stab wounds, thready pulse, blood loss," one technician shouted into a walkie-talkie, "BP is ninety over sixty." He continued talking as the stretcher was brought to waist height on wheels and removed from the room. The EMT called "Mercy" to Wyatt, who nodded.

Cops swarmed the room. With one of their own on a stretcher and headed to the hospital, the mood was solemn but charged with anger. I was actually worried about Fiona's safety. Fiona was on her knees with her hands laced on her head, a female cop standing over her with her gun drawn. After a few minutes, Sally Hiney came over, pulled Fiona's arms off her head, and tightly cuffed her hands behind her back. Sally, roughly twice Fiona's size, dragged her through the chaos. Fiona turned and looked at me. "I'm sorry," she cried, as another officer by the door joined in hauling her out, lifting her by her armpits so that her feet were a few inches off the floor.

Wyatt bent down and picked up Crawford's bloody shirt and my slip. He held the slip/tourniquet aloft and looked at me, one eyebrow raised. "What's this?"

"He was bleeding and I needed something

to stop it," I explained.

"Good thinking, Nurse McSmartypants." He opened a Ziploc bag and put the shirt in it. He got another bag and put the slip in there, marking both of them as evidence.

I looked at him. I had told Crawford about my alter ego; he must have passed this information on to Fred. I let it go. "She killed Kathy Miceli."

As if on cue, I heard Fiona's voice in the stairwell protesting to someone else. "It was an accident!" she screamed.

I pointed to the paper, still a bit caked with train muck.

Wyatt picked the paper up between the tips of his thumb and index fingers of his gloved hand. "You puke on this, too?"

Instead of laughing, I burst into tears. Wyatt muttered, "Oh, jeez," and took my arm, steering me toward the open door of one of my colleague's offices, which was on the other side of the office area, and the farthest away from the action.

I fell into the plush office chair in front of the desk and rolled back a few inches. Wyatt pulled up one of the chairs that was used for students visiting during office hours, his immense frame filling it. He leaned in, his hands hanging down between his legs. I think he was waiting for me to stop crying.

As a precaution, he took the waste can from under the desk and put it by my feet.

Connie Burns is another English professor and the most meticulous person I have ever met. Her office was neat, orderly, and clean. A full box of tissues sat at the edge of her desk, right next to the picture of her neat, orderly, and clean children. I pulled out six or seven tissues and blew my nose loudly. She would be disinfecting for days.

"You all right?" he asked.

"I'm fine," I said, pulling more tissues out of the box and wiping my eyes. I balled all of them up until they resembled a wad of papier-mâché and threw them in the spotless waste can.

"Tell me what happened."

"Where do you want me to start?" I asked.

"Start with why you're here tonight and end with how my partner ended up stabbed." There was an edge to his voice that told me that given the chance, he might tear Fiona apart, limb from limb. He took a small notebook from his back pocket and from Connie's desk grabbed a pen that I knew she would never see again.

I started my story. He stopped me a few times for more details, but I finished a complete retelling in under ten minutes.

"That it?" he asked.

I nodded.

He snapped the notebook shut. "That's a shame," he said, and shook his head. The tough veneer crumbled, and he wiped his hands over his face, rubbing his eyes. He stayed silent, composing himself. I looked away, focusing on Connie's desk — the datebook, the stack of papers on top of a grade book, and her calendar of meaning-less aphorisms. Today's was from Oscar Wilde: "Man is a rational animal who always loses his temper when he is called upon to act in accordance with the dictates of reason."

Wyatt looked at me. "You're friends with Father Kevin, right? Call the padre. Tell him to meet me at Mercy Hospital."

I picked up Connie's phone; it smelled like disinfectant. I called Kevin and, giving him the shortened version of the horrible story, asked him to meet Wyatt at the hospital. Kevin is used to calls like this; he didn't ask questions and hung up quickly.

I took a couple of more tissues and blew my nose again. "Can I go, too?"

Wyatt pondered my question for a few minutes. He looked at his watch. "I guess now is as good a time as any." He stopped himself. "Sure. Let's go."

There was a knock at the door, and Wyatt

reached back around him and opened it. A young man, whom I vaguely recognized, stood in the doorway, his blue NYPD uniform throwing me off momentarily. When my head cleared, I recognized him as the skateboarder who called me "ma'am" at the Starbucks a few weeks earlier. I did a double take, and he smiled sheepishly at me.

"Ma'am," he said, and gave me a little salute.

"You're a cop?"

He gave a little shrug. "Yes, ma'am."

Wyatt laughed. "Derek was on your tail for a few days. Good undercover work, huh?"

I continued to stare at him. With the uniform on, he looked slightly older than the eighteen years I had given him when we first met, but not much. "Excellent undercover work."

Derek cleared his throat. "Detective? We need you."

We left Connie's office and went back into the main area. Max was standing by Dottie's desk, her arms folded across her chest, chewing the inside of her mouth nervously. When she saw me, she ran down the length of the office and threw her arms around me. "What the . . . ?" she yelled, at a loss for words. She was so loud that the officers in the room stopped and looked at her. "Are you OK?"

"I'm fine, Max," I said. Never forgetting my manners, even in times of extreme stress, I turned to Wyatt. "You remember my friend, Max Rayfield?" I forgot that they had spent some time together the night before.

He was back to normal. He peered down at Max from behind his glasses. "Who could forget you, Ms. Rayfield?" he said, rather charmingly and without any sarcasm.

She blushed, something I had never seen Max do. Blushing was my department. "Call me Max."

He held out his hand. "Call me Fred."

"Is that your real name or just what you want me to call you?" Max said, smiling.

"Real name."

I cleared my throat. Apparently, I had become invisible. "I'd like to go to the hospital, Detective."

Max reminded me that she had her car. "I'll drive you. I've canceled my dinner plans, obviously," she said. She took a business card out of the wallet inside her pocketbook and jotted down her cell-phone number with a pen that she walked over to Dottie's desk to get. "If you're ever in

Tribeca, Detective, please give me a call." She handed him the card, which he accepted, read, and then put in his pants pocket.

Max exchanged a last look with Wyatt, fraught with some kind of meaning lost on me.

Wyatt smiled and called a uniformed officer over. "Get them to their car." The officer nodded and opened the blood-spattered office door for us with rubber-gloved hands.

The officer walked us to Max's car, which was parked in the dorm parking lot, behind my building. We got in, and Max locked the doors with a thunk, nearly scaring me half to death. I grabbed my throat. "I'm a little jumpy."

"I'll say," Max replied, and started the car. "What happened in there?"

I told her about going to look for Fiona and our debate over the paper and how she finally revealed to me that she, not Vince or Ray, had killed Kathy.

"Did she threaten you?" Max asked, maneuvering the car up the main drive and off campus.

"No." I felt my eyes well up again. "But God knows she's in enough trouble now to ruin her life forever."

We pulled up to the hospital entrance, and Max told me to get out while she looked for a parking space. I went inside and waited a few minutes; Kevin arrived, holding a small leather bag and wearing his black shirt, collar, black pants, and black shoes. No more Stoner Priest. We stood in the bright lights of the hospital admissions area, his arms around me. When I was done crying, he went up to the nurses' station and spoke to a woman at the admissions desk. After a brief conversation, he motioned to me, "Come on."

We walked down the hall and got into the elevator, which was empty. He pushed the button for the fourth floor and turned to me. "You're covered in blood," he said.

I looked down and saw that my neck, arms, and dress were covered in dried, russet-colored blood. Kevin touched my jaw. "There, too."

The door opened on the fourth floor. Several uniformed police officers were clustered together in front of the nurses' station; they all turned when the doors opened. I recognized Simons from the day before. He came over and took Kevin by the arm, leading him down the hall wordlessly. When they were a safe distance away, Simons told Kevin something, and Kevin nodded like he understood. He returned.

"He's in surgery and will be for another hour or so. The shoulder wound isn't too bad, but the other wound was close to the heart and nicked an artery. The doctor is also concerned about infection, so the next twenty-four hours are critical." He looked at me, his eyes huge behind his Coke-bottle lenses. "They want me to stay. Do you want to stay or go home and get some rest?"

"I'll stay."

"You want coffee?" he asked, as we walked to a bank of plastic chairs against the wall.

I shrugged. I didn't care.

He put his bag down on the chair. "No fooling around with the holy chrism," he admonished, shaking his finger in my face. When I didn't laugh, he turned and went to find coffee.

A tall cop, about fifty, in knee-high leather boots, jodhpurs, and a leather bomber jacket approached me and knelt next to me. He held a round helmet with a visor under his arm that had "Motorcycle One" printed on it. "Are you the professor?"

I nodded.

"Jack Panebianco. Motorcycle." He held out his hand.

"Cannoli rider?" I took his hand, which was rough around mine.

He looked puzzled for a moment and then laughed. "Cannoli rider," he confirmed.

"We never got to eat them. They're still in my refrigerator," I said, and sobbed.

He looked uncomfortable. Of all of the cops I had met in the last several weeks, none could handle tears. Crying Witnesses 101 needed to be added to the cop school curriculum, too. "You can eat them when he gets out."

I shrugged. "I guess."

"He's tough."

"I know."

He looked around. "I just wanted to say hello. I wouldn't cart cannolis around on a motorcycle for just anyone." He walked back to the nurses' station and leaned against it, turning to talk to one of the nurses.

Kevin came back with two cups of coffee and handed one to me and the other to Max, whom he had met up with in the elevator. "I spoke with one of the nurses, and she said that you could clean up in the bathroom behind the nurses' station if you want," he said.

I didn't answer.

"Do you want to?"

I shook my head. "I'll do it when I get home." The three of us sat in silence for two hours, Max and I sipping coffee that tasted like battery acid. I decided that whatever they taught Kevin about silence in the seminary was well learned; he didn't feel the need to fill the space with chatter. Even Max had adopted the code of silence and sat quietly, just holding my hand.

Well into our second hour of silence, I spoke. "He has kids. Twin daughters."

Kevin nodded. He knew.

Wyatt showed up an hour later, looking drained. He fell into the plastic chair next to Kevin. "How we doing?" he asked.

Kevin answered. "Don't know. We're waiting for him to get out of surgery."

Wyatt nodded. "When he gets out, go in and do whatever it is you Catholics do to sick people. It'll make him feel better even if he doesn't know."

Kevin smiled. "You're not Catholic, Detective?" he asked.

"I'm half-Samoan. We send our dead out on surfboards to the great beyond," he said, almost serious. "My grandmother is probably in Antarctica by now."

I shot Max a look and whispered in her ear, "Your kids will be a quarter Samoan."

The four of us sat in the plastic chairs, an odd quartet: a blood-covered woman, a priest, a sexy sprite, and a half-Samoan, half-something-else detective. Every time the elevator opened, we tensed, looking for the stretcher that would hold Crawford's body. Finally, after fourteen or fifteen false alarms, the doors opened and he was back from surgery.

I started to get up, but Wyatt took my arm. "Sit down," he commanded, and for some reason, I did. "Wait until they get him settled. I'll ask the doctor if we can go in."

I sat back down.

"Besides, the nurses here eat college professors for breakfast. If you break the rules, they'll toss you out and you won't be coming back."

"I get it," I said impatiently.

Wyatt got up and loped down the hall slowly, his long arms swinging back and forth. He stopped outside the door to Crawford's room and turned back, giving me his version of the sad face.

The doctor came out, a short Asian woman with waist-long black hair. She had on blue scrubs and plastic baggies covering her clogs. She looked up at Wyatt, her head bent back at an uncomfortable angle. I saw her hold up one finger and give directions, and then all five fingers. She walked away a minute later, leaving Wyatt standing in front of Crawford's room.

Wyatt whistled. "Padre!" he called to Kevin.

Kevin leapt up and flew down the hallway, the leather bag clasped in his hand. He entered the room while Wyatt waited outside.

I got up and joined Wyatt in front of the window outside the room. Kevin was standing over Crawford, who was shirtless and had oxygen tubes up his nose and a jumble of tubes going into his right arm. A thin white sheet was pulled up to his waist, and the wound was covered in a thick pad of gauze that was taped down. He was unconscious. Kevin leaned over, his lips moving, and put his thumb into a small, open canister of holy chrism. He put his thumb to Crawford's forehead and drew a small cross as he performed the anointing of the sick.

Wyatt turned to me. "She said you can go in. For five minutes. That's it. Got it?"

"I get it."

"No lap dances."

"You're an asshole, you know that?" I asked him. It figured he would pick today to be funny and personable, but I wasn't in the mood.

He smiled. "I know. I work really hard at it."

Kevin finished up and put everything back into his leather bag. "I'm done, Detective. If you need me, please call me." He looked at me. "Same for you." He put his arms around me and kissed me on the forehead.

Wyatt held his hand out, showing me the way to the door. "Five minutes."

"He's unconscious, Detective. I don't think I need that long."

"You're welcome, Your Pissiness."

I went into the room and stood at the foot of the bed. A nurse tucked the sheet in tight around his body and picked up his limp wrist, holding her finger against it while looking at her watch. "Wife?" she asked.

I shook my head. "Friend."

She dropped his wrist and went to the bottom of the bed to take the chart off the hook on the bed frame. She noted his vital statistics. "Five minutes," she said.

"Do you think he'll recover?" I asked.

"Don't know," she said noncommittally. "The first twenty-four hours after an injury like this and surgery are really critical."

"So I've heard," I whispered.

She surprised me and put her hand on my shoulder before she left. "He's got kids," she said. "Clean up before they get here. I'll give you scrubs."

I nodded to her back; she was already out

of the room before I understood what she meant. I turned back to the bed.

His skin had a ghostly pallor except for the ring of yellow around his shoulder and chest. I turned and looked out the window of the room, but Wyatt had turned his back to the room. I inched closer to the top of the bed. I put my hand on his forehead; it was hot to the touch. His eyelids fluttered slightly, but his eyes didn't open. I wondered if I would ever see his eyes open again.

I leaned over, kissed his cheek, and laid a hand on his hair. "I'll see you later. I'm going for a ride in a cruiser." No response. "You were right about one thing: they do cut your pants off."

I thought I saw his eyes move slightly under his closed lids, but they never opened.

"But I protected you from the emergency tracheotomy."

I moved my hand to his cheek and kept it there, leaning down to kiss him after a few minutes.

I left the room; Wyatt was a few feet down the hall talking to Max. Like the little doctor, she had her neck craned at an uncomfortable angle, staring up at him. They both stopped talking when I joined them.

"I'm ready to go."

Max took my hand and interlaced her

fingers into mine.

Wyatt looked down at her and then at me. "I'll call you if anything . . ." He paused. ". . . changes."

I nodded and took Max's hand, walking past the sober-faced cops clustered in front of the elevator. We got on and she pushed G to get us to the ground floor.

"I'm so sorry, Alison," she said, and put her arm around my waist, pulling me close. "He's going to be fine."

"I hope so, Max."

"Those big Irish ones have good genes. You can't take them out that easily."

"And you would know this how?" I asked, running a finger under each eye to wipe away runny makeup.

"He didn't come into your life to leave this quickly."

I hoped she was right.

TWENTY-FIVE

The phone rang off the hook most of the day, but no calls from Wyatt. Sister Mary, the *Journal News,* the *Daily News,* Max, the president of the college. Kevin McManus. Not a word from Ray.

After going through the day in a semi-stupor, I decided to take off my clothes and get back into bed at four in the afternoon, wearing only my underpants and the huge NYPD T-shirt that Crawford had given me. I held the bottom of it to my nose, hoping for a whiff of the clean-laundry scent, but all I could smell was eau de cranky cop. I drifted off into a restless unconsciousness and was awakened at six in the evening by the ringing of the phone next to my bed. I picked it up, groggy and still mostly asleep.

It was Wyatt. "He's awake."

My breath caught in my throat.

"But he's got a hundred and three temperature, so he's isolated. He wanted me to call you."

I started crying. "Thank you, Detective."

"Call me Fred," he said.

I used Max's line. "Is that your name or just what you want me to call you?"

"Has anyone ever told you what a funny lady you are?"

I wiped my nose on his T-shirt and thought for a moment. "As a matter of fact, yes."

"They've got visitation restricted to immediate family, but when you get to the main admissions area, tell them that Dr. Chin has given you clearance."

"Thank you, Fred," I said. He paused for a moment, and I didn't know whether or not we were done. "Fred?"

He let out a breath. I waited. "Bye," he finally said, and hung up.

Max had dropped me off the night before and left her car, calling a car service to pick her up and take her home. "You may need transportation," she said, as we stood at the bottom of my stairs, waiting for the car to pick her up. She put the keys in my hand.

I jumped out of bed and into the shower. When I was awake and clean, I put on jeans, a T-shirt, and a sweater. I pulled on sneakers and ran a comb through my wet hair before I headed out the front door.

The trip to Mercy took thirty minutes. I

went through the main entrance and gave them Crawford's name. An older woman, wearing a pink smock and a badge that said, "June, Volunteer," sized me up as she peered at the computer screen that listed all the patients' names and room numbers. She got to Crawford's name. "Immediate family?"

"Dr. Chin has given me clearance." I looked around, tapping my foot nervously on the floor.

Behind her bifocals, her eyes narrowed. "There're already three up there."

I smiled, hoping to disarm her.

She let out a long breath. "All right. Five minutes." I started off. "Wait!" she called after me. She handed me a badge to clip to my sweater. "You have to wear this."

I clipped it on. "Thanks, June."

I ran down the hall and found the bank of elevators, pushing "4" when I entered. The door opened on the floor, and it was a different scene from the night before, with no cops in sight. I guess word had gotten out that he was going to survive; no vigils necessary. I headed in the same direction toward the room he had been in the night before.

A nurse behind the desk stopped me. "Crawford?" she asked.

I nodded.

"He's in isolation." She pointed to her left.

"That way. You can only look through the window. There're two in there already."

I started down the hall, my badge jostling against my chest. I looked in every window until I saw him. He was in a room, plastic curtains around all four sides of the bed, with two young girls next to him on the outside of the bubble. He was still shirtless, and the wound was covered in the same thick gauze from the night before. His arm was in a sling.

The girls were on the side of the bed that faced the window to the hallway; one was standing and one was sitting. They were in full scrubs with masks, their hair covered. The one who was standing had Crawford's face and build — she was six feet if she was an inch. The other one must have looked like her mother, because she had brown eyes and judging from the wisp of hair falling out of the side of the cap, black hair.

He looked up when he saw me and waved weakly, a strange look passing across his pale face.

I put my hand to the glass and pressed it there, smiling. He turned to the girls and said something. The one that looked like him looked at me and smiled, while the other one kept her full attention on him. He pointed at the tall one and mouthed

"Meaghan," and then to the short one: "Erin."

A bank of chairs faced the room. I sat down, waiting to see if one or both of them would emerge from the room. I exceeded my June-imposed five minutes and sat for twenty.

A woman came down the hall toward me, holding a cup of coffee. She smiled and sat down next to me. She was smaller than I — about five-foot-five — and slim, with short black hair, a light complexion, and dark eyes. She had on a white T-shirt and jeans. "Hi," she said.

"Hi."

She took the lid off her coffee and tested it with her finger to see how hot it was. "I'm sure this will be delicious," she said, jokingly.

"I've had the coffee here, and it's more akin to sludge than a beverage."

She got up and went to the window, tapping on it gently. She motioned to the girls and mouthed to them, "Wrap it up in there." She returned to her chair and sat down.

"My name is Alison Bergeron," I said, offering my hand.

"Christine Crawford," she said, accepting it.

"You came a long way," I remarked, staring straight ahead at the window of his room. I figured with the last name "Crawford," she was either his sister or his sister-in-law. I guessed sister because she resembled one of the women in one of the pictures I had seen at the beach.

"We're in southern Connecticut, so it's not that far."

"Oh, Crawford said you lived in northern California."

She turned to look at me. "Bobby's sister lives in northern California." She took a sip of her coffee and grimaced.

I got that feeling in my stomach that indicated something I didn't want to hear was coming my way. "Then who are you?" I asked, laughing nervously.

She looked at me for a second before answering, as confused as I was. "I'm his wife."

Twenty-Six

The nuns at school went into full-blown novena mode every year prior to graduation, getting together and having group-prayer sessions at which they prayed for sun. On sunny graduation days, the ceremony was held on the great lawn, the majestic Hudson glimmering in the background behind the dais. When it rained, we had it in the auditorium, which was not quite as majestic; the auditorium was old, smelly, and badly in need of a complete renovation. As an added bonus, the chairs had an equivalent comfort level to concrete. With the river as a backdrop, the president of the college would speak, diplomas would be handed out, and the valedictorian would give his or her address (the old "believe in yourself" maxim usually being employed). Parents would smile, thinking, "I got my money's worth." Everyone was happy.

At six in the morning of graduation, bright sunshine was streaming in my window. It had rained lightly the night before, but the storm moved quickly, a mere sprinkle falling around the time I ate dinner.

It had almost been two weeks since I had last seen Crawford. Once I had met his wife, I had tried to leave the hospital gracefully; citing Volunteer June's five-minute rule, I thought I got out of there pretty quickly and without making a scene. The sobs were a bubbling cauldron in my chest. Once in Max's car, I let it all out. I cried and banged my head on the steering wheel, mad at myself for having allowed myself to develop any kind of feelings for him in the short time in which we had known each other. I vowed never to allow myself to be hurt again and put another layer of bricks and mortar on the wall around my heart. My anger was like a white-hot ball of steel that I had swallowed and that burned in my gut. I unleashed its heat on anyone who crossed my path, Max receiving the brunt of most of my rage. I was in a funk, and I wasn't getting out of it anytime soon. The last time we spoke, she recounted with glee and sparkling insensitivity her first date with Detective Wyatt, which had been a success and which — unlike almost every other date

Max had recently — hadn't ended up in bed.

She finally took herself out of my way, telling me to call her when I was done being mad at Crawford. It had been a week since we last spoke.

Crawford had called me at home a total of twenty-seven times, but I didn't answer the phone anymore. The voice mail on my cell phone became full of messages of his recorded voice. I only kept the most contrite and least pleading of them.

Considering everything that had happened over the last several weeks and how stupid I had been, I came to the conclusion that I had spent way too many years with my head in books, missing life's little clues, missing what was right in front of me all the time. I had stayed married to a man who didn't love me and lied to me with regularity, never mind his "sexual addiction" as he came to call it; I had carried the Shakespeare papers around for days, not realizing that they held the key to solving Kathy's murder; I had put my full trust in Crawford, ignoring the fact that he remained closed to me, never telling me anything about himself — either who he was or how he felt. I guess I wasn't as smart as I thought. Or, maybe I just knew a lot about James Joyce and nothing else.

What I did know now was that knowing a lot about James Joyce really didn't do me a whole lot of good.

I got out of bed and opened my closet. A red-linen dress, sleeveless, very fitted, and knee-length, hung in a dry-cleaning bag. I took it out and removed the plastic, hanging the dress on the back of the door. I had hours until I needed to be at school, so I took a leisurely shower and shaved my legs, using the shower gel that I had bought on my last shopping trip with Max. Now I was an angry, depressed woman who smelled like coconuts.

Along with being incredibly angry, I never slept. I went to bed after midnight and was up at dawn. I ate only when I felt hungry; usually about every two days. I was thin and exhausted.

School had not been the same since the incident with Fiona in the office. Where it once pulsed with joy and excitement at this time of year, it was now dead. It was as if the heart of the school had been removed. Although classes continued and grades were assessed and recorded, nobody was the same. The student body was sad and subdued; all of the senior week activities were canceled in the wake of Fiona's arrest. Sister Mary left me alone, accepting all of my grades via e-mail with nary a comment. Dottie eyed me suspiciously, waiting for me to either lash out or collapse in hysteria; we reached détente and greeted each other with a smile and a pleasant hello but left it at that. One day, she came into my office and gave me an awkward hug, but I managed not to break down until she had gone back to her desk. I saw a police cruiser parked outside every once in a while, and assumed it was Moriarty waiting for her.

Kevin stopped by every day and asked me if I wanted to talk. I didn't.

I had the feeling that I was being watched, but I never actually saw Crawford. If he was doing surveillance, he had gotten a lot better at it.

I spent hours reliving every encounter and conversation that we'd had because if I knew anything, it was that liars don't only lie about one thing. Lying is a habit for them, an epidemic. I came to the conclusion that he had used me to solve the case and nothing else. He had gotten close to me to see what I knew; he was no better than Peter Miceli, who at least had the decency to act in character and just kidnap me. I knew there had to be a reason why we had never slept together; turns out he wasn't interested in me or attracted to me.

That solved the riddle of why every time I had given him the opening, he had slept on the couch.

As I dressed for graduation, I thought about my recent trip to the City to buy my outfit: the red dress and a pair of red slingback pumps with a very high heel. They were Manolo Blahniks — very Max — and the price of them equaled the cost of two credits at my school. Although I had no plans for any postgraduation festivities for the first time since I had joined the faculty at St. Thomas, I had even had my hair cut and colored. I was single, and my best friend wasn't speaking to me, but I looked fabulous.

I pulled the dress on over my head and attempted to get the zipper all the way up; the length of my arm wrapped around my back left me with a two-inch gap near my neck. I took a hanger and bent it, trying to hook the curved part into the zipper. After five minutes of effort and much sweating, I gave up. The zipper remained zipped up only three-quarters of the way.

I left my hair down, blowing it straight and spraying it until it was smooth. The layers had grown out to a point where I felt comfortable getting it all cut to one length; it was now shoulder-length and dark brown with auburn highlights. I put on my diamond earrings and a swipe of "Jennifer."

So many events were taking place at school, I was back and forth every single day. I finally broke down and leased a car: a brand-new, black Volvo sedan that sat in my driveway, the spanking-new cousin of my old 240. Every time I looked at it, I felt sad. I took my pocketbook from the counter in the kitchen and made my way out to the car.

I pointed the key tag toward the car and unlocked the doors. An envelope sat on the windshield, my name scribbled across the front. I pulled it out from under the wiper and was about to open it when I heard a male voice say, "Hi, Alison."

I looked up and saw Jackson standing on the other side of the hedgerow that separated our driveways. I shoved the envelope into my pocketbook. "Hi, Alison," he repeated.

I wasn't in the mood for chitchat and I wanted to get to school so that I could get a few things organized in my office before the summer started. I looked at him and didn't respond.

"Nice car." He looked uncomfortable. "Is it new?"

"Yes." I stood on the driver's side of the

car, peering at him over the roof.

"Where are you going?"

"Graduation." I opened the car door.

"You look nice."

"Thanks."

"She told me," he blurted out. He blinked a few times as tears came to his eyes.

I looked at him, not caring. I put my elbows on top of the car and clasped my hands together.

"We're working it out."

"Good," I said.

"I'm sorry," he said quietly. His face went sad.

My eyes filled with tears; he was kind, and I was a bitch. "Me, too," I said, and hastily got in the car, slamming and locking the door. I backed out of the driveway quickly and headed down the street, wiping my eyes on a balled-up tissue that was on the passenger's seat. I was finding a lot of them around lately.

I got to school and parked behind the dorm next to my building. I took my pocketbook and walked the length of the parking lot to the back stairs, treading carefully on the unevenly spaced steps behind the building.

I let myself in by the back door and walked the short distance between the back door and the office area. It was early — about four hours before graduation — so nobody would be in the office for at least another two hours. I pulled the door open and entered, my thin heels making a clicking sound on the hardwood floors.

Crawford stood in front of my office and turned when I entered. I stopped at the end of the table where, just two weeks earlier, I had laid his head when he had lost consciousness. He turned and looked at me, a mixture of despair and confusion on his sad, handsome face.

His arm was still in a sling and he was a little thinner. His color was better than it had been in the hospital though, and his hair, slightly longer. He wasn't wearing the sad face or even the really bad-news face; this was clearly the "I'm a shithead" face, and it became him at that moment. He had on baggy jeans and a Lavallette PD T-shirt, untucked. He was holding a paper bag. No gun, no badge.

I put my bag on the table. "Doing surveillance?"

He shrugged. "I'm awake, aren't I?"

I pointed to his shirt. "Where'd you get the shirt?"

"Ted," he said. "I went down to the shore for a few days. He left it in the mailbox for me after he read in the paper about what happened." He smiled. "He left one for you, too." He offered me the bag. I took it and opened it to find a light blue LPD T-shirt.

"I can add this to my collection of police-issue clothing," I said, almost forgetting how angry I was. "Tell Ted I said thanks."

"You look beautiful," he said.

I looked down.

"You cut your hair."

"You don't miss a trick."

"You've lost weight. When's the last time you ate?"

"I had four frozen cannolis and two martinis on Tuesday," I said, my tone cutting. He winced. I think I was madder than he expected me to be after two weeks.

"Graduation is today, right?" he asked.

I nodded.

"What time?"

I got angry. "One. What do you want, Crawford?"

"To find out why you never took any of my phone calls. To explain. To say I'm sorry."

"For what?" I asked. "Lying? I don't even want to hear it." I headed toward my office, taking my keys out of my purse. The words were caught in my throat, but I managed to get out, "How could you?"

He looked down at me, and I almost felt sorry for him, but I pushed those feelings aside. I started crying, furious at myself for letting him see me lose control. "After everything I told you about Ray, and what he did to me, and how I felt, how could you?" I rooted around in my bag for one of the handy balled-up, used tissues, but I didn't have one.

He handed me a neatly folded, pressed white handkerchief. "Here."

I blew my nose loudly and handed it back to him. He laughed. "I don't want it back." He finally took it after I continued to hold it out; he put it in his pocket. "Can we go in your office?"

I opened the door and waved him in. He waited until I entered and then followed me in, closing the door. "Sit down," I said.

"Your zipper isn't all the way up." He came up behind me and zipped up my dress. He let his hands fall onto my bare shoulders, but after a few seconds passed, and I didn't turn around, he took his usual seat across from me. I sat behind the desk. It was my turn to ask questions. "Yes or no. Are you married?"

He let out a breath and went pale. "Yes."

I caught a sob as it tried to escape from

my throat by swallowing hard.

"Technically," he amended.

I rolled my eyes. "That's like being a little bit pregnant." I went for the jugular. "You're sounding like Ray."

He closed his eyes and leaned forward in the chair, wincing as his bad arm caught the armrest. "I can explain."

I looked at my watch. "You've got five minutes. Go."

He put his good hand under the elbow in the sling. "We're separated."

"Oh, thank God," I said, rolling my eyes in disbelief.

He ignored me and continued. "We separated six years ago. It just didn't work out. She hated the job, the hours, the danger, and ended up hating me because I wouldn't give it up." He held his elbow, his right hand dangling uselessly in his lap. "That's simplifying it. There's more to it than that; I wouldn't choose my job over a woman I loved." He looked out the window, unable to meet my eye. "I moved out and left the girls with her. I knew I couldn't raise them alone and do this job. We agreed to be friends and make it work for them. We were always better at being friends than we were at being married anyway." He took his hand out of the sling. "A lawyer drew up an agreement, and we decided to share custody."

"So, why didn't he draw up divorce papers at the same time?" I asked, having a little familiarity with these things.

"He did. I have the divorce papers in my desk at home, but I never signed them. My wife . . . Christine wanted me to agree to an annulment."

I looked at him.

"She wouldn't give me a divorce unless I agreed to an annulment at the same time."

An annulment in the Catholic Church basically gives you a "get out of marriage free" card; it certifies that your marriage was null and void. Never happened. The end. Regardless of whether or not there were children, who usually served as evidence that a marriage had happened. That was simplifying it, but that was the gist. Kevin later explained to me that the Church defines an annulment as the dissolution of a marriage between two people who were incapable of "informed consent" at the time of their union. I thought it was one of the most bogus aspects of the Church and even though receiving communion as a divorced Catholic could get me excommunicated, I didn't give a rat's ass and marched up to communion with all of the other sinners. I didn't think the Vatican had its own police force to monitor these sorts of things.

If you wanted to remarry in the Church, an annulment was mandatory. Since divorcing Ray, I didn't think I would ever remarry, much less in the Church, so an annulment was a nonissue. Especially since I thought they were a load of crap.

I repeated what he had said, and asked, "So, why didn't you just give her one?"

He looked at me. "I think they're a load of crap."

I almost liked him again, but I stopped myself.

"We have two beautiful daughters. Our marriage . . . well, it just didn't work out." He leaned back and stuck his hand inside his sling to scratch his arm. "I wasn't going to pay some priest two grand to wipe the slate clean. There's a lot of writing on that slate. Some of it is even good." He closed his eyes. "I also never thought it would be an issue. I work eighty hours a week and spend another thirty with my kids. Sometimes I sleep. I didn't think having a nonexistent, yet legal, marriage would be a problem. I guess I was wrong, huh?" He opened his eyes and looked at me. "I never thought I'd meet anyone worth compromising for."

I softened slightly but I had hardened

myself so much in the past few weeks that I was incapable of a complete thaw. "She's still in love with you."

He shook his head. "I don't think so."

"Then why would she introduce herself to me as your wife?" I asked.

"Because she is," he said quietly.

He should have kept his mouth shut, but I guess he finally felt like he had to tell the truth. She was his wife. He was married. I started crying again. "Can I have the handkerchief back, please?" I asked.

He reached into his pocket and pulled out the soggy piece of linen. He handed it to me across my desk. I blew my nose again.

"I really don't want it back this time," he said, smiling, but I could see that his eyes were moist.

I crumpled it up in my hands and held it there.

He looked down at his shoes. "I'm going to sign those papers."

I looked back at him. I wasn't sure what that meant, but it was probably good news. The way things were going, I was having a tough time separating the good from the bad.

"Do you think Father Kevin would help me with the annulment?" he asked.

I shrugged. "Hard to say. If I were you,

I'd stay away from Father Kevin for a while. He's pretty mad at you."

"Go out with me tonight so we can talk about this," he said. "Or let me come over."

I shook my head. "I don't think so."

"Tomorrow?" he asked hopefully.

I stared back at him.

"So, that's it?" He looked at me for confirmation.

I crossed my arms on my desk and put my head down on them. After a few minutes, I looked up. "I'm sorry. I just can't get past the fact that you lied," I said, my voice hoarse from crying.

He got up and came around to my side of the desk. "I'm sorry. I didn't mean to hurt you. When you asked me the question that night in the restaurant, I really didn't think it would ever be an issue. I guess I was wrong." He put his hand on my cheek. "Will you forgive me?"

I stayed in my chair. I took his hand from my cheek. "I don't know. I can't see you again until you're divorced or annulled or whatever you need to be to not have a wife. I know that." I stood up and took his left hand in mine. "Good-bye, Crawford."

"Wait," he said, putting his arm around my waist and pulling me close. "This will all be over in a few months. How do we stay together until then?" he whispered, leaning toward my face.

I extricated myself from him. "We don't. You're married."

A knock at the door put more space between us. I called, "Come in," and the door opened. It was Kevin. He eyed Crawford warily. "Detective," he said, nodding.

Crawford cast his eyes down. "Father Mc-Manus."

Kevin gave him the priest version of the evil eye. "You look good. Are you feeling better?"

"Yes. Thank you."

Kevin looked at me, taking in the red nose, the bloodshot eyes, and runny makeup. "I saw your car. You're in early."

"Trying to get some work done," I explained.

"Call me when you're done. I need help with my homily for today's Mass. I thought I'd talk about 'new beginnings.' I'll be in the chapel," he said, and closed the door.

I stared at the closed door, and Crawford stared at me. "So, that's it?" he asked, his tone surprised and full of hurt. "After everything we've been through? That's it?"

I nodded. "That's it." I wanted to add "for now," but didn't. "Can I give you a tip, Crawford?"

"Put a ten on Almost Divorced in the fifth at Belmont?" he asked, trying to get a smile out of me. It almost worked, but not quite.

I stared back at him impassively. "The next time a woman asks you if you're married, say 'yes.' "

"There won't be a next time." He put his free hand to his head and rubbed his forehead.

I wasn't sure if I had the fortitude to remain on this moral high ground I had constructed. When he put his hand on the doorknob, the finality of everything hit me. I stood. "Crawford, listen. Give me a couple of weeks. Gas up the cruiser and drop by when you're feeling better."

"It's not a cruiser," he shot back. He pulled me close with his good arm and kissed me.

I pulled away.

"I'll be back," he said, and turned to leave. He gave me one last glance and left my office, closing the door behind him.

I waited until I saw him go up the back stairs and then whispered to no one but myself, "And I'll be here."

EPILOGUE

It was three days later that I found the envelope that had been on the windshield of my car. It was shoved deep into an unused pocket of my pocketbook, wrinkled, but still intact. I pulled it out and opened it, reading the brief message aloud:

Alison,
Remember. I owe you.

Peter

ABOUT THE AUTHOR

Maggie Barbieri is a freelance textbook editor as well as a mystery novelist. Her father was a member of the New York Police Department, and his stories provide much of the background for her mysteries. She lives in Westchester County, New York.

The employees of Thorndike Press hope you have enjoyed this Large Print book. All our Thorndike and Wheeler Large Print titles are designed for easy reading, and all our books are made to last. Other Thorndike Press Large Print books are available at your library, through selected bookstores, or directly from us.

For information about titles, please call:
(800) 223-1244

or visit our Web site at:
www.gale.com/thorndike
www.gale.com/wheeler

To share your comments, please write:
Publisher
Thorndike Press
295 Kennedy Memorial Drive
Waterville, ME 04901